S0-BDR-205

From Porn to Poetry

Clean Sheets Celebrates the Erotic Mind

Edited by
Susannah Indigo and Brian Peters

Samba Mountain Press
Colorado
2001

Samba Mountain Press
P.O. Box 4741
Englewood, CO 80155
www.sambamountain.com

ISBN 0-971-66230-4

FIRST EDITION: DECEMBER 2001

Printed in the United States of America

Contents

Fiction

Essays

Poetry

Introduction

From porn to poetry and everything else in between, *Clean Sheets* has been publishing a weekly zine on the Web for over three years. A devoted staff of more than twenty people from around the world volunteer to make *Clean Sheets* happen with a sense of joy—we work with hundreds of writers, new and established; we laugh; we cry; we are charmed; we get heated up; we fuss over the real meaning of "sex-positive" at least once a year; and we all love what we do.

Our diverse and thoughtful readership is literally global in reach, and we are forever grateful to every one of our readers or their attention and their participation. In honor of them, we keep a full three years of feedback about *Clean Sheets* always available on the Web site—they praise, they complain, they cheer, they differ wildly in what they think is *really* sexy, and most of all they let us know that sexuality is the most fascinating topic in the world.

So we bring you our best in this book—brand new stories mixed with our favorites from the Web—and we hope you'll get a sense of the joyful, passionate, and thoughtful erotic world that we live in. We celebrate every bit of the thighs shivering, clothing torn away, nipples painfully erect, cocks glistening, and pussies dripping that follow—and if you find it amusing that we propose to do all that on clean sheets, you're our kind of reader.

Susannah Indigo and Brian Peters
December 2001

From Porn to Poetry

Clean Sheets Celebrates the Erotic Mind

Perfect Pussies

Janice Callisa

My cats like to watch me while I masturbate.

Perhaps they are jealous, perhaps they are curious, or, some days, I think they are just happy for me. They both curl up close, so close on either side of my spread legs that I can feel their breath on my skin. Gloria is a golden tabby, and she begins to stalk me the moment I reach for the vibrator drawer—she knows what's coming. Jerome is a black Bombay and he is a bit cooler about it, pretending he doesn't care where we're going, but he never misses an orgasm.

I stack at least three CDs on random—Van Morrison for Gloria, the Grateful Dead for Jerome, Jeff Buckley for me, and then I strip, and we dance. I have always danced naked with every cat I've ever had since I was a little girl. There was safety in cats in my childhood—I told them all my terrible family secrets, we played, we danced, I held them, they kept me soft. I slept with my cats every night of my young life, close to my face like a pillow, and some days I would wake up with my long red hair tangled and pulled by their claws, but I didn't care.

We dance, and then I hold them close and spin them around in my own tribal dance of love. If their claws dig into my breasts or my shoulders I don't care, it is a kind of foreplay. I have silver rings pierced through both of my nipples, and sometimes Stella will bat at them—it's not truly sexual, it's play, but it sends a tingle straight down to my clit.

When I am tired from the dance, I lie down on the blue oriental rug on my hardwood floor, my head propped up by a soft pillow. If I have forgotten to grab the vibrator from where I left it on the armchair, one of the cats will find it and roll it toward me.

It may be the buzzing sound that they love so much—they do not watch as closely when I am with a man and getting sexed-up. One night my lover put leftover sushi on my nipples and tried to get them to nip and lick at my nipples, but they only snatched the food and ran. It may be that they want me all to themselves. I have often been tempted to try spreading catfood tuna on my cunt to see what would happen, but I have a secret fear that I would like their tongues better than my lover's, and then where would I be.

I listen to the music when I touch myself, and I disappear into it. *Let the music put you in the zone, I am lost, lost inside a rhythm.* I become a little girl when I touch myself, traveling back to the world of an imaginary perfectly-loved child, a little girl hiding quietly under the bed on the hard floor, hugging herself, holding her kitten.

The feel of Gloria's claws on my thigh mix with the vibrating pulse on my clit. *We are free, we can fly, we have more than nine lives and they are all meant for sex.* I imagine I am in a room full of cats and they all love me and they are quiet and warm, and I am warm and quiet and then I am hot—and when I come, I am still quiet, but they begin to purr.

Afterwards, Jerome comes up to nuzzle my face, and I think he almost tries to kiss me, and then I know I am safe for another day.

carolina rain

Donna Michele Hill

we awake to the sound of morning drizzle
and for what is to be the last time
in a long while, hold each other near
touching as only we do
silent good-byes
etching deep within our gaze
like native cave markings

a sunlit mist of smoky blue clouds
will soon carry me on to atlanta
then home to canada
my blurred hand pressed against
the plane's window, framed in loss

but in this moment I lay still
your breath and tongue washing
over my body, like a soft carolina rain

What's Abstinence Got To Do With It?

Jeff Beresford-Howe

I want to talk about abstinence for a moment.

I don't mean "I've been fucking way too many people and I need a break to cleanse my palate," and I don't mean "The Lord Jesus told me that the pleasures of the flesh will put me smack on the cast iron skillet of the Great Fry Cook," either.

I'm talking about the kind of abstinence our local school boards and Algore and W and Bill Clinton think should be taught to impressionable 15-year-olds.

This is the new wave in sex "education" and there's something in particular I want to say about it: if we believe in it, even for our beautiful daughters who are growing up way too soon, we're running the risk of killing people.

We all know the endless research data which shows that giving kids practical help with disease and pregnancy prevention helps bring significantly lower rates of those problems than does the absence of such instruction. That argument is hard to bring home into your heart, though.

What we care about is our kids, and the kids around them.

We want our kids not to fuck. Not to fuck anyone from the opposite sex and, though we'd never admit it at a PTA meeting or even to our spouses—unless you are, as Sen. Bob Kerrey might put it, in an "unusually bigoted town"—we definitely don't want them fucking someone of the same sex.

And who can blame us? Geez, we're all grown-up, and we look back on how little fun we had fucking when we were 16, how rushed and ignorant and pressured we felt. How incompetent we were, how (if you're a girl) painful and unorgasmic it was, and you think, "Why would anyone risk AIDS, or pregnancy, or herpes, or whatever other nightmare you might have in mind, for *that*?"

So why did you?

You have your garden variety "I was drunk at a party" fucks and your "I just wanted to lose my virginity and get it over with" fucks, but mostly what I think you have is, "God, that (guy or girl) was so hot and I was in love." Looking back, what you felt in your own personal Dark Ages little resembles the intensity and depth of what you feel now. But you had to start somewhere, and at the time it seemed like the right thing to do. At least for a few minutes.

And that's the problem with abstinence programs: sex is a natural process, emphasis on both words. It requires growth, both physically and emotionally. It requires practice for it to become a whole statement of yourself and your feelings for someone else.

When we teach kids not to start that process, we leave them in a horrible box. They can either distance themselves emotionally from their objects of desire and learn how to close themselves off, or, when they have those feelings, they can go the other way and tell themselves, "If I'm feeling sexual, the only acceptable context for that is deep and profound love, so that's what must be happening to me."

The consequence of the first, of course, is denial. The kids won't learn how to talk about their deepest feelings, not with themselves or anyone else. When they end up having sex—which they will because hardly any kids have the kind of impulse control it takes to bottle up that flood of hormones—they'll have to do it with an absolute lack of self-awareness.

That means getting drunk. Or high. It might mean, if they're a gay boy, a stranger who no one will know or see. It means no precautions because precautions would mean a consciousness of the act. And you know what? That boy will probably get away with it a few times; he won't get the HIV virus because getting it isn't like falling off a log. But some of them will. More of them will the fifth or twentieth time they do it, and those people will die.

And there are the girls, of course. They're vulnerable to the HIV virus, too, but even more than that, they're vulnerable to a starry-eyed marriage at 19 and, shoot, since they're in a love that will last forever, let's get started having kids at 20. That route often leads, as we know, to divorce at 28, and often to brutally truncated and poverty-stricken lives, for those girls and for their children.

There are a few kids who will take abstinence to heart, and abstinence is the fantasy we have for all our children: a risk-free world in which they never come to harm. But the hard truth is that our kids will learn about love and sex with or without our help. They will take risks to do it. If all we do as parents is simply tell them to wait, our kids lose a chance to get our help, to have a source for facts and a sympathetic ear in school or at home, and we will have missed a serious opportunity to teach our children well.

The Secret Life of Humphrey Milquer

J. Hartman

1504, 1506, 1510 . . . Humphrey Milquer eased off the accelerator, peering at the dim building numbers under flickering street lamps. There it was: 1592, at the corner of Addison and Huxley. A discreet wooden sign declared the grey concrete building to be The Secret Garden. A tough-looking motorcycle cop was parked on the broad sidewalk in front, facing the street.

Humphrey drove slowly past. The cop stared at the street, as if he'd been instructed to see nothing.

Humphrey parked a block away. His hands trembled as he set the parking brake. He shut off the engine, sat with his fingers on the keys for a long moment.

Finally he took a deep breath and yanked the keys from the ignition. He got out, locked the car door, and strode toward The Secret Garden.

A middle-aged man in a leather jacket, carrying a gym bag, emerged from the grey building as Humphrey approached. The man scurried around the corner and disappeared into the shadow of the tall wooden fence that extended from the grey wall.

The cop continued to stare dead ahead, still as a mannequin.

Humphrey pushed open the pneumatic door and found himself in a grimy, bare entrance way. A dim incandescent bulb dangled from the ceiling. Straight ahead was a window of thick glass, with a hole in the base for the exchange of money. A bored-looking young man, tall and thin and blond, stood behind the glass.

The man looked up as Humphrey stepped forward. Humphrey cleared his throat. "I'd like, uh, a one-time membership?" he croaked.

"Ever been here before?" asked the blond man. He pushed a form and a pen under the glass.

Humphrey shook his head. He wrote his name on the form, conscious of the blond man's cool gaze.

"Over 18? Picture ID?"

Humphrey pried his wallet out of his tight jeans pocket and slid his driver's license under the glass.

"All right. Here's a key to locker number 82. Grab a towel from the stack just inside the door, then leave your clothes in the locker."

Humphrey picked up the key. It was on an elastic cord, just big enough to fit a wrist. The young man pressed a button; a door to Humphrey's right clicked. Humphrey pushed through it.

A locker room. A dozen men of assorted shapes, ages, and skin colors were showering or stripping. The room looked just like the one Humphrey had suffered through every day in high school.

> . . . It was the bottom of the ninth down, in the final game of the World Series Cup. The Catalina Fighting Eels were trailing by a single goal. Star halfback Humphrey Milquer— "the most promising sophomore this game has ever seen," according to CNN—faked left, faked right, and ran fifty yards with the ball before a dozen burly players from the other team converged

on him. He chucked a wild pass up into the air, and only then noticed that everyone else on his team had already been tackled. Squaring his broad shoulders, he plowed through the initial assault, shrugging off opposing players like rain, and charged forward just in time to catch his own throw. He raced another hundred and twenty yards to make the game-winning touchdown.

The cheerleaders from both teams propositioned him en masse, but Humphrey, steely-eyed, square-jawed, turned them down. "My team awaits," he said.

In the locker room, the players had stripped down to their towels and champagne was flowing freely. Tom Studds, a broad-shouldered senior, affectionately snapped a towel at Humphrey. Humphrey grabbed the end of the towel and reeled Tom in; before Tom could react, Humphrey's lips were on his. Tom melted in his strong arms; Humphrey could feel Tom's cock spring to attention against his belly. As the kiss ended, Tom moaned, "Oh, Humphrey—I always wanted you, but I thought you were too much of a man for me."

Humphrey grinned. "I am. Good thing the rest of the team is here to help you out."

A spontaneous cheer rang out. Several team members lifted Humphrey to their shoulders and pulled away his towel, revealing his thick fourteen-inch cock in all its standing glory. Jack Ace stepped forward and licked . . .

"'Scuse me, that's my locker."

Humphrey jumped, then moved aside to let the other man pass. Where—oh, yes, locker 82. He stripped, eyes downcast, and wrapped the towel tight around his waist. Then he piled his clothing into the locker and locked it.

He padded through the locker room and through a swinging door into a wide lounge area. A big TV mounted high on the wall showed a tight closeup of an enormous cock sliding rhythmically into and out of an asshole. Grunts and moans issued from the TV's speaker. Three or four older men sat near the TV on padded benches, wearing nothing but towels, half-watching the video action.

Humphrey looked away, but stole a fascinated glance at the TV as he walked past. In, out, in, out . . . he fixed his gaze on the floor. From somewhere deeper in the building he could hear a Top 40 radio station playing; he walked through an open doorway toward the music.

On his second pass through the lounge, Humphrey sat down gingerly on a wooden bench to rest. He hadn't sat still for more than a minute in any of the other half-dozen areas of the Secret Garden—the outdoor hot tub, the weight room, the other lounge (complete with a pair of pool tables and a fireplace), the steam room, the video room (with five different TVs showing five different videos at once), or the maze of narrow corridors blanketed with doors, each leading into a tiny spartan bedroom.

In each area, men wearing towels (or sometimes nothing at all) lounged against walls, or sat on benches, or conversed among themselves. Eyes darted back and forth. Some of the men had an air of forced casualness; others seemed genuinely at ease. They were a mix of whites, Latinos, and Asians, of all ages—one or two looked barely eighteen, and a few weren't going to see sixty again. Skinny and fat, tall and short, balding and bearded, muscled and nerdy. Humphrey had never seen so many men without clothes in one place before. It was disconcerting—he couldn't tell who was a businessman, who was a computer programmer, who was a waiter, or a bus driver, or a street person. All just men, and all there for the same reason.

But Humphrey couldn't see how it was done. There were scattered couples here and there, but most of those not coupled were engaged in light conversation, or sat silent, watching the other men. Humphrey never saw the moment of contact, never figured out what two men said to each other to get things started. And he felt sure that if he sat down without some excuse—like this TV to watch—those who walked by would find him out, would see that he wasn't a Cool Guy who knew what he was doing but just a scared virgin.

Out of the corner of his eye he saw someone looking at him. Giving up on pretending to watch the video, he stood, gathered his towel around him, and strode from the room as if he'd just remembered an appointment.

In the pool lounge, a gorgeous young angel with a halo of red curls bent provocatively over a table, contemplating a shot. He glanced over a shoulder and smiled as Humphrey entered the room. Humphrey stumbled to a padded seat by the fire and sat down to watch.

The man took a leisurely shot and sank a ball. He ambled to the other side of the table and sank another. Every sway of his hips declared that he knew he was being watched.

For his next shot, he positioned himself directly between Humphrey and the table, then bent forward until his tight ass stood out against the towel.

. . . "He said he wouldn't surrender to anyone but you, Lieutenant."

Police Lieutenant Sam Milquer stood at an alley entrance in his trenchcoat and battered fedora, a stump of cigar dangling from his lip. It had been a long night—three murders, a case of gay-bashing, and now this.

In the harsh glare of a police spotlight, a sneering pale-faced youth in a kilt stood defiantly, fists on hips. Behind him was a cherry-red Nissan sportscar. A ring of police officers surrounded him, but kept their distance, respectful or afraid.

"Are ye Lieutenant Milquer?" the youth challenged, flashing his steely grey eyes and tossing his mop of red hair.

"Yeah," Milquer said. "And you're Tom McStudds, right?"

"The same." The boy's thick Scottish brogue was unmistakable to anyone who'd watched a news broadcast that month. "Th' leader of Caer Lomond." The dreaded Scottish youth gang had instilled a reign of terror on the city for weeks now, ever since their leader's 18th birthday. They were proud and dangerous, and nobody knew what they wore under those kilts.

Milquer squared his shoulders. "So you'll only surrender to me?"

"Ye're the only one o' the police that's man enough to take me."

Milquer stepped forward, out of the shadows and into the actinic glare. "All right. Turn around. Hands on the roof of the car."

With the air of a man going to a firing squad but haughty to the last, McStudds flicked the toothpick from his mouth. Then he turned languidly and put his hands on the car.

Milquer stepped forward and with practiced ease kicked the boy's legs further apart and away from the car. McStudds was leaning forward now, but still stood firm and defiant.

Milquer bent and with one quick motion flipped the boy's kilt up over his head. A gasp came up from the assembled officers as a perfect, rounded white ass glowed in the spotlight.

Milquer opened his trenchcoat. He wore nothing underneath—always ready for just such an occasion to arise. His fourteen-inch cock was already stiffening, seeking like a hungry arrow for its target. He stuck one hand in his coat pocket and squeezed out a gob from the tube of lubricant he always kept there, then quickly greased his cock with it.

He grasped the boy's hips with both hands. The boy's clenched lips let forth a stifled gasp; Milquer could see the shadow of McStudds' narrow cock as it stiffened against the front of the kilt. With a firm thrust, Milquer was inside the boy's tight little ass. McStudds couldn't help himself; a full-throated moan emerged from his proud mouth. Milquer thrust deeper, his arousal swelling. He'd wanted McStudds since the first time he'd seen him, on a barricade two weeks before. And he was clearly the boy's first; this asshole was too tight to have ever been entered before. Milquer thrust again, and again, harder and harder, barely stifling his own groans as . . .

"Hola, amigo!" A cheerful young Latino man slapped the pool player's ass in a friendly way. The pool player turned, grinning, and rested his cue against the table; then, with a quick glance at Humphrey, he kissed the new arrival passionately. The two walked off entangled in each other's arms.

Humphrey stepped up to the table and picked up the cue stick. He was terribly aware of the eyes of the men who walked by, glancing at him and at the table. He took aim and shot but the stick slipped; the cue ball spun out of control and into a corner pocket. Blushing, he set down the cue stick and escaped through the sliding glass door into the darkness outside.

He stood still for a moment as his eyes adjusted. Half a

dozen men lounged in the big hot tub. Towels littered the nearby deck chairs. After a moment of hesitation, Humphrey whipped off his towel, dropped it in a heap, and darted into the water. Murmurs of conversation went on around him. There was no sign anyone had noticed his arrival.

> . . . Captain Jacques Milquer—the French pronunciation, if you please—stroked through the warm Caribbean water. Coral reefs fanned out below him in rainbow colors; small sharks and eels dodged playfully in and out among vast schools of bright tropical fish. Catfish, dogfish, angelfish, devilfish— fish of every size, shape, and color. Milquer's steely grey eyes glinted. He took a deep breath through his snorkel.
>
> Ahead, a human form loomed in the dim water. It was Milquer's first mate, Tom Studds—broad of shoulder, firm of thigh, with smooth skin the shade of Colombian coffee. The rest of the crew of the *Nautilus* were on shore leave, resting up from three long months of filming an underwater documentary for the Discovery Channel. Milquer and Studds alone had remained behind. It seemed Studds had taken advantage of his captain being off on an afternoon swim to go skinny-dipping. The mate's hairy chest and firm stomach stood out against the murky water beyond him. Milquer grinned to himself and attached the special SCUBA rebreather that left his mouth free. He'd seen Studds' covert glances at his ass during that documentary; he knew what his mate wanted.
>
> As stealthily as if he were wearing water moccasins, Captain Milquer approached Studds with an effortless underwater crawling stroke. Studds was floating upright, relaxed, unaware of his captain's approach. The mate's cock, not long but thick, swelled above his

balls. Milquer swam closer, eddies of water drifting from his moving hands, then reached out and gently brushed Studds' hairy balls.

Studds stiffened at once but did not move. *Perhaps he thinks I'm one of the dreaded Cock-hunting Eels of Madagascar,* thought Milquer with a grin. He touched the mate's cock, then moved closer still and licked at it from the side.

Studds' hands, limp at his sides, flexed involuntarily. Through the water, Milquer heard the mate moan.

Captain Milquer licked the other man's balls, then reached around with both hands and squeezed Studds' ass hard, pulling his crotch closer. With one quick move, he engulfed the mate's broad cock in his warm mouth, feeling it stiffen into full erection as he did so. He began to bob his head back and forth, pulling Studds' warm body toward him with every stroke. The mate's hands twitched again, then buried themselves deep in the Captain's steely grey hair . . .

A man who'd been sitting on the edge of the tub, near Humphrey, stood, scattering water, and left the courtyard. The tub had grown uncomfortably hot. Humphrey blushed ferociously at his own erection and glanced around to see if anyone had noticed. Nobody had. He crept from the tub and pulled the towel around him again, then went back inside through a different door, dripping.

The maze of hallways was dark, with one or two men lurking in nearly every corner. Doors stood open here and there, each with a man lounging on a cot inside. Nobody spoke. Rhythmic thumps came from behind one door, and a wet slap-slap from behind another. The idea of standing in a doorway and examining the merchandise inside was too much for Humphrey—he fled deeper into the maze.

. . .Errol Milquer, rapier at his side and cocked hat aslant his brow, slipped like an eel through the dank stone corridors of Doom Castle. From somewhere far off came the sound of water dripping, drop by slow drop, into a stagnant pool. Milquer stopped at an ironbound oaken door; a burly guard leaned snoring against the cold stone arch. Without waking the guard, Milquer used his rapier tip to lift the iron key ring from the man's belt; then he twisted the key in the rusty lock and pushed on the door. With a squealing moan, it opened a few inches. Milquer held his breath, frozen in the flickering light of an ensconced torch, but the guard only paused in his snoring for a moment, mumbled to himself, and slipped back into the depths of slumber.

Milquer wriggled through the narrow opening and crept onward into the maze of passageways beyond. At last he came to another door. This one had a single barred window in it; a quick glance told him that he'd found his way all right. Within the moldering, fetid cell, Prince Tom, rightful ruler of the land, hung in exhausted sleep from chains and manacles bolted to the wall. Milquer unlocked the heavy door and entered the room.

Prince Tom awoke with a start, eyes wide with fear. "Who—" he gasped, but Milquer was beside him in a flash, and covered the boy's mouth with his hand.

"Fear not—'tis I," said the dashing young blade. His steely grey eyes flashed in the dim torchlight, and the Prince relaxed.

Milquer removed his hand. The Prince's eyes shone. "Oh, Errol—I thought you'd never come!" he said.

"The Duke has harried me through the greenwood," Milquer said. "But I'm here now. Once you're free, the Duke will pay for his treachery." He tried the keys on the Prince's manacles as he spoke.

"With every stroke of the Duke's whip I thought of you," said Prince Tom.

A cold sneering voice, like a steel rasp, came from the doorway behind them. "How sweet. It seems my bait has captured a mouse!" Milquer whirled. Framed in the doorway stood the powerful form of Duke Doom, arms akimbo, studded leather gauntlets on his fists.

"You're mine at last, Milquer!" continued the Duke. "And you shall be punished for your crimes against the State. Guards!" A pair of giant brutes stepped into the cell. "Chain him well. I shall return to whip him in a few moments . . ."

Humphrey rounded a corner and stumbled into a brightly lit hallway. A bald man covered in tattoos caught him and helped him regain his balance, then smiled at him and moved on. Humphrey could still feel the man's cool touch on his shoulders. Shivering, he walked past the mirrored weight room and into the video lounge. A wildly improbable scenario was being played out on screen, something about an airplane pilot and a handsome young hijacker. Humphrey moved on, into the steam room.

As he walked in, steam jets hissed to life. He could see no more than a couple of feet in any direction. Whispers and grunts from all around were the only sign that he was not alone. He groped his way to a bench and sat down, letting his towel shift to show more of his leg to the invisible room.

. . . Sherlock Milquer stalked through the narrow streets of the seaside town of Muddleton, magnifying glass in one hand and meerkat pipe in the other. His deerstalker cap was firmly settled on his handsome head.

In the distance, the muffled moan of a foghorn sounded. The fog was thick tonight in Muddleton; the Grey Eel would be out tonight. The Eel was a slippery devil who would approach innocent young men on foggy nights and do unspeakable things to them. Milquer had determined to bring the criminal to justice.

He stopped at the entrance to an alleyway. The fog was thicker in the alley, and darker, but he'd heard a faint sound, as of labored breathing. He stepped cautiously into the alley, and was enveloped in thick billows of fog.

Suddenly, Milquer's plaid cape was plucked from his shoulders. He whirled—but there was nobody behind him. His jacket split down the middle of the back, cut by an invisible knife, and slipped in two halves down his arms.

Milquer spun again but there was no sign of the Eel. "I know you're out there," Milquer said. His suspenders parted, sliced through, and his trousers dropped to the ground. His shirt split the way his jacket had, and Sherlock Milquer, master detective, stood nude and defenseless in the fog.

And then the Grey Eel's touch was all over Milquer's body, like a thousand feathers brushing against his skin. Milquer gasped, eyes closed, mouth open, engulfed in sensation. Warm breath in one ear, then the flicker of a tongue, soft and warm, on the other. The briefest of sharp nips at the nape of Milquer's neck; his breathing quickened. A light flickering touch, snake tongues and butterfly wings, down his spine, and across the tight-curled hair of his chest. Another tiny sharp bite on his left nipple; Milquer made a small sound, almost a whimper. His cock pulsed, hard and upright. The soft touch flickered across his firm stomach, almost touched his cock but then slipped past, down the front of his thighs. A momentary pause, and then a soft, warm exhalation made his balls shiver. He opened his eyes, reached forward, but all he could see or touch was mist. That teasing tongue again, flickering oh so briefly around his asshole, and then licking once hard along the undersurface of his balls before vanishing again. And then, when Milquer felt he could bear it no longer, the sudden shock of a warm wet mouth engulfing his anxious cock. Milquer felt dizzy at the rush of warmth. He kept his hands at his sides, afraid the mouth would vanish again if he reached out. Any idea of apprehending the Eel had vanished, along with all other rational thought. The master of rational deduction surrendered to pure sensation as the superbly controlled tongue, lips, and teeth worked their magic. Milquer's cock fit perfectly into the other man's mouth. He bucked against the invisible presence, and the Eel's mouth and head shifted in response, sliding up and down along the shaft, swirling tongue around the head and glans and then down again swift and inevitable as a waterfall. Milquer came to the edge of orgasm and hung there, suspended in a world of mist that had narrowed to this single point of time. Then that amazing tongue flicked, once, precisely, against the eye of Milquer's cock, and a flood tore through him, releasing his pent-up cum in a thick spray that . . .

"Hey, guy, watch where you're pointing that thing," a voice said from the steam next to Humphrey. The voice was friendly, but more amused than interested. Humphrey, mortified, his cock shrivelling in his hand, wiped up cum with his towel and beat a hasty retreat.

Humphrey pushed open the outer door of The Secret Garden, and wandered dejectedly to the curb, where he stood for a moment gazing unseeing at the dirty street.

Finally he glanced at his wrist, then remembered he'd left his watch at home. Damn. He looked up and saw the motorcycle cop still seated impassively in front of The Secret Garden doors. Humphrey took half a hesitant step forward. "Uh . . . excuse me . . ."

The cop glanced up—not at all stern and angry as Humphrey had expected, but with a look of friendly interest.

"Excuse me, I was wondering . . . that is, I left my watch at home . . ." He gestured at his empty wrist, feeling his face flushing. "Um, could you tell me what time it is?"

"Sure." The cop lifted a muscular arm and looked at his wrist. "It's five 'til midnight."

"Oh. Okay. Uh, thanks." He'd stayed in there long enough, he'd given it a good shot, it just hadn't worked out. Humphrey turned to walk back to his car.

"Hey, hold on a sec," the cop said from behind him.

Humphrey stiffened. It wasn't illegal to go in there, was it? Couldn't be—the cop had been here all along. What had he done? Flushing, he looked back.

The cop was smiling. "Listen . . . I'm getting off shift soon, and I'm horny as hell from hearing all these guys go by all night. How about a drink?"

Humphrey swallowed, looked at his feet, glanced up at the officer's broad friendly smile, looked at his feet again. "Uh . . . I . . . I guess so. Sure." He started to smile as the words sank in. He looked up again, grinning now. "Yeah. That'd be great!"

"Great," the officer said. "It'll just be a couple minutes 'til my replacement comes—by the way, my name's Tom—what's yours?"

The Final Fuck:
The Parting of Legs and Ways

Cher Ladd-Vuolo

You said it was over.

Accepting of this.
Accepting of you.
I never could say no to
your bizarre requests.
And so, a parting of our ways
includes the parting of
my thighs.

No blood or sweat.
Just tears.

Come then say goodbye.

And as your urgency grows and
presses into my belly,
so does the notion that
I am being
fucked goodbye.

Emotions emerging from
blackened jeans
and I give you the last of me.

A wet, warm place in which to enter,
a long, hard way
to say we're through.

You never knew the way to
my heart,
taking this route over and over
like a misguided traveler.
Yet I guide you into me knowing
this will not last,
nor will we.

Plummeting into the depths of
warm, stirring waves,
I am convinced you are trying to
reach my mind.
Convinced you are probing me
to know what I am
thinking.

Coming means going
and that is all I know.

I know with this fond farewell,
I am truly fucked.
Mind, body and soul.

You flip me over to take the
road less traveled,
and my gentle curves provide
the map that leads you home.

Home, to where I bleed.
Home, to where I need.

In the pulling of my red and raven locks,
I pretend you are pulling me
back into your life.

Pull harder and call me "bitch",
how dare I leave you.
Pull harder and say my name.
How dare I walk out that door.

Pull harder . . .
and leave behind a souvenir of
seed and sorrow that you
plant in this,
my rainforest.

When the door clicks in the lock,
I play in a puddle of you.
Splashing in the rain of
white ribbon on my
satiny blue bed.

I cannot see beyond the waters
that flow from my eyes,
my thighs.

And then, the realization,
I've been fucked goodbye.

How To Make A Strawberry Sundae

Bill Noble

Years ago, when a dear friend bicycled off to campus to turn in her thesis—the product of years of struggle—we set the phone tree going.

In ones and twos, friends slipped in the door of our big, stately, shared home in the Berkeley hills. The heat was cranked up; a fire crackled to life in the fireplace; candles were lit. The table was dragged into the middle of the kitchen and transformed with foam pads, rolled towels and a red gingham tablecloth. Our purpose? The creation of a human strawberry sundae.

Nancy and Sam brought the berries, a stewpot full of them, sliced and layered with sugar, and set in the sun for a day to grow syrupy and lascivious. They rewarmed them, to blood heat, on the stove. Terryl, Bobby and Maya, stripped to the waist like a ripe-breasted press-gang, whipped sweetened cream to a satiny froth. George, our resident aesthete, cycled Brahms, Saint-Saens, and Joni Mitchell on the stereo until, finally, the muted guitar of John Fahey rippled along our senses. Jackie, the backyard farmer, with her black, bobbed hair and luminous eyes, filled half a dozen pipes with resinous homegrown, and slender glasses with her elderflower wine.

We piled all our clothes in a corner of the living room and congregated before the fire for a ceremonial hug. Our doctoral candidate would soon return.

The surprise was ready.

That was the first of many culinary-erotic adventures, and perhaps the most memorable. It was the 60s. Love was in the air. Discovery and experiment were nearly full-time professions. Safe sex meant slowing the car to thirty as you came.

Here's how to transform someone you love into a strawberry sundae.

First, the setting. Sad as it may seem, indoors is best—mosquitoes, fruit flies and yellow jackets add unwelcome texture to any dessert time, especially one so exposed and prolonged. Have the room at 75-80 degrees. The light should be warm and a bit subdued. And these days, you have the choice of thousands of indistinguishable, inoffensive New Age albums as the background for your libidinous gluttony (though my preference is still Bach solo cello). One thing we didn't do that long ago night, and should have: cover the floor with a plastic sheet. It avoids finding your Persian cat permanently glued to the tile next morning.

Be sure of a minimum of two or three hours, undisturbed.

Next, the fruit. It's hard to beat strawberries, though dicing in a few pears and mangoes is an option. (Remember, no mango skins. They'll give you a precise equivalent of poison ivy in all your tenderest places.) It takes 6-8 pints of strawberries to slather a human body satisfyingly, or one to two pints per licker and slurper. You'll be surprised how much you eat.

Slice each strawberry into 2-4 pieces. When you have an inch-thick layer in the bowl, sprinkle it with sugar. Add another layer and sprinkle again until the berries are done.

Set them in the sun, covered with cheesecloth, for about four hours. (Alternatively, warm them gently on the stove to blood temperature. *Don't* cook them. Wrap the bowl in a thick towel for 3 or 4 hours.) The sugar will draw the juices from the berries, making exactly the right amount of a magnificent blush-red syrup.

To a quart of heavy cream, add 4 tablespoons of sifted confectioner's sugar and a scant tablespoon of vanilla extract. Whip the cream to the soft peak stage.

Undress the sundae person in a teasing, ritualized way. If their hair is long, put it up carefully, and keep it dry. Give them a sensual, languid shower—being careful, of course, not to get too carried away this early in the evening. The exact details of this part of the preparation will depend on how many bodies your shower can hold, though it will hold more than you think. Ask the sundae person to close their eyes from here on. Dry them with thick, warmed towels as if their entire skin surface is erotic (it is, of course).

Lead them to the table. Lay them down. Make them comfortable, but don't give them any hint of what's about to happen; ideally, you'll have been building mystery and anticipation for hours. Remind them to keep their eyes closed. Give everything a bit of an edge, a whiff of danger, a heady uncertainty.

The strawberries are blood-warm. How you begin with them should be utterly tuned to the person on the table. Do they like to dive right in? Do they need to be enticed, seduced? Are they a little intimidated, or are they shivering with arousal? How many climaxes, how quickly or slowly?

I might ladle half a cup of warm berries into, or onto, their navel.

Then the person dearest to them might slurp up a mouthful from their navel to feed to the sundae person, mouth to mouth. *Aaaah, this is about strawberries!* They will begin to understand.

Strawberries can be ladled on, or spread by hand or mouth. Hold a leisurely pace: you want the feast to last a long time. Keep feeding the sundae person with mouths, fingers, berry-laden breasts. Use your imagination. Use theirs!

You'll know when it's time to add whipped cream. Let it be a cool contrast to the warm berries and mouths. Cool, but not shocking. The whipped cream will cling to places the sugary berries wouldn't, so new possibilities open up. If you have access to erect penises at this point (and you may), they're nearly perfect for dolloping cream on nipples, or sliding a sweet, other-worldly taste onto a receptive palate or a hungry tongue. Whipped cream in eye sockets guarantees no peeking, and licking it out is as tender a thing as one of us can do to another.

The recipe stops here, at the place where the vast mathematics of imagination and arousal take over.

Strawberries inside vaginas may not be a great idea, so be cautious (I'm assuming you already know that no one involved in this feast has a strawberry allergy). A fairly ripe, peeled banana is a lovely thing to stroke any species of genitals with—and then to slide, strawberry-slippery, into a panting mouth.

Before I lose your attention altogether (you're getting very distracted, aren't you?), a few alternatives. If your feast progresses to full-on lovemaking, another sensual shower might be a good idea along the way; it'll save you hours of cleanup the next day. And bear in mind that interaction between pleasure-deliverers is always encouraged. Don't get too narrowly focused. A final whipped-cream suggestion, too: an erection can be concealed entirely in a huge, floating, snowy cloud of it. This may be the time to have your victim, female or male, open their eyes. It's an amazing way to be penetrated, and an equally amazing way to be vigorously fondled.

I'm sure I don't have to tell you about chocolate syrup, the fragrant flesh of sun-warmed apricots, painting bellies with dull-ripe ollalieberries, or any of the things that can be done with peeled grapes and toes. You'll have already thought of those.

Feast well, love well, and blow out the candles before you sleep.

Flash Poetry

Gary Blankenship

Crowded elevator,
crowded to the back,
wall to left,
another body behind.

Perfume,
after shave,
cologne,
baby powder,
sweat
mingle by the 5th floor
29 to go.

Stop at 6,
one off—two on,
at 7, two off, three on,
27 to go.

Stop at 8,
delay as the front shuffles,
a hand caresses my butt;
at 9,
fingernails stroke my thigh.

Stop at 10,
an argument over
"you sure this is *really* the right floor?"
The hand forces my legs open
until it touches my balls,
at 11,
someone coughs,
the sound of a zipper hid.

Stop at 12,
the hand,
long fingernails,
run along my cock;
at 13,
the nails touch skin.

Stop at 14,
a whisper from her throat,
"Don't move or turn around."
The nails prick my head.
"Or I will quit."
At 15, her hand begins to move
my foreskin
slowly.

Stop at 16,
then faster, as she said,
"I want your cock in me."
I shift.
"No," the whisper urgent,
"Don't move at all."
At 17,
the skin moves faster.
"And you to suck my nipples."

Stop at 18,
"But not before I lick your balls."
My cum rises,
a leak appears.
At 19,
her fingers urgent.
I nearly stop breathing.

Stop at 20,
"And your tongue is in me."
The leak larger,
I shudder.
"Oh, the man is ready to squirt."
At 21,
she squeezes.
The elevator still crowded,
but not packed.

Stop at 22,
"Come in me, baby.
Come in my cunt."
I lean back
before I fall.
She smells of Opium.
At 23,
the leak is steady,
my tip is wet.
"Hold, it, my man.
Wait."

Stop at 24,
several out,
she squeezed.
"Fuck me harder,
NOW!"

At 25,
"Get out at 29,
my stop is 31,
and I don't want to be caught
with your cock in my hand."

Stop at 26,
she rubs my cock
from head to balls.
Her tits felt through our coats.
At 27,
the elevator half empty,
"Meet me in the stairs at 30."
My juice leaks.

Stop at 28, her hand
squeezes one last time.
"We'll finish fucking on the stairs.
At 29, her hand
releases me
and withdraws,
quickly.

I rush past
the others to the stairs
and wait
and wait,
my zipper open,
my cock hard,
my pants stained.

Until in the men's room at 30,
I find an empty stall.

Go Large

Mike Kimera

I watch my new lover as she studies her body in the mirror. I am in the adjoining bathroom, and she is not aware that I can see her as she hefts one breast, pouts and splays her thighs to display the sticky evidence of our recent coupling.

Lois has a substantial body, and she revels in it. She knows that she looks much better naked than clothed. Her pale skin is soft and smooth. No bones are visible, only bold curves and luscious folds of flesh. Her nipples are psychedelic pink snowcaps atop mountainous breasts. The space between her formidable thighs and the escarpment of her belly is thickly forested with shiny dark hair.

Yet it is the warm pastures of her buttocks that I yearn for, to sink my fingers into that elastic flesh and feel her strength, to lower my mouth to her upraised invitation and navigate by tongue the dark, aromatic crevasse.

We have been lovers for only two days. I am infatuated.

I shouldn't even be here, but my secretary, Sarah, who mothers me even though I am older than her, engineered this working vacation. Having decided that I had been working too hard, she accepted an invitation for me to attend a technology briefing here in Cannes. Even more deliberately, she booked me on a Sunday flight although the conference won't begin until Tuesday. Even in November, this is a pleasant place, though a little empty. I could almost believe that all the fashionable people left when they heard I was coming.

But wait. How rude of me. Here I am sharing this story and I haven't yet introduced myself. My name is Clarke Kent. No Really. My mother was a slightly scatty woman who chose the name because it sounded familiar. She had no idea of its provenance.

At 39, I have never been married, although I have had two relationships with women and one rather discouraging hour with a prostitute.

The first of my lovers was Joan. She and I were at school together, but she left me after 4 years. I was a nice man, she said, "but boring." After Joan, there was Sally. We worked together, and she wooed me and bedded me, then left me to move to a new position in the company's New York offices. She said I was too afraid to grab hold of life, and that was the end of Sally. Mandie, the prostitute, just said "Never mind, luv—it happens to people all the time." She even offered to charge me a lower fee.

I tell you this so that you will realize that, even when I take my glasses off, I am not Superman.

Two nights ago, I found myself in Cannes, dining alone in the hotel restaurant, with a romantic view of the sunset that seemed completely wasted on me—and Lois came into my life.

"You don't mind if I join you, do you? I don't speak French and I like to talk while I eat." All of this was said as she seated herself between me and the setting sun.

She was wearing a red T-shirt dress, big but still clinging to her form. The words, "GO LARGE" were printed across it at a 45 degree angle, in huge jagged black letters. As I struggled for a suitable response, trying not to show how pleased I was, I was transfixed by the nipple of her right breast. It formed a prominent punctuation mark in the center of the letter O.

"And how did you know I spoke English?" I asked.

She laughed and said, "Well, you could hardly be

French."

She noted my raised eyebrow (too many Roger Moore movies in my youth I'm afraid) and understood the interrogative interjection that it was meant to be.

"Well, Watson, firstly you have no wine on the table," she explained. "Dining in France and drinking only water with your food is like getting to an orgy and then declaring your celibacy. Everybody wonders why you didn't just stay home. Secondly, there is the matter of the clothing: this season's GAP you-can-wear-this-without-offending-anyone range of casual wear, not a typical French choice. But, the most obvious sign of course is the English language copy of *Harry Potter and the Goblet of Fire* that you've put on the table to keep people from joining you."

"!" I said, silently.

"I take it you're here for the conference," she continued. "You have that nerd-made-good look. My name is Lois. Lois Lewes. My mother valued alliteration."

She looked away from me, summoned the waiter by raising her hand and, in the process, rearranged the topography of her dress. I couldn't take my eyes from her breasts. I knew it was rude, perhaps even pathetic, but I was hypnotised by the sheer mass involved.

"That was your cue. You're supposed to tell me your name now," Lois said. "My face is up here, by the way. "

"Clarke Kent," I said, and my cheeks reddened as I struggled to keep my eyes focused above her neck.

"Yeah, right. That's a new line. I haven't heard that before," she laughed.

"No, really, it's my name," I replied, with an it's-not-my-fault tone.

"Cool. Now I feel like one of those characters in '*Magnolia*,' linked by some huge chain of coincidence that challenges the nature of free will. Watch out for flying frogs."

Now it was my turn to laugh.

"I'm rather afraid that our waiter, who probably hasn't seen the movie, thinks that you've just used a derogatory term in reference to French pilots," I said.

"Screw him."

"I'd rather screw you," I said.

The moment the words left my mouth, I wondered who had said them. I wanted to look around for the culprit and give him a good thrashing. The easy, rapid pace of the conversation, combined with the impact of Lois's physical presence, had made me giddy. What had I done? I almost expected her to toss my glass of water in my face.

"I'm sorry . . ." I started, lamely.

Lois was no longer smiling. She was looking into me, carefully, as if searching for something. I felt like she was the one with X-ray vision, and I had no secrets. With speed surprising for her size, her hand moved under the table and found my erection. The sun seemed brighter than ever. I breathed.

"Oh," she said. "If this is you on mineral water, just wait until we get to the Bordeaux."

Then her hand was gone, back on her side of the table, but the place where she had touched me still tingled, and I knew there was now a wet spot on my GAP easy-fit chinos.

The conversation slowed to a canter after that. Over the next three courses, I learned that Lois was an MIT graduate, with technical expertise that made her a hot property in the telecommunications market. Like me, she was here for the conference. Unlike me, she had no intention of attending. She was going to "scalp some data," as she put it, give her name to a few recruiters, and have a damned good time. In our conversation, there was no mention of a significant other.

I charged the bill to my room. Lois checked the room number and said, "We'll go to my room. It has a better view."

I paused, surprised. Women don't react this way to me. Oh, sure, they have dinner with me, because I'm a "nice man," and a good listener. But, at the end of the meal, it's traditional for them to find someone who will show them a good time.

"Are you sure?" I said, sounding prim and ever so English to my own ears. "We've only just met . . ."

"No," she said. "So far, we've talked. We'll meet when we get to my room and take our clothes off." The waiter chose that moment to pick up the bill. I blushed.

Lois was standing now. "So, have you changed your mind?" she asked. "Or are you waiting for us to be formally introduced?"

She was smiling, but I glimpsed some vulnerability there. For once in my clumsy life, I did the right thing. I kissed her. Then I did it again.

Her room was a suite with a beautiful view of the Mediterranean. I didn't notice. As soon as we entered the room, Lois pulled the dress up and over her head. Her body glowed, and I was blinded by the heat from her. She smiled and knelt in front of me, unzipping my trousers without comment. I was about to have oral sex and I hadn't even had to ask, never mind beg. Then I came, all over her hand. I was mortified.

Lois laughed, a hearty, full-blooded sound, still holding my shrinking cock. If she had let go at that moment, I think I would have run from the room.

"Well, Clarke, that was faster than a speeding bullet," she mused. Grinning, she licked my sperm from her hand. "Now, let's see if we can find the man of steel." She moved her mouth onto my cock and flicked the underside with her tongue.

I should have been ecstatic, but in truth I was deeply depressed. I knew what would happen now. I would stay soft, she would get frustrated, then angry. And then she would tell me that I was a nice man, but it was time for me to leave.

"Ah," Lois said, sitting back on her heels, letting go of my cock. "It's like that, is it?" I felt dismal. She had gone from lust to leave in a couple of seconds.

She stood up. I took a last look at her glorious body and prayed that my limp flesh would choose that moment to show its appreciation. It didn't.

"I should go." I said.

"No," she replied. "You can't go until you come; and you will come."

"What?"

"I know what you need. We'll soon get rid of the Kryptonite effect. Just leave it to Lois." She folded her arms and let one hip jut out. "Now *strip,*" she ordered.

No one had ever spoken to me like that. It felt weird. It felt good. I undressed. Lois tapped her foot impatiently as I started to fold my clothes, so I just let them fall to the floor. After a few moments, I was standing naked with my hands demurely held over my shrinking genitals.

"Put your hands behind your back and kneel", Lois commanded. I didn't question, but did as she asked.

Lois reached out and grabbed my nipple, twisted it briefly. "Good boy," she said, pushing her thumb into my mouth. I suckled obediently.

"I'm going to tie you now, Clarke." Lois was circling me, and from somewhere produced three scarves. She used one to tie my hands behind my back, pressing her breasts against my shoulders. Her luxuriant pubic fur brushed against my hands as she bound me with the scarf. Still pressed close against me, she folded a scarf and placed it over my eyes, tying it securely behind my head.

I felt excited, yet surprisingly relaxed. I gave myself up to Lois and her three scarves. Thus blindfolded and bound, all I could do was wait.

I must have sighed. Lois whispered in my ear, "One more, and you are mine."

Her fingernails scraped over my chest, down my belly. I felt her fingers move around my balls, pulling down gently but firmly. When she tied the final scarf there, my cock rose like a balloon filled rapidly with helium.

"You're mine now Clarke, until you come. And that won't happen for a long time yet."

Her voice was in front of me now. "Open wide, Clarke."

I did, and my mouth was filled with the satin-smooth warmth of her breast. She pushed into me until I was overcome by her flesh. It became difficult to breathe, as she held fast to the back of my head with one hand, and twisted my nipple with the other. But it was wonderful. My cock was so hard now that it throbbed in time with my pulse.

"Much better," Lois purred. "Now let's see if you're a good fit."

She withdrew her breast, allowing me breathe but gaping blindly for more flesh to suckle. Effortlessly, Lois pushed me onto my side, then rolled me onto my back, trapping my arms beneath me.

I smelled her cunt as she lowered herself to my mouth, and then I tasted it. Tangy. Salty. Like the earth and the sea combined. Without waiting for her command, I started to lick. Her thighs tightened against my cheeks. Her moans reached my ears as tremors rather than sounds, each one exciting me more. Just as my tongue began to tire, she moved down my body and took a firm grip on my cock. "Is it a bird? Is it a plane?" Lois murmured, stroking my swollen flesh with each question. "No! It's Supercock!" she proclaimed, lowering herself onto me at that instant.

Her muscles were a surprise, holding as tightly as a handshake, but slick and hot. Lois rode me and rode me, and then rode me some more. She was relentless, and I was her flesh dildo, her sex toy. And I loved it.

As she felt her orgasm approach, she released the scarf that bound my testicles. My cock erupted. I found myself yelling "*YEEEEEEEE GODDDDDDS*." I had never come so forcefully before. Never.

Lois pulled off the blindfold and the light hurt my eyes.

When I finally was able to look at her, she smiled down at me, pink and sweaty.

"Well" she said. "Do you still want to leave?"

"It would be rude to leave now," I responded. "I've only just come."

After two days of room-service and continuous sex, I'm exhausted but happy. Lois is just getting her second wind. I'm certain that neither of us will be going to the conference.

Sorry, I'll have to go now. I can hear Lois moving around, getting out of the bed. And any minute now, she will release me from the towel rack I'm handcuffed to.

Sex in Space: Finding The Zero-G Spot

Naomi Darvell

Space—the Final Frottage, er, Frontier, I mean. This intrepid reporter recently explored sex in space and discovered—a NASA document about doing the wild thing aboard the Shuttle. A quick read-through revealed that, as with more Earth-bound foolings around, the two main difficulties were—you guessed it—controlling thrust, and trying to keep your partner from drifting away.

"The female's buttocks were against the male's groin, while her knees straddled his chest. Of the approaches tried with an elastic belt, this was by far the most satisfactory. Entry was difficult, but after the female discovered how to lock her toes over the male's thighs, it was found that she could obtain the necessary thrusting motions. The male found that his role was unusually passive but pleasant."

Elastic belt? All that the high-tech inventors at NASA apparently could come up with to prevent "no gravity drift" when coupled was . . . an elastic belt? Sheesh! That's when I began to think "Wait a minute, could this NASA document be . . . faking it?"

Of course, the article wasn't the first to deal with rocket-ship rogering. As early as 1973, Isaac Asimov published a paper called "Sex in Space." Recently, more people have been speculating about weightless sex. Elaine Lerner actually tried to sell NASA the design for a sex belt she called the "Belt to Paradise." Another space-sexer suggested a pair of underpants made to fit two people, complete with four leg-holes. As I got more into it, my exploration began to feel like The Three Stooges Meet Major Tom.

Back at the now suspicious NASA document, I read that another proposed method of navigating some space nookie was a foam tunnel that the horny astronauts slid inside like a womb room.

"An inflatable tunnel enclosing and pressing the partners together. The partners faced each other in the standard missionary posture. The tunnel enclosed the partners roughly from the knees to waist and pressed them together with an air pressure of approximately 0.01 standard atmospheres.

"A general disadvantage of the inflatable tunnel approach was that the tunnel itself tended to get sticky with sweat and other discharges. We feel that the difficulty of keeping a tunnel clean in zero-G makes these solutions most unsatisfactory."

Oh, yeah, I almost forgot about "discharges" in zero-G gravity. Floating sticky stuff like blobby clouds would sure spice up the video transmissions back to Houston.

Another source chimed in that a good solution to the zero-G problem might be to have more than two people: an extra to hold one partner in place while the other did the fucking. Hmmm, zero-G sex began to sound like an opportunity for real experimentation.

The qualities for future astronauts might have to radically change. "Do you have strong voyeuristic urges?" "Have you ever held someone down while another screwed them silly?"

The more I thought about it, the more the physical aspects of weightless sex seemed to be only the beginning. During a long space mission, usually with more men than women, real sex and relationship issues are bound to arise. Lack of privacy, jealousy, and clashing of values will have to be negotiated in ways that will challenge people's inner space in outer space.

In the course of finding solutions to sex in space, who is to say our paradigms of sex won't change? When "plain vanilla" boy-girl sex suddenly becomes the least feasible kind — because the person on top is apt to float away—people determined to have sex will be going in alternative directions. Solitary sex or group sex might look suddenly attractive. Or astronauts might try Tantric sex, orgasmless sex or—why not?—various forms of cybersex and virtual sex.

After all, cybering has changed many people's entire experience of sex here on Earth. They go online as another gender; have intercourse that's not physical intercourse; commit adultery that's not adultery.

People have been imagining innovative space sex for some time, in literature and especially online. Think of the long tradition of Star Trek fan-fiction, in which women writers use the bodies of Kirk and Spock to enact their fantasies. Something about space travel has always made people think of transcending the more mundane barriers like male-female and hetero-homo.

No wonder the putative NASA reports were solid-fueling everyone's fantasies. Allegations even floated around in the media for awhile of two female cosmonauts going at it on a Russian ship, and of a British woman drifting within Mir in a pink nightie.

NASA quickly disclaimed the reports. But sex educator Raymond Noonan just as quickly pointed out that they sounded like they were in denial. NASA just doesn't want to talk about sex in space. Has the old "don't ask, don't tell" policy in the U.S. military invaded space? Such an attitude of Puritanism seems like a refusal to see that people are sexual even when they are in government-sponsored programs.

Investigating further—it's what we reporter-types do—I

soon discovered that the NASA document in question, elastic belts and all, was really a well-written satire. Darn—just another urban legend. But I wasn't alone in being taken in at first. In a book titled *The Final Mission*, Pierre Kohler claimed to have discovered a report about sex experiments on the Space Shuttle. Yep, same document. Oh, well—maybe somewhere, like in that big mysterious government warehouse where Indiana Jones's Ark, Mulder's space ships, and a few other top-secret goodies are kept, there really *is* a NASA report on Sex in Space.

In any case, there's something too provocative about sex in space to dismiss the idea just like that. In a way, it's like the excitement people felt over John Glenn's latest mission. Glenn changed our view of aging when he went back into space after so many years being earth-bound. And the freedom to re-imagine sex, especially as we all age and keep looking toward the stars, is an appealing one indeed.

I couldn't resist a last look at the document that had fooled me for a few enticing moments. Heck, maybe it did fool me a little longer. I saw something I'd missed before. This was the very last of the sexual positions supposedly tried in the Shuttle experiments:

"10) Each partner gripping the other's head between their thighs and hugging the other's hips with their arms. This was the only run involving non-procreative marital relations, and it was included largely because it provided the greatest number of distinct ways for each partner to hold the other. This 4-points redundant hold was good enough that we found this solution to be most satisfactory. In fact, it was more rewarding than analogous postures used in a gravitational field."

Leave it to the writer of "NASA 14-307-1792" to describe my favorite position without once mentioning the number 69. Enough with the future stuff: I wanted to blast off in the present. I tossed the report to one side and got out my own personal "Buzz Lightyear." It's shaped like a rocket ship, too. As enticing as Sex in Space may be, it's always good to know you don't need to leave your own bedroom to travel to Infinity and beyond.

Arianne

Helena Settimana

I am sitting on the beach with my hand shading my eyes, watching as Arianne emerges from the sea. Her skin is the colour of cinnamon and is sprinkled with diamonds; the water is showering gems off her fingertips, between her legs. She is walking up the shingle toward me, naked, gorgeous, like a water weed, swaying, serpentine, sinuous.

Arianne is beautiful. She says that she does not see it, and thinks that she looks horsey, but she is not. She is strong, with wide shoulders that are not bony or overly big. Light brown hair sprinkled with copper where the sun catches it, and gooseberry green eyes. Freckles, too, across her nose. She looks like a classical goddess, or one of those heroic women in the sculptures of the Reich. That itself embarrasses her, as does her name. She is always trying to say that she is not really German, not born there, but her looks, her name and her presence all contradict her. I don't get into it with her, that's her bag. But sometimes I wonder if that is why she is hanging with me, because I am so different from her. Perhaps she is atoning for a sin she did not commit, except by association. Aryan guilt. But I never ask, as if by asking, this intoxication would vanish like the smoke rings I am blowing into the air.

I am in love with Arianne. Somehow I can't tell her, and I doubt she knows just how. She comes and sits with me, familiarly. The pebbles on the beach are exceedingly hot where our straw mats do not reach. We are drinking cold retsina from a thermos, smoking Marlboroughs, and gazing out over the hazy sea, slightly drunk. There are hills all around this little bay. They look like mounds of bleached bones, bristling with cypress and pine. Across the water we can see a chapel, stark white against the ecru-coloured peninsula, which juts across the cove like an accusing finger.

She smells good. The light is very strong, and the scent that is rising from her is the scent of skin baked by the sun. You know? Like the smell of rain hitting a hot dusty pavement. We are talking close, sitting side by side. There is really no one around here at the end of summer, when most of the tourists have fled. Some nights we ride into town where there is still a raucous night life. We walk past the tavernas on the quay and scores of heads turn to watch us as we go by. They look hungry, these watchers. Hungry, dangerous, aroused. Once or twice we have witnessed a couple making love in the shadows in a bar, or off the road under the trees. It feels like the last days of Rome in this place. The country is quieter.

There is a pesky kid hanging around us—a local. We hurry to cover ourselves when we see him approach. He's wearing blue jeans cut off at mid-thigh and appears to be about fifteen or sixteen years old. He has dark curly hair and the face of a young satyr, like some boy from a Caravaggio painting. Give him a few more years and he will look positively corrupt. He wanders by a lot, splashing in the water and then back out. He runs up to us, poses, laughs, and dashes down the beach. We laugh at his antics. Earlier in the day he brought us a snake that he had captured. I think he wanted to see if we would scream and run in panic. Arianne said, blowing smoke from her nostrils, "Oh, cool," and looked away. He went off, looking disappointed, and disappeared from sight.

To save money, we took a pension room, with one bed. It is wide enough, raised on a dais in a corner of the whitewashed cell. For ten days I have lain beside her, shoving aside my desire to reach out and touch her; fearful that I might send her bolting like a doe into the night. When I hear her breathing become regular and deep, I roll over and watch her sleep. Lying beside her torments me so. I hazard a gentle touch, a caress. Her skin feels like chamois, rich, smooth. If my desire is too strong I will make myself come, imagining that velvety skin, her mouth, her hands there, there and there. Once I woke her, with my cries. She mentioned it to me the next morning. I told her that I had a dream.

So we are here on the pebble beach, alone, scanning for dolphins breaking the horizon, telling little jokes and secrets. We are laughing, and my face is in the curve of her neck, tickled by her hair. I kiss her there, quickly and playfully, and she looks at me with something like alarm in her eyes. I turn away and say, "Sorry, sorry, must be the wine," or something like that. The colour is high in her face.

She is on her feet, saying that she is hot and needs to cool off again. She lopes toward the water, through the shallows until just deep enough to dive in. I follow her. She is floating on her back, with her hair fanned out around her face, like a mermaid. Under the surface there is so much life, little brilliant fish, spiny sea urchins, a lone, candy-pink jellyfish. I dive under her, and splash her, and she splashes back until we are shrieking with laughter and I think the moment of discomfort on the shore has been forgotten.

It is just shallow enough to stand here, if one does it on tiptoe. When a large swell tumbles through the bay, it lifts us high off of the bottom and we glide with its current like seahorses, then dive together. The water glides over our skin like oil, neutrally warm on the surface, cooler beneath. We surface face to face, en pointe. A swell rolls through us again, and when we come to rest once more, we are touching; belly to belly and breast to breast. She slides one arm around my waist. Then the other. She is pressing the small of my back where my buttocks merge with my spine, pulling me closer, tighter. Her legs twine around mine as she pulls herself up so that I can feel the velvety softness of her sex on my thigh, and her mouth is seeking mine. She is saying, "Oh, Mimi, tell me it is true, tell me that you love me, tell me that this is what you want." My eyes are feathered with kisses that feel like the beat of a moth's wings. I kiss her mouth and explore the soft centre, the hard edges of her teeth, her tongue. She tastes like pine trees and cool groves. I can't speak and I can scarcely move, crippled with such a heaviness in my legs, in my womb. We move like sleepwalkers, back toward the beach.

The boy is there again. He is standing amongst the pine trees and scrub that is growing where the shingle ends. I can see him, watching us, his face congested with blood and his mouth slack and wet. He is not really hidden, but this time I doubt he will rush up to us to pose and flirt and run away. He looks catatonic. His erection is showing clearly under his jeans, and he is clutching and squeezing it through the denim. It seems far too big for his adolescent frame. When Arianne sees him, she takes my hand firmly and we collect our clothing and our things. It is a short walk to the pension. Taking the path back to the village, I look over my shoulder; far below in the shadow of the trees, he is standing, watching us ascend.

The stark room has an icon over the door, illuminated by a single green light like the ones used to decorate Christmas trees. It is of the Virgin in an attitude of benediction. Lucky us. Arianne stands still in the middle of the room, and raises her hands above her head, to help me pull her cotton beach shift over her head. Light filters through the louvered wooden shades, and casts a pattern of sun and shadow across her body. I stand close to her, inhaling her scent, tracing the contours of her body with my fingertips, blindly. My hands look dark, walnut brown, against the cinnamon toast colour she has achieved under the sun. She comments that we are as a reflection of the light and shade from the window.

I am kissing her face, kissing Arianne whom I love and

desire. On a silver chain she wears a small blue glass eye which rests between her breasts. It is to keep away the evil eye; for protection. I trace the contour of her shoulders with my lips; trace my way with slow deliberateness to the spot where the amulet lies. When I begin to suckle at her breast she begins to moan and gasp, her green eyes rolling under fluttering eyelids, and she grasps one of my hands with hers, placing it firmly between her legs. She is warm and fluid, slippery, tumescent. I roll her clit between my fingers. It is hard and prominent. More than anything, this pleases me. It is so obvious, and unlike most women's. Her hips are rocking into the palm of my hand and my fingers are opening the mouth of her sex, gently.

I tell her that I want to taste her, that I want to taste her loving what we are doing. Her breath catches and her hips rise harder into my hand. I slide down her length, to the thatch of tawny hair bristling between her legs. She is glistening. Little beads of moisture festoon the fine hair there. She smells musky and watery. She tastes like the sea, brilliant little fish. Her lips don't need parting, she is wide open and they lay back like the wings of a butterfly. I lick her clit, trace its hooded length, down both sides and underneath; she responds by pushing it up closer to my mouth. She is murmuring something ecstatic, like a mantra, the same words over and over again. I can't make them out. It sounds like an incantation, a prayer.

I slide one, then two fingers inside of her, pressing upward, firmly. She pours honey into my palm and I put my wet fingers to her face and mouth saying, "Smell . . . taste . . . that is you, that is your desire." My lips are in her ear telling her how much I have wanted her, and how beautiful she is, and that I really want to love her right here on this bed at the end of summer with only the icon over the door and the whitewashed walls as our witnesses. She is inarticulate. I'm saying to her, "Squeeze your tits, push them up so I can see them real good. I want to rub my clit on your nipples." And I am climbing her; straddling her chest so that I am brushing her breast and the pit of it is running into the groove of my lips, I buck on it and then slide down so that I can feel it in the opening of my sex. Her breast is slippery where I am riding it. She pushes herself down, down to where her mouth finds me pink and wet, her breath hot and moist.

She is saying that she is going to come real soon and that she wants it to be together, with me. She says that she wants to feel my lips on hers and is begging me to help her that way. I lie down away from her and our legs twine until we can feel the heat and the wet come together. She is holding my hands and rolling her hips. I can feel it all. I can feel her wetness and the thickness of her swollen lips, the hard knot of her clitoris, all of it sliding into, across and around me. Her head is back, and her mouth open, panting, *"ah, ah, ah, AH, AH!"* her breath more and more ragged, irregular.

I am coming. I can't help it: this feels so good, riding Arianne's velvet mouth, sopping wet. It starts way down deep inside and moves in a rolling wave, crashing in harsh and guttural cries that seem to come from outside of me. Arianne is screaming, crying, but I can see it is not distress, it is delirium. She is there with me thrashing and clutching with her thighs, calling for her god and her mother in the same breath; then my name louder and louder and louder, still.

There is a commotion outside of our room in the courtyard. A man is shouting hoarsely and angrily and there is the sound of overturning pails and baskets . . . a clattering across the cobblestones. We venture a peek through the shutters. Our landlord is home and has confronted the boy from the beach, who has been in the yard. The boy is lying on the cobbles under our window, trousers undone, exposed, and quite insensible. The shouting has drawn other men to the courtyard, as well as the landlord's wife who is pacing anxiously, alternately weeping and angrily shaking her fist at the kid. It is quite a scene. The men drag the boy to the street and out of sight. The landlord and his wife knock at our door, offering their apologies for the unfortunate incident, but I get from the look in their eyes that they wonder about what happened and what our role in it might have been.

No matter. In a week we are gone, skimming across the water, passing the bony whitish hills, the windmills, the chapels of this island, on our way to another, and another after that at least until the rains come. Flying fish are skimming the water off the prow of the boat, and the dolphins we had sought now run along side. It is the end of summer, and Arianne is mine.

Storm Blind in Bohemia

William Dean

Like, dig this scene. Blind in the alley as a piss-drunk dog, the supernova scribbler of the ages, man, was hanging on to the bricks and scuttling along, arched and inky fingers as crabbed as Mother Jones and twice-bit bitter. Drunk as skunks, drunk as hunks of derelict old men, dig? And like the rain and the wind were washing him away; like, the sand of his castle of lit, you know, was crumbled and drifting into the mud of his waiting nowhere. But he was game; what a game cat. And the sluice of sky juice had gripped his right thigh jeans taut around his boner because drunk as the funk of a barroom floor, he wanted to fuck.

Cats and chicks, no matter; like, what is gender when you're on a bender? Sex is king, the thing, the ring of brass or golden queer queen, dig? Old sheets and repeats of fumbles on the sandy shore with this whore or that. Copulation and fellation, sodomy was stirring in his San Francisco fogged-up brain and the rain, well, man, like the rain can't wash that clean and so he stumbled.

Out of the alley—man, this can't be Bleeker, I'm out on the other coast, can't get bleaker—on the shuffled cardboard decks of the sidewalk, soggy, sodden as some fateful drowning pack of cards some Alice tossed, he came titanic as the promise of The New Beat, simply wanting to fuck.

Upward looking, he came, eyes dripping, the sky's pelting, yeah, well, what's that? He could wear the wet welts easily; somewhere back behind were welts from the Old Man's belts, dirty old enraged and beating, beating, beating on the son that sneered. "Beat me, Daddy-o," his brain engaged itself in saying, "for I don't break I only bruise and the Old Man was just planting seeds to grow out tender plants of rhythms for my words."

"I am the thing that stalks. I am the chalk that bleeds pale dust. I am the fuck that comes out of the alley and makes you cry some other names like the low litany of lost lovers," he said softly to the rain that hit him, and then the sidewalk lurched and the building fell on him, but, dig, it was only him and the body's sudden stutter from his often grace in walking. As drunk as a circus geek on chicken blood, he lay in the close street gutter and curled himself around the question mark of who will I fuck tonight.

Whitman would have dug it in his manly hairy way. Poe would have nodded, muttered "Shit, get up and write some more, you lazy dog." There were old men poets in Europe that would have kicked his arse and so he kneed himself up and crept along the splashed curb, blind as hell and fumbling but moving still, mind aflutter with stanzas and rant.

"Goddamn, I need some soft tit to lean on," urged his raw cheek, unshaven for some weeks. "You'll get yours, but I need nipple to kiss and lick," his lips argued back. The separate pads of him—each messy, unkempt but, dig, so free from the bourgeois clamor—shouted at his mind and pushed him from behind until he stood, a weaving wreck that, desperate, pushed itself against the pushing wind. "I'm not crying, it's this pissing rain," he mumbled, and the inner riot grew quieter.

Down the block, in the halo of a storm-bent street light, ran a chick in an old battered raincoat, tucked beneath a rain-pouring umbrella, ragged as the smile of the Man in the Moon: coalesced, you dig, into every angel any writer imagined could come. Racing, one shoe after the other, wet clicks that hammered and got lost in the night.

"I am," he whispered, "the goddamn Writer of the Ages. I am not afraid," and staggered on. The beat of his heart was breaking drumsticks, was pounding fists through soft skinned bongos, was hitting, like, the world, man. "You are a beauty I have known," he recited, "on cross town buses' smoke that chokes and . . ." Christ, he lost the thread and thought abruptly, "I wanna fuck you so bad my eyes are crossed."

Down the slippery slide of the block—halved now by her momentum—she saw him stumbling and stopped. Dig this scene. Her lifted head, all shadow and blonde hair, Nordic cool eyes that hurt as they undress with vision, mouth a line of red, red wine, red roses, red fingernails that dart to her face, and, dig, not shock, you know, but recognition paints her face so suddenly softer in the oblique glint of rain. Silently—who can hear such words in the wind— her lips form the oval shapes of "Oh, baby."

Yeah, man, it was her that night. One night spent in wet caresses on his bed, one sharp delirious blowsy night with the jazzy marching raindrops assaulting the crystal panes beside the bed, with them on the bed, limbs all akimbo, tongues and mouths craving all over the hastily-toweled skin. And, man, what do you think, such scenes last forever or just are soon-chopped fodder for the grazing beasts of the beat, beat, beat that he scribbles on the sheets when he's not stumbling from the alley, drunk again?

Pussy Galore

Deborah Bacharach

The first day I wore
my Pussy Galore t-shirt
in public no one hit me.
No one spat.
A man on the bus stared. I'm sure
I saw him licking his lips.
I stared back.
A clerk told me the woman on my chest
was none other than
Nancy Sinatra strutting her
60s bikini, thigh high white boots.
The owner told me
she would have gone except.
On the street a clown
stopped juggling to read
every word about fetish a-go-go,
live sex acts women only please.
Sounds like fun
he said looking me full
in the face. I grinned,
totally naked under these damn clothes.

Body and Soul: Confessions of a Kinky Churchgoer

Rebecca Brook

A few years ago, my husband and I moved from New York, one of the centers of BDSM scene activity in the United States, to a far more modest (in every sense of the word) city out west. The landscape's a lot prettier where we are now, but only lately—literally, as I write this, in the last few weeks—have we discovered any signs of a leather community. For the past three years, we've been back in the closet, at least socially. My husband has kept himself busy working on *Prometheus* over the Net, but I found myself hungering for physical and social community. So I started doing something really kinky —going to church.

Actually, my spiritual journey began long before our move, and I might well have become a churchgoer even had we stayed in New York. Public worship wasn't a conscious substitute for scene activity. It wasn't a repudiation of it, either. All too many people in both cultures, I suspect, would consider them profoundly incompatible. But the more I think about the two worlds, the more traits—both positive and negative—they have in common.

Radical Speech

To begin with, faith and sex are both extremely fraught

subjects. Each is central to the human experience, but also very difficult to discuss openly. If you try to talk about what you do in bed, or how you worship, with anyone who doesn't share the same practices, the conversation is all too likely to end in embarrassment, anger, or hurt feelings. I've always talked about sex more openly than many of my peers, and until I joined The Eulenspiegel Society (TES), I often found myself shunned for it. I've been much shyer about discussing my faith, but when I did begin telling friends about my long, meandering conversion, a number of them, from different spiritual traditions, said, "Oh, it's such a relief to be able to talk about this! There are so few people with whom we can discuss religion!" Their voices sounded the way mine must have, when I finally joined TES and could say the word "orgasm" in public without being treated like a pariah.

The reason both faith and sex are so hard to talk about is that they both carry huge amounts of cultural and personal baggage. Each is surrounded by thickets of stereotypes; each summons forth so many wounds, fears and insecurities that it's a wonder anyone ever manages rational discussion on either topic. If you tell people you're kinky, they may assume you barbecue babies for breakfast; if you tell people you go to church, they may expect you to begin spewing fire-and-brimstone Bible verses. Whatever the judgment, too many people will pass it first and ask questions about your personal experience later. It doesn't help that both kink and faith offer such a wide range of actual practice, even once the cobwebs of prejudice have been cleared away. Sexually, I'm a married het switch; churchwise, I'm a liberal Episcopalian. Being a het switch doesn't mean that I'm not "a real player," or that I scorn, say, gay male bottoms. Being Episcopalian doesn't mean that I'm socially chilly ("God's frozen people," as a friend put it), or that I'm intolerant of my Jewish, Buddhist, Presbyterian, or Atheist friends.

In the face of so many stereotypes and so much judgment,

why do any of us do any of this at all? Why not just stay safely home on the couch? Well, because we gain so much when we get out, whether to play parties on Saturday night or to church on Sunday morning.

Radical Acceptance

For me, both the scene and the church offer the comfort of communal ritual while affirming the sacredness of the body. Many people in both cultures would find that statement startling. Too many people outside the scene believe that it's about abuse, about the degradation of women, about self-destruction. Too many people outside the church (and, indeed, a tragic number within it) equate organized religion with hatred of the body and hatred of sexuality.

As a newcomer to the scene, I was particularly nervous about going to public play parties at SM clubs like Hellfire and The Vault. I expected to see lots of men leering at scantily clad women, and I was afraid that I'd see women being scorned and objectified, treated only as fantasies and not as real people. Part of my fear stemmed from the fact that I wasn't comfortable with my own body—in the United States of Advertising, few of the women I know are—and I was afraid to expose it in public. But once I'd gone (fully clothed and cautious) to a few clubs, I found myself in a world nearly one hundred eighty degrees away from my preconceptions. At Hellfire and The Vault, I saw all kinds of bodies, in all states of dress: old and young, thin and wide, buff and drooping. And I saw that I was in a world where it didn't matter what you looked like: what mattered about your body was what you did with it and how that felt. As a result, I was finally able to begin accepting my own body, even though it was a bit too flabby here and a bit too skinny there.

At its best, the scene moves beyond mere acceptance of the body (as important and radical as that is) into love and reverence, into sacred space. One of the first times I got the courage to bottom in public, I was lying on a bondage table, blindfolded and still mostly clothed, while my husband gently spanked and flogged me. I was vaguely aware that there were people nearby, and that we seemed enveloped—in the midst of a crowded, noisy play party—in a hush that deepened as the scene went on. When it was over, when the blindfold came off and I opened my eyes, I found myself surrounded by a ring of people, women and men, all beaming at me as tenderly as if I were the most beautiful thing in the world, as if I were infinitely precious. I've rarely felt more loved, or less leered at.

A few years later, after a string of similar experiences, a scene friend and I talked about how healing it is to be cherished this way. "Most people never get that kind of attention once they're out of infancy," my friend said. "It's like being a baby again: everybody loves you and just wants to look at you all day long. I think most of us become starved for that as we grow up."

I think the watchers are healed by this kind of love, too. Once, at The Vault, I saw two women do a long, involved, intense scene which culminated in one of them using a strap-on dildo on the other. Now, this is the stuff of porn movies, perfect leering-guy material, and indeed, the roped-off play space was surrounded by watching men. But nobody was leering, and nobody was trying to get too close. The men were perfectly silent—with that same hushed reverence I'd felt during some of my own scenes—and when I looked at their faces, I saw vulnerability—wonder and yearning, rather than lechery.

At the end of the dildo scene, the bottom came. A few seconds later, the top came, too. The audience's hush held through both orgasms: only when both women were spent did the crowd begin, very gently, to applaud, a sound like soft spring rain.

The top looked up and around at the audience. She was crying. "I don't usually let myself come in public," she told us quietly. "I couldn't hold back this time." I looked around at the watching men. Several of them were crying, too.

Have I ever seen anything like that in church? Well, no, not exactly. But because my denomination stresses the importance of the incarnation—the belief that God became flesh, assumed a suffering, mortal, human body—our services tend to demonstrate a very similar love and tenderness, one I've found hardly anywhere else except the scene. I've seen newly baptized babies being carried up and down the aisle as congregants reached out gently in welcome, touching the child's hand or smoothing back a curl of hair. I've seen everything stop while we waited for an elderly woman, using a cane and leaning on two priests, to make her way slowly back to her seat. One Sunday, I shared a pew with a very old man who seemed insensible to everything around him. His wife unbuttoned his jacket and patted his hand, but he just stared ahead, mouth open slightly. I wondered if he was blind. He didn't sing with us, didn't stand or kneel for prayers; when everyone else made their way to the altar rail for communion, he stayed in his seat, his gaze vague and unfocused.

At the end of the service, as everyone else was leaving the church, the old man was still in his seat. I started to ask his wife if there was anything I could do to help them, and then I saw the priest and the deacon coming down the aisle towards us, carrying the host and the chalice. They knelt down next to the old man and fed him communion, as one would feed a child: folding the bread into his hand and guiding it to his mouth, holding the chalice to his lips and tipping it, ever so slightly, for him to drink. There was no impatience in any of this: it was an act of love, a gift. Watching it, I cried, and I realized that my definition of God is of a being who looks at us as tenderly as the people in Hellfire had looked at me, as tenderly as the priest and deacon were looking at that old man, who was holy and beautiful to them even though his imperfect body was failing.

Radical Trust

Growing up, I learned from the culture around me not to trust, and especially not to trust men, who would take advantage of me if I gave them the slightest opening. I learned to watch where I walked, what I wore, what I said, because if I sent off the wrong signals, I would be raped—or at least humiliated—and it would be my fault. The message made me angry, even back then, but even back then I was often too afraid to try to challenge it. The summer I was eighteen, a family friend, an older man I liked and respected, took me aside and warned me sternly not to wear such skimpy shorts, because boys my age couldn't control their sexual impulses, and I might get hurt. I remember looking at him and thinking, "Does that mean you were a rapist when you were eighteen?" But I was afraid to ask the question aloud, because I was afraid of what the answer might be.

I really wanted to believe that the messages I was getting were nonsense. I wanted to believe that men, as much as women, were capable of taking responsibility for their own behavior. I wanted to believe that people who cared about me wouldn't hurt me, no matter what I wore. But these were difficult propositions to test, because I couldn't do so without putting myself into situations that I'd been told, over and over, were dangerous.

I think this dilemma was largely responsible for the fact that I didn't act on, or even consciously recognize, my true sexual nature until I was in my late twenties. If having power over another inevitably involved inflicting harm, only harmful people would willingly play with power dynamics—and I wanted neither to harm nor be harmed.

This conundrum made coming out, to myself or anyone else, very difficult and frightening indeed. But when I did, I learned at last that I could be vulnerable without being hurt. I learned—from direct physical experience, and not merely intellectual conviction—that someone who loved me wouldn't take advantage of me: not even if I were tied up and helpless, not even if he were standing over me with a whip, not even if I were so deep in bottom space, so blissed out on hormones and endorphins, that I could barely remember my own name. Someone who loved me wouldn't do anything to me without my consent. And if my husband didn't suddenly become a leering rapist, unable to control his own behavior when I was tied up, neither did the men at Hellfire. I learned that I could walk around naked, or be bound to a table, and be perfectly safe, even in a room of people I didn't know. I learned that the scene is a far more trustworthy place than the surrounding culture that so often reviles it.

This discovery had a profound effect on my view of vanilla power exchanges, politics, and sexuality. I no longer buy the "my hormones made me do it" argument, nor the "my political power made me corrupt" argument. I know now that power needn't inevitably take the form of irresponsibility. On several occasions, this knowledge has allowed me to challenge vanilla misuses of power I would simply have accepted before. I've learned that sometimes, even people outside the scene can hear safewords, and heed them. And I've learned that when people refuse to respect safewords, it's an indictment of them, not of me—a statement about their arrogance, not my weakness.

These insights helped lay the groundwork for my faith in God, a state which can be an even scarier prospect than faith in other people. Many of us have been raised to believe in a punitive God, the deity of plagues and thunderbolts, the one who ignored every safeword Job could summon. This is God as dangerous top; who could trust such a being? I count myself fortunate not to have been raised with that image of the divine, but in its place was absence, for I grew up in a family that practiced no faith at all. My journey into belief has been a series of gradual discoveries that I've been the recipient, all along, of attention lavished by a benevolent power. Looking at the trials of my life, examining the times when I've been hurt and confused and in danger, even mortal danger, I've come to believe that neither an indifferent universe nor a cruel one can explain my continued survival and well-being. Nor do my own merits explain the richness of my existence; too many of the things that have sustained me have been completely outside my personal control. I'm still here, simply put, because I'm loved. God is a caring top, not a rapist.

Every Sunday in church, we confess our dependence on God, the power in whom we live and move and have our being, whom we praise and thank for all good gifts. We kneel in joy, not terror. To the people who sneer at such submission, who claim that church is a crutch, my answer now would be a simple shrug and the response, "Yes, sure it is. So's breathing." The scene taught me that it was safe not to be totally guarded and completely self-sufficient; church teaches me that in fact, I never have been, and that the collar of my submission, far from being a mark of shame, is cause for gratitude and rejoicing.

Radical Stewardship

The tops I respect in the scene don't abuse their bottoms. The clergy I respect in church don't push over old women with canes, or scoff at old men who need help taking communion. In both places, power expresses itself most properly as service and compassion, not cruelty. Both cultures call on me, likewise, to be fully responsible, fully trustworthy, fully present to those I serve: either when I top or when, at the end of the church service every Sunday, I heed the deacon's admonishment to take God's word into the world, "to walk in love as Christ loved us."

If bottoming taught me that someone who loves me won't hurt me, topping taught me that I can be similarly responsible to and caring of a beloved partner, that I won't turn into a monster if I pick up a riding crop or a pair of handcuffs. The scene challenges me to put the needs of my bottom before my own ego; church challenges me to love my neighbor as myself—even when my neighbor happens to be someone I don't like very much—and to forgive my enemies. Both cultures demand that I care for other people, rather than harming them. In a society that has fetishized nonconsensual violence and looking-out-for-number-one individualism, this isn't a trivial task.

Both the scene and the church should be, and very often are, havens for outcasts, places where people come for healing. Jesus ate with lepers; the scene welcomes those whose sexuality would cause them to be ostracized elsewhere. But all too often, both places replace such ideal tolerance with entrance and qualification requirements every bit as exclusive and petty as anything dreamed up by a secular, vanilla country club. This is understandable; it's human nature. It's also very painful. I'm sick of hearing certain players suggest that I'm not "real" because I switch or use humor in scenes or don't follow a 24/7 lifestyle; I'm sick of listening to religious institutions, including the Episcopal Church, squabble over whether to ordain gay and lesbian clergy and bless gay and lesbian unions. The bad stereotypes about both cultures are there for a reason: all too often, they're true. I have to keep reminding myself that leatherfolk I dislike don't invalidate my sexuality, and churchgoers I dislike don't invalidate my faith.

Episcopal preacher Barbara Brown Taylor has issued a passionate call for compassion within the church:

> If there is anyone in the world equipped to care for people body and soul, we are. We are God's baptized, who have been given the gift of second sight. We can see spirit as well as flesh. We know there is more going on than meets the eye. When we look at people, we see them whole, the way God meant them to be. When they are not whole, it hurts us, as if we are missing something we need for ourselves. Because of this,

disciples cannot take part in anything that diminishes the soul of another human being. Disciples cannot stand by while anyone is called names, or talked down to, or cast out, because all those things wound the soul, perhaps even murder it, and it would be better for us to chop off pieces of our own bodies than to let that happen to us or to anyone else.

I wish more churchgoers tried to live up to this responsibility, but I wish more leatherfolk did, too. We can also see spirit as well as flesh, if only we look, and most of us have experienced firsthand what it feels like to be called names and cast out. Let us remember to be good stewards; let us treat each other as we would wish to be treated, whatever we call the spirit we honor. If we can learn to accept one another, then maybe one day the wider world, including its churches, will learn to accept us.

A Jewel of a Woman

Mary Anne Mohanraj

You ever wonder what women think about when they're grabbing the goatee? I bet you hope they think about you—about the smell of you, or the taste of your slightly salty come, or how much they want a nice, thick cock slamming into them right about now . . . well, sorry to disappoint you, but I don't think about men when I'm jilling off. Maybe other women do—I don't know, so you can still keep hoping—but I'm a little strange. You know what I think about?

Jewels. That's right. When I'm fluffin' the muffin, buffing the beaver, airing the orchid—you know exactly what I mean—I'm thinking about rubies. Rubies and diamonds. Rubies and diamonds and emeralds and sapphires and I'm getting wet just thinking about it. Here, let me get more comfortable—undo this silly bra and spread my legs so I have lots of room to work with—ah, that's better.

So as I was saying, I don't know what other girls do when they're dousing the digits, but me, I get myself off with gemstones walking through my mind. Before I even start, I open up my jewel case and adorn myself with some pretty or other—not that I can afford real jewels, but at least I can pretend. Sometimes I wrap imitation pearls around my waist, or put a string of bangles on my naked arm. I've thought about getting my nipples pierced, so I can hang earrings from them—don't you think that'd look cute? And at Christmas, I could hang little ornaments there.

I once tried that trick you read about, where you stuff a bunch of pearls deep into your pussy and then pull the strand out slowly, one by one. It drove Mike (my ex) crazy at the time, and it felt so good, so fucking good as those pearls came out, grinding against my clit one by one, but it totally ruined those imitation pearls. I need real ones, baby . . . real strands of pearls. And topazes and opals, and amethysts, and garnets—I'm not picky—I'll even take semi-precious if it's the best I can get.

Mmm . . . just thinking about it makes me want to fuck. And since you're not here, well, I'll have to do the best I can myself. Let my fingers do the walking, from my hard nipples down to pet the pussy, oh yeah. Uh huh. Just a little tickle here, then a little jab there . . . pull those labia apart so I can really get to strumming the clitar, oh yes. I left my vibrator at the office—silly me—but hey, I've had years of getting off without it. Just takes a bit more work. Just think of diamonds, girl, diamonds in your hair and ears and around my smooth white neck —a diamond in my belly button and another in my pubic hair. They say that back in olden times, ladies used to grow their pubic hair extra long so they could tie ribbons in it. Wouldn't mine look cute with a couple diamonds attached?

Maybe I'd just stuff a handful up my pussy—though rubies would be better for that. Oh, yeah. Nice, big, goose-egg rubies, cold and hard at first and then warming up inside me. I could walk to work like that, and all those rubies would be jangling around in my pussy, and strange men would look at me in the street, wondering where that strange knocking noise was coming from. And I would smile . . . "Diamonds on the soles of her shoes?" She ain't got nothing on me, baby.

God, I'm soaking now, at the thought of all those rubies inside me. I wish I did have something inside me, something big and hard. Rubies would be best, but I wouldn't complain at a cock right now, no I wouldn't. My fingers are getting wrinkled, and it would be nice to have someone else take over thumbing the button, waxing the saddle. You could buy me jewels—the kind of jewels I can't afford with my $7.75 an hour as an Arthur Anderson file clerk.

How 'bout that for a deal, huh? Buy me rubies and pearls, black onyxes and opals—hell, I'll wear an opal in my ass; I'll deck myself out in jewels from head to toe, like those exotic harem girls over in Arabia. And you can lick me from head to toe, lick right around and over and under all those pretties, and take 'em off one by one to leave a clear path for you to fuck me, *oh yeah, oh yeah, oh yeah*—wrap your fingers in my hair and pull me down to the bed naked and wet beneath you—just leave me my pearls, my string of pearls wrapped twice around my waist and I will fuck you like you've never been fucked before, oh boy, oh God, yes—I will fuck you until you scream.

You're Welcome

Nola Summers

I want something from you and I want it tonight.

I made sure you were comfortable. I rubbed your feet, cooked your dinner and served it to you.

Now, you will serve me.

I am going to go and prepare myself and you will be ready when I return.

You will disrobe. You will, naked, clear the table. You will lay out an assortment of whips and paddles, and you will pick one.

You will pull on a leather pouch and adjust it so it holds your already hard rod tightly in place.

You will attach cuffs to your ankles and wrists, then stand and anticipate my return.

I hear you moving about in the other room and I wait until I know that you are standing, ready, before I begin to prepare myself. It's better that you wait for me.

I pull on my black Victorian corset. It fits snugly under my breasts, presenting them on a shelf of leather, forced up and out. The back ends just where my ass splits. It is framed, white and round, by the black stockings I have attached to the leather garters. I will wear boots tonight, knee high with stiletto heels. The dog collar that I fasten around my own neck will eventually be worn by you, but for now, I'll wear it.

After dressing, I sit at the table to apply my makeup. I spend extra time on my lips, outlining them and painting them a deep red. I comb my hair and pin it up.

I stand to assess myself. Almost as an afterthought, I change the ring that pierces one nipple to a stainless steel one that matches the metal in the collar.

I can feel the warmth at the top of my thighs as I approach you. You stand between the table and the chair and wait for me to decide where I will tie you. Tonight I prefer the table.

First, I instruct you to take off my collar and put it on yourself.

I direct you to the table, place your feet by their respective table legs, and attach them firmly. I tell you I love you, then force you face down and pull your arms across the surface and tie them to the other legs.

I see that you have chosen the small whip. Silly boy. We'll use your little whip a little later.

I choose a medium sized paddle.

I stand behind you and admire your tight, smooth, unmarked ass. I caress it and bend to kiss your cool skin. There is usually some evidence that I have been there, but tonight it is an empty canvas—mine to paint and color.

I begin.

I hold the paddle against you and rub it in a slow circular motion. You moan quietly, in anticipation. When I see the muscles tense in your legs I know you are ready. I lift the paddle and begin a quick succession of strokes. Ten, then I stop. A slight pink blush creeps up your backside. A little harder, ten more. I make you count. Rosy, and warm. Harder—ten more to produce the shade of red I prefer.

I stop for a moment and sit in the chair at the side of the table that your face is turned towards. I tell you that you are being good and you thank me, even though you know that I'm not done just yet. I return to your ass, pleased with the remaining color. I apply a few more vigorous slaps with the paddle, just to see you flinch with each contact.

I place the paddle where you can see it and pick up the small whip. I start at your head and slowly drag the tails down over your back. I swirl them down between your legs and pay special attention to the straining bulge of your rigid cock, still held in its leather pouch. You feel the hardness of the handle being dragged back up between your ass cheeks.

About now you begin to realize that I am going to whip your already heated rear. You indicated your choice when you picked this little one. I simply chose something else first.

The tails are short but sting nicely when they come in contact. I lay them across your backside, producing a nice pattern of raised red welts. I ask you to decide how many more strokes you need. Not less than five, I suggest. You ask for five and begin to count.

One.

Two.

Three.

Four.

And the last one—with every effort.

Five.

I bend and draw my tongue along the whip tracings. I can't help it, they are a wonderful sight. I touch my face to your ass cheek, absorbing the heat. You beg to be let up and I will, of course, release you after I've finished admiring my work, proud that I have made some marks that will last till the next time.

I undo your arms first and let you straighten up. When I kneel to release your ankles I again lick your red marked derriere.

I stand up and turn you around. As I undo the pouch, your still hard cock springs into my hand. The dripping juice betraying your need for punishment, and your need for me.

You thank me.

I tell you that I did not do this for you and guide your hand between my legs. You find that I am wet, my juice running onto your fingers. I tell you that I do this for myself. I like it. Seeing you tied off, excites me. That you are man enough to take it makes me want you. That you accept your role pleases me. Your occasional defiance intrigues me.

I turn around and bend over the table, taking the position that you so recently held.

You enter me in a rush of pent-up frustration. Hard and furious, making the same noises you did earlier. I grip the edges and hold on as you bang into me. I know that it won't be long before you come, and I allow you to take what you need. I am coming myself when I feel you pull me roughly back against you and your hot come splash inside me.

You may thank me now.

Now That I'm Done

Scott Poole

I'll take a shower. No, I'll take a shower outside in the leaves. I'll take a shower among the leaves with three naked women. In a thunderstorm. Yes, I'll take a shower with warm water and cold water and the leaves steaming around four naked bodies. I'll watch. I'll watch the three nymphs bathe in a raging ancient forest under a hot-springs waterfall. Then I'll join them with coconut milk. Wait, I'll take a shower in warm coconut milk with one woman and some lightning and a waterfall to watch in the distance. We could have our clothes on, wait for them to soak through with coconut milk, then rip them off in a crack of thunder. There will be drums and parrots. There will be drums and eagles. There will be a string quartet and screeching osprey. There will be nightingales and a small acoustic combo. There will be Robert Bly reading my poems, drunk on coconut milk, declaring me a genius, while a screeching raptor pecks out his entrails. I'll take a shower with milk and a nimble nymph under a waterfall at all times of the day and people will pay money to see it. The monks will join and throw rose petals. I'll take a shower with a coconut covered nymph and a choir of Krishnas to the music of the New Criterion Banjo Orchestra. The whole populous of Toronto will take a shower with the whole populous of Buffalo in Niagara Falls and I and the nymph will watch from a leaf-covered cliff drinking coconut milk from a cistern in the shape of Robert Bly's head, while the screeching eagle will become the symbol for international peace and harmony. No, I'll take a bath.

How to Suck

H.L. Shaw

I want to tell you about sucking cock.

I love it.

I've written long, long letters to boyfriends, describing for them in detail just how much I love the feel of the tips of their dicks on my lips. It's like putting on lipstick with a big, velvet applicator. It's best if there's a bit of pre-cum viscous to slip through, but even without . . . God, I love cock.

So, I'm going to tell you how I swallow it.

In Monty Python's *The Meaning of Life*, an English school teacher tells his chaps in sex ed: "Don't go diving straight for the clitoris, boy! Warm her up with a nice kiss first!" The same is true for cocksucking: at first, the objective is not to touch the cock. At all. No matter how much your lips ache to wrap around it, no matter how much you drool to lube it up. No touch there. Yet.

Kiss him. Kiss him with your mouth open, jaw dropped, as if you're sucking honey off a piece of peach. Explore the perimeters of his lips, lick along the inside lightly and revel in the different texture there. Breathe in when he exhales, share his air. Once you've achieved shivers through this small self-tease, suckle his bottom lip between yours. Gently now. Ah, ha-huh . . . that's it. Let the little intimacies of what you're doing here tickle your senses.

I always get a rush of warm wet between my legs now.

With this level of intensity, kiss his neck. Don't give in to the urge to fall into large, slurping sucking kisses here. Treat the skin as softly as you would a baby's cheek. Let the fine hairs along the back of his neck pull lightly on the skin of your lips. Exhale here; he should shudder.

Now it's time to work down the body. You can do this on any side, and I recommend experimenting often to change it up a bit. Occasionally it is necessary to start at the arch of the foot or ankle for this change of pace. Never begin with the toes. It's like diving for the clitoris, really.

If you're doing the basic neck-down route, you'll want to stop and see that collarbone before you get down too far. Trace it with the tip of your tongue—take it to the other shoulder, pausing at the hollow of the neck. Repeat, exhaling to cool the wet spots you just left. If he shudders, allow yourself a shiver or two to share. An idea to keep in mind is that his arousal turns you on. Let it. Things will get very intense.

Another point not to miss are the nipples. These vary immensely, and if you don't know whether his are very sensitive or not, I'd suggest you start as if they are. Besides, we're still in the "light touch" mode. The barest touch should produce the biggest results. Save heavy nipple-sucking for a nice break later.

Navels are nice, but again, his ticklishness is a serious variable. Make sure he likes what you're doing, and is not made too uncomfortable. I suggest skirting the navel for now. Take a left to the hip bone, one of my favorite spots. If you're at all lucky, there's a little ledge there. Mouth it. Kiss it. Gnaw, if you're feeling devilish. This is a good spot to introduce the hands, as it's a pleasure to feel the solid shape of the hipbones against inquisitive fingers.

From the hip, there's an old favorite bypass I like to take that seems to work every time. Make a biting line (with lip-covered teeth if necessary) down the top of his leg to the knee. Kiss the top of the knee, avoiding the underside. Slowly, as if you were following melting ice cream on not-that-warm a day, lick from the underside of the knee up to the top several times. Then start up the inner thigh.

Another route from the hipbone involves underwear (if he still has those on) and can be very erotic as well. Run your index finger along the inside of his waistband. Kiss the waist band. Pull it back with your pinky an inch or so and kiss there. Put it back and smile up at him. If you can pull it off (and you should have a feeling at this point just how well this is all working), lick your lips when you look at him. Turn your head back and lick along the inside of the waistband. You can repeat this with the leg openings (especially with unfortunate underwear such as tighty-whities), or you can pull the band down to the base of his cock. Either way, it's now time to nuzzle.

Smell him. Yeah, yeah, just shut up and do it. Do it again, this time getting close enough for your nose to touch it through the cloth. Uh-huh. Work up until you're rubbing your face along his prick. It really helps if you can enjoy this, as he'll undoubtedly get off on the thought of your pleasure when you do. Feel his scent travel into your mouth. Drag your lips along his length and compare their softness to his rigid cock. Nuzzle his velvet knob. Love it.

When you yank his undies off, be sure not to catch him in them. Your courtesy will assure him you can be trusted with his baby. Follow the undies down, then lick your way back up until you're at his balls. Lick, nuzzle, suckle. Linger in his puckered globes. Learn their ridges by heart.

Two good techniques to use just about anywhere are the *Up and Down* and the *Side to Side Tongue Flicker*. Pull your lips back and stick out your tongue. For the *Up and Down*, you'll need to use the muscles in the back of your tongue for speed and control. Flicker up, flicker down, letting the quick strokes lap at his balls. You'll have to practice to make this look pretty, but for now he doesn't care. Trust me. The *Side to Side* is easier, as it uses the mid to front tongue muscles, and can be performed while resting slightly over either the bottom or the top lip.

There's one more essential we should learn now: the lip-covered teeth. Roll your lips around to cover the sharp edges of your teeth. Let's practice on the balls. Keeping your teeth carefully covered, gently take one of his testicles into your mouth. Feel the roughish texture of his sac against your lips, your face. Look up at him, if you can, and hum. Or better yet, let out a long, high-to-low sigh of longing. The more sound, the more vibrations rock his tender testes. Repeat for the other ball. When you're ready to move up, lick from the underside, along the cleft of his balls.

Now we need to work on that pole. First you'll want to nuzzle again, this time letting the soft skin of your face rub directly with his own satin jewels. Compare textures; breathe on him. Then you can wet him. Unless your boy has an unusual amount of pre-cum, these things don't come pre-lubed. Take your tongue and moisten him.

You can do this slowly, side-flicking along the ridge on the underside of his cock; or you can take the flat of your tongue and draw it up the entire length, washing him like a cat. Or combine the two with an up-and-down-flicker. Either way, you must stop before the head. On uncircumcised guys, the foreskin will pull up and cover it on those flat licks, so you needn't worry as much. But save that bud for later.

Now you need to wet the other side. Keep in mind that this side is not as sensitive; I recommend playing with his balls in your fingers or even light ass-play, if your boy is into that. (Most anal play works beautifully with cock-sucking and can add heightened sensation.) Be sure you know the limits, if you tickle his asshole. Penetration should really only be approached with a standing invitation; but then again, there's something to be said for unexplored territory. Are you still licking his cock? Good. Again, avoid the head.

Go back to the underside and do whatever you didn't do the first time. If you flicked, now lick flat and vice-versa. Play with him and drool; this part has a function.

In some slow fashion of your choosing, make your way to the tip. Run your tongue around the little ledge there. Lick around the head. Notice the cleft on the underside and french kiss it. Follow that up and lick the hole. Insert the tip of your tongue if there's room. Savor him.

In a swirl of saliva, take only the head into your mouth. Suck in your cheeks, then let go, staying close enough to leave your upper lip attached. Breathe in to draw air over this area. Hold your mouth over the end of his cock and twirl your tongue around it. Suck him in a little, twirl again. When he's in far enough that you can't move your tongue, let him out a bit.

If you need a break at any point, you can go back to the flicks along the underside. After heavier cock-sucking, you can break to other parts of the body, such as the neck or the aforementioned nipples. If you're female, nipple-penis contact is a hot way to let him know you'll be back soon. Try spanking your breasts with his erect penis. Fuck his hole with your nipple. Making a large break away from mouth-genital contact for too long can be a signal to "move on" to intercourse. If this is not your intention, make sure you keep charge and always return your lips to his prick.

Where was I? Ah, yes. Now you're ready for some heavy-duty snake swallowing. So. What are you waiting for? Suck him in. Now, let's see just how much of that juicy prick you can stuff in your pretty little mouth. Ah good. The trick here is to open your jaw. Relax, and extend as far as a yawn. Farther. OK, now pull back and let your jaw rest. We still have vacuums and swallows to do before the last leg.

The vacuum starts at the end of the prick, lips slightly apart. Suck him to your lips. Let your suction help him penetrate your lips; let him feel as if he's the one pushing through. You can suck him down part way or all the way. When he withdraws, it should be against the pressure of the vacuum trying to keep him in. Repeat several times.

The swallow is one I like to think of as a specialty of mine. Pull him down to the back of your throat. Swallow a couple of times, letting the back of your throat close around him like your lips were earlier. Now, slide him back, down your throat if you can manage. Now swallow. Oh, trust me, he'll go nuts.

Speaking of, make sure you don't ignore them once you're on the main thrust. Even if you're tough and don't take a break, you should at least cup his balls in a free hand. Tickle them a bit; many guys like that. Ass-play is also very nice here, but be sure it doesn't get him too close to orgasm. The goal now is to have sensation in as many places at once as possible.

When are we going to let him come? Ah, not yet. There's a strategic move in taking a break. You let him cool down. Not all the way, but shift the level of intensity from HOT to shivery again. Kiss his neck (yes, you can slurp and suck; just don't mark, if you can at all help it. It happens, but it still can be considered tacky if done intentionally or painfully). Then work your way down his body, a tad bit quicker and in a way you didn't explore last time. Bring him to a simmer several times, starting from lower and lower down the body until "pulling back" means to the inner thigh or even testicles. It will make him boil quicker when you're ready for him to. The control you can have here is amazing, and can be quite an arousing experience.

Ah, the finale. If you've worked him up right, you're wet from sharing his arousal, wet from your own arousal over what you're doing and the delicious effects it's having on him. If you've done him up this next part will be simple and quick. Now, most guys need that constant in-and-out (up-and-down) motion to come. You need to maintain speed and intensity for as long as it takes. Hold on for dear life this time. You can suck and try to lick, but I find the rhythm often leaves me behind, and I just concentrate on breathing through my nose and keeping my teeth covered with my lips so as not to nick the eager boy. But, once you feel those balls tighten . . .

Hey! Get back there! You're going to miss out on one of the most erotic male experiences women can share: Having a guy come in your mouth. Oh, it makes me drool. And I'm not a fan of the taste, either (although I will admit vegetarians taste much better than heavy meat-eaters). In fact, you shouldn't taste it. When he comes, have him come in the back of your mouth. Let it pulse down your throat in hot frothy bursts. Feel each jet spurt down the length of his dick, past your lips, by your cheeks, pumping at your tonsils. Practice your swallow technique (see why it's good to be able to swallow with your mouth open?) and drink him down. Let him grow small and soft in your mouth and cradle him like a baby bird. Be gentle, as it's sometimes extremely sensitive at this point and that hard sucking you were doing earlier will almost certainly be painful. Slowly draw him out of your mouth, and set him gently back against his body.

Look up at him and smile.

And lick your lips.

Fantasies in Rush Hour

Brian Peters

Two cars, two lives, one traffic jam—five-oh-three p.m., headed home. Perhaps headed west into a smog shrouded sun still a few hours from sunset. Maybe headed east with a nearly setting sun glancing off the rear view mirror. It's hard to tell for sure. The turnpike is parked solid with a lonely mass intent on travel, and stalled in place. A still life of humanity crowds the road nearly touching, but desperately isolated, perhaps by the proximity itself.

Meet Dusty Smithson: CEO, single, fourth decade and a year, sport utility vehicle four months from purchase, cell phone, tailored suit, NPR, lonely.

And meet Leslie Tolly: between jobs, failed marriage (second), third decade and eight tenths, simulated wood paneled station wagon quickly becoming rust, want ads, stained work shirt, AM radio on local talk, desperate.

That's about all I can say for sure—you'll have to fill in genders and colors and brand names. The more I concentrate, the fuzzier that gets. I can't say why.

Then meet their fantasy, within sight of each other: a fantasy of love, perhaps.

The car door opens. "I can't believe I'm here."

"Neither can I, but I've wanted this for so long." An uncertain smile probes the now broken isolation.

Broader smile. "Who'd have thought it, all these weeks

across from each other in traffic jams?"

A desperate hand brushes across the distance between them: barely touching.

A lonely hand touches fingers to the other's chin, and guides the two of them gently into the softest of kisses. "Ah, that was it, altogether right." A deeper, greedier kiss follows, then an anxious, tentative pause.

"Do you think . . ."

"No. The timing's just right."

"I think so too."

One button released, then two, as each extends a hand, one lonely, one desperate, to trace the midline between hidden breasts, pausing insistently at buttons still resisting, but no longer secure. A slight flush is growing on their necks as adrenaline accelerates what curiosity began.

"So open here, I don't know . . ."

"Only as open as we will it to be."

"Hundreds of eyes . . ."

"Staring ahead at hundreds of windshields, ears locked to hundreds of cell phones."

"Touch me again . . ."

More buttons give way, and hands slowly search beneath shirts, tracing paths of first fireworks around their breasts, centering toward—then touching—hardening nipples. Eyes slowly blink as the light seems brighter through dilated pupils, and hearts beat louder.

"Look at me world, I'm flying."

"They can't look, they're on hold with . . . ah, no fair. Don't stop."

"Kiss me again."

There follows a kiss felt to the toes, arms insistently tightening and roving over arching backs and through tousled hair, to clenching buttocks and across backs again, zippers opening quickly to allow eager hands between their legs.

"Ah, if you'd only—how did you *know*?"

"Just curve your finger so it . . . no touch has ever . . ."

"Cup your hand and stroke so . . . so . . . oh . . ."

Slowly, brake lights flash, drivers lean ahead, and the traffic begins to move. Legs rubbery, their hearts pounding in their chests, Dusty and Leslie move forward with the traffic: Dusty in a sport utility vehicle four months from purchase, and Leslie in a simulated wood paneled station wagon quickly becoming rust. Two cars, two lives, two lanes apart—headed home.

River of Butterflies

Bill Noble

Not a sound—she'd swear it. The equatorial sun lay heavy on the day; the Talaanu ran clear and silent, warm as blood. At intervals, a bird *wheeered* mournfully from the midday jungle. But she knew. She felt it in her flesh.

Eyes were watching.

In a half-conscious gesture, she cupped her hands over her breasts before she turned toward the riverbank.

He stood at the edge of the forest, motionless beneath an enormous Gunnera leaf. His dark eyes were unwavering.

The water tickled the fine hair between her legs, making her aware of her nakedness, of her slender height, her long pale hair, even, somehow, of the gray of her eyes. She felt her nipples crinkle against the palms of her hands.

"*Twi,*" she said, "*Tanu tatwani*?" Twi, friend, why are you here?

"*Su'uma mesami. Ge wegado, wegadi Diana.*" I was going to a honey tree. I thought I heard a capybara, but it is you, Diana.

"*Twi,*" she said, struggling with the still-unfamiliar sounds of Wa'atani, "I am bathing."

"*T'u,*" he said solemnly. Yes.

She saw that he did not understand. "In my village, we bathe alone."

"*Polasu?*" Why?

She looked at Twi's broad, puzzled face, at the delicate

line of his lips. Her gaze traveled down his compact body, over his shining young skin struck with mahogany highlights, at his meticulously hairless, satiny genitals, set off only by the intricately twined sash around his hips. She held her breasts more tightly. Perhaps there was a Wa'atani word that could convey Boston modesty, but she didn't know it.

Suddenly he smiled, a radiant smile that lingered at the edge of laughter. He turned to pluck a long, curving Heliconia blossom. With the thorn from a *chunta* palm he arrayed the flower at the center of a large waxen leaf, then knelt at the river's spangled edge and sent it sailing toward her.

"*Matu,*" he said. Beautiful. And vanished into the forest.

Diana had been in the village eight days when Twi sailed his flower, but her arrival among the Wa'atani already seemed remote.

It had been less than two weeks since the last good-byes to her parents in Connecticut, the moving out of her tiny office in "Animal Crackers," her final dinner with ecologists from the Bio Department in Cambridge. The long flight to Lima and the journey to Wa'atani had an aura of unreality: the rattling buses and trucks over the Andes, the squalid river towns, the succession of dugouts and near-naked men that paddled her deeper and deeper into the forest. She had had nothing to guide her but a thirty-year old aerial survey and her GPS receiver.

For five days, the river had been all that existed. It was at first muddy, but two days out, her guide turned their prow toward the Rio Talaanu, a tributary whose waters ran crystal clear. Armored caiman longer than the boat basked indolently on sandbars. Morpho butterflies the size of birds flashed scintillant blue as they crossed the river. When she found the village, miles from its last documented location, she felt a sudden apprehension at leaving the boat for land. Her guide set her ashore just below the village, mumbling, as best she could tell, that the Wa'atani were sometimes unfriendly. He backpaddled, turned, and vanished downriver.

She hoisted her backpack and tugged an ungainly duffle through a labyrinth of vines and fallen trees. Disoriented and exhausted, she stumbled into the longhouse clearing to call out one of the half-dozen Wa'atani words recorded in the literature.

"*Naandi!*" Hello!

Every sound in the village ceased. Two dozen naked men emerged from the high-peaked longhouse and came toward her, weapons at the ready. They stopped a bowshot away, silent and expressionless.

The silence stretched for what seemed a long time. A graceful young woman stepped out of the shadow of the longhouse with a bowl in her hands. She approached the line of men, spoke to them, then made her way to where Diana stood. She addressed Diana, offering the bowl of food. She swirled two fingers in the thick, pale paste and put them into Diana's mouth. Diana thanked her in English and took the bowl, but the woman spoke again to her with greater urgency. She touched Diana's cheek and smiled, then held her own breasts up and gestured toward the men. Diana had no idea what to do.

The woman spoke again and waited for a response. When none came, she reached with slender fingers to open Diana's shirt. Diana froze—terrified in equal parts by the stone-faced warriors and by this public undressing at the hands of an incomprehensible, confident young woman. Harvard Yard seemed very far away.

She tugged the shirt down to Diana's waist and exposed her breasts. After a moment, the men burst into easy laughter and set their weapons down. Women flooded out of the longhouse, children clinging to them. Everyone converged on Diana and the smiling young woman. One of the men offered her a handful of small red bananas. The women touched her shoulders and her hair. Children stared. The young woman spoke her own name, smiling: *Munai.* No one paid any further attention to Diana's pink, bare, bewildered breasts.

One month among the Wa'atani. Brief tropical twilight filtered into the longhouse as Diana rearranged her few possessions beneath Munai's hammock: the carefully folded clothes; the laptop and the notebooks that would record the two hundred days of her stay. *I thought these months would be about my research, about kilograms of manioc and swidden rotations, but that's incidental, just what I do with six or eight hours of every day.* She sealed the last Ziploc and let her mind rest among the people that had come into her life.

Hammocks were the center of Wa'atani existence. Forty hung in the longhouse, side by side. Sometimes a married couple shared a hammock. Sometimes each maintained their own. Two very social young men slept in one together nearly every night. Invitation to another's hammock was a profound offer of friendship. Munai had invited Diana to sleep in hers the first evening.

Privacy was precious in the longhouse. Couples making love, someone sleeping, or two friends conducting a negotiation were granted a kind of invisibility. Several times in the first week Diana discovered herself standing within a few feet of intense lovemaking. She was surprised how quickly she learned to stifle her shock (though she had the blushing suspicion that she might be the only villager who peeked).

As Diana emerged from the longhouse, Munai caught her eye. Munai had skin of deep burnished gold, angled cheekbones, and quick, glowing eyes. Her breasts were perfect cones. She sat with three women, stirring a cauldron of manioc beer; the others roasted peccary and prepared thick white yuca paste for the evening meal.

"*Hanatapu'u, Diana, patani.*" Come to the fire, Diana.

"*Malimunai polatani.*" I am happy at Munai's fire.

Young and old, the women smiled up at her. "*Lataan.*" We are happy.

Munai and her sweetheart, Twi, were Diana's best friends among the Wa'atani. The affection between them transcended their frequent, and mutual, incomprehension: they understood from the first that much of what the other did, or felt, or thought, would be mysterious.

Diana had felt the fiery heat in Munai's breasts, pressed against her back in their hammock, and had noticed with concern how tender and sore they were. Munai was in the earliest stages of pregnancy: when her breasts and belly began to swell visibly she and Twi would join officially in one hammock —by Wa'atani custom, they would be married.

At the evening meal, Twi presented Diana with a hammock he had labored over all the previous week. Diana sensed his dual motives. He was honoring her, and he wanted more time with his sweetheart.

Two nights after Twi and Munai helped Diana hang her new hammock, Twi was away on a hunt and Munai again invited Diana to sleep with her. The two of them nested together, each with a hand gently cupping the other's breast. They chatted in the darkness for a while, then slipped toward sleep. The sounds of breathing, the quiet murmurs, were a soft lullaby in the longhouse. One of the pet macaws in the roof peak clappered its wings. Someone turned in their hammock; the longhouse's limber frame of bamboo and palm transmitted the sway to every other sleeper in the tribe. With Munai's breath warm against her cheek, Diana slept.

She woke in the night. Bodies were moving against her. The hammock swung in a wide, unsteady arc; a muscled leg lay over her thighs. Munai's breathing was ragged. As Diana groped to get her bearings, her hand encountered a thick, moist-headed penis. She jerked away and heard Twi's gasp.

Should she climb out of the hammock? Should she pretend to sleep? Was she horrified? If she was, why was her face so heated, why did she tremble? Munai's body grew slick and sweaty. Twi's skin burned Diana where they touched. Kisses were vivid in the blackness, astonishingly detailed: breath sighing, sometimes against the smoothness of a neck, sometimes hollowly against an open mouth; the wet, urgent smack of lips; the low, easy sucking sounds of mouths and tongues. Diana's leg was under Munai's back; her mound rested against Munai's hip. Twi lay on the other side, his pelvis tucked under Munai's legs, thrusting into her. As the lovers' breathing accelerated, Diana was startled to feel Munai's slender hand reach for hers. She took Diana's hand and pressed it hard against her belly. Unmistakably, Diana felt Twi's penis moving inside Munai, felt its thrusting length under her hand, felt the tension rise in the young woman's clutching hand. Munai gulped air. Her belly ridged. She began to vibrate in breathless silence. The pulses of Twi's ejaculation started deep under Diana's fingertips; without volition, her mouth opened in a voiceless cry; her hand reached to clutch at Munai's breast, then slipped down her belly again toward her genitals; the smell of sex became overwhelming; the hammock, swinging violently, seemed about to overturn. She began to cry out in the darkness of the longhouse, fearful at the echo of her own voice in the silence. Her body worked itself frantically against Munai's satin hip. Her fingers raked Twi's back. She came.

At the end of her second month, Diana perched on the trunk of an enormous kapok tree, fallen across the river. Her solar array lay beside her as she clicked at her laptop, correlating information on the manioc harvest. She closed the computer and let her eyes drift shut. She was now regularly brave enough to shed her clothes—not just for baths—and the sun soaked into her skin. Toucans flew overhead, croaking. A pair of antbirds hooted antiphonally. She heard the crash of a distant troop of spider monkeys moving through the gallery forest. She slipped silently into the water, her hands roaming her breasts and stomach, savoring their sun-warmth. Pushing aside a pang of Bostonian guilt, she brushed her pubic hair and began to caress her clitoris, undulating in the enveloping water. More and more she sought time like this, away from the village, for pleasure. She made herself come daily now, sometimes dreaming of home, but more often drifting with quiet images of the Wa'atani, naked along the Talaanu. Often, it was visceral recollections of the night with Munai and Twi that sent her cries echoing down the river.

With one hand, she stroked herself. With the other, she explored her breasts, traced her ribs, glided down the long rigid line of her thigh. She remembered the heat and sparse hair of Twi's leg working against her, felt how close her fingers had come to touching the place where he plunged into Munai's slick body. Her body arched, pulling her head suddenly beneath the water. She convulsed, over and over in the drifting, breathless, blue-green light.

She floated in the afterglow. The gurgle of the river filled her ears. When she emerged from the water, another sound came to her from the forest. A voice. Munai's voice, she realized with a start. "*Pa tuii. Twa'ao. Aa, twa'ao!*" Touch me. Touch my doorway!

Without thinking, she started toward the call, her heart racing.

Twi lay sprawled head to toe beside Munai, sheltered between the buttresses of an ancient strangler fig. Munai's belly was round and golden, her breasts full and fruitful. Their eyes were closed. Twi held two fingers inside Munai's body, his penis glistening wetly on his belly. Diana knelt and kissed Munai full on the mouth, then leaned across and tenderly kissed the underside of Twi's penis just below the cleft. As she stood, their wide eyes found her. She knelt again and kissed each of them open mouthed, then fled back toward the river, a fire between her legs, her heart hammering in her throat.

One afternoon Munai took Diana to the river and laid her half in and half out of the warm water. She rubbed garnet-colored, pungent oil into her blonde-furred genitals until they swelled with gentle heat. With a pair of pearly shells as tweezers, Munai removed every hair. She kissed Diana's pink, hooded clitoris and smiled. Diana was now a proper Wa'atani.

It was halfway through her time with the Wa'atani. Sometimes, lying with Munai in her hammock in the languid afternoons, tears would well up; she would pull the woman's swollen body fiercely against her breasts and stroke her long black hair. Once Munai braided her own hair and Diana's together, wheatstraw and ebony. She made a brush of the end of the braid and stroked Diana's breast until she shuddered.

Eight weeks remained. She and Munai sat and kissed at the edge of the water. The river lapped and suckled their legs, tugged their swelling lips. Twi lay full length in the water between them, gazing up at their two faces, one umber and broad-planed, the other long-nosed and pale. Diana yearned to kiss like a Wa'atani, like Munai kissed, with a relaxed focus she felt any Cambridge Buddhist might have envied. Munai kissed as if breath were the soul of kissing, mouth wide, yet her mouth and tongue moved everywhere, swirling against Diana's eyelids, washing her cheeks with moist air, devouring her neck and shoulders. She wet the whole inside of Diana's ear and then caressed it with her soft-breathing nose. She sucked the lobe of an ear into her mouth until little jolts of sensation traveled down Diana's core. She breathed into the silky hair behind

Diana's ear to make her mew with pleasure. And all the time, focused on each other, the two women stroked Twi's full penis, glimpsing his joyful eyes. Diana felt the deep structures of Twi's sex being graven somewhere at the base of her brain; she had never known a man's body with such intimacy or such ease. She thought of Twi full and slow inside her, and remembering, wondered at the new heat that had grown in the last weeks in her breasts. A sigh welled from between Twi's lips and semen poured in waves over his belly and chest. The two women washed him with their tongues, and then the three of them slept, tangled, rocked by the living waters. As they slept, hundreds of inch-long iridescent tetras came and darted between their bodies, flashing blue and red in the light.

Twi gave her a tiny canoe carved of balsa, loaded with painted fruit and fish. She gave the two of them a series of Polaroid photographs taken through the pregnancy: Munai and Twi at the river, Munai and Twi sitting in their marriage hammock, Munai and Twi proudly holding a fat, black-feathered currasow after the hunt. She longed for a picture of them making love, and felt almost brave enough to ask.

Munai's baby would be born a week after Diana left. Her vision blurred as she thought of it.

One week remained. After a violent thunderstorm boomed and sluiced its way over the forest, Twi and Munai found Diana in the longhouse, bent over her notebooks. When they pulled her to her feet, her eyes were red and teary.

"*Paataniu.*" We are going swimming.

"*Waasu ge.*" I am working.

Twi broke into a grin. "*Paataniu, Diana. We'esuli paataniu.*" We do not swim alone, Diana.

They led her on an upriver path farther than she had

ever ventured. When they emerged from the forest Diana forgot to breathe. Before them, a broad sandbar stretched for a quarter mile along the emerald river, covered everywhere with a trembling carpet of butterflies. A hundred thousand, she thought. No, more. Yellow sulfurs and blue swallowtails, emerald and turquoise charaxins, nymphalins of amethyst and burnt orange, heliconiins and glass-wing butterflies, more than the eye could take in, fluttering and rising, settling, drifting across the clear reflecting waters.

Something was shifting, Diana knew. She felt the power in this place, saw the grave attention in her two friends. *My lovers,* she thought. Something like fear tightened her gut. As they took her hands, one on each side, she understood that this was no longer a dalliance, an ecologist's adventure in a far-away place. A voice, her own perhaps, tugged at her: *I'm going back to Boston. My life is in Boston.*

Munai and Twi brought her to the edge of the river. The blood rushed to her face, tingled in her lips. With great solemnity they undressed her. They knelt before her, Munai holding her own great round belly in her hands, and began to kiss her breasts. Twi was rigidly erect, hot where his arousal brushed her leg. They suckled her not with the hurried fever of college lovers but with nurture, holding her sun-dazzled eyes with their own dark ones. Her hands twined in their shining hair, traced the intricate bone beneath. Her fear grew with her arousal. After a time her legs would no longer hold her, and they lowered her to the sand. Her tears overflowed. Butterflies rose and swirled, brushing them, lighting on their flesh to sip the salty juices.

Munai held her breast to Diana's lips. Something sweet and watery, not milk but ineffably sweet, flooded her mouth. She saw Twi's penis, the bright pink tip peeking from its dark foreskin, and she took him, heavy and pulsing, into her hand and brought her face to his to kiss. Twi plucked his scant beard daily; his face was as smooth as Munai's. She pulled Munai over her and raised to kiss her between the legs. Amazement filled Munai's face: strange as Wa'atani caresses were to her, so were hers to Munai and Twi. She let her tongue search Munai's deep places, tasting her, drinking of her salt, losing herself in Munai's body, until the young woman opened against her face, then clenched, then opened again, over and over, calling Diana's name.

Diana felt Twi put his mouth against her, a look of wonder on his face. She felt her pelvis bell open to him. Noisy, wild, delicately attentive, he devoured her. Diana laughed as her climax seized her, and felt her fears move to stand somewhere outside herself. She wrapped her hands tightly in Twi's long hair, and made him begin again

They made love for hours. She could no longer tell if it was Twi's taste on her lips, or Munai's. When her eyes were closed, she lost all ability to distinguish between their three bodies, arms and legs, and dizzy kisses. But still her fear stood, downriver, along the water's edge, waiting. Boston, her fear whispered.

When they were spent, utterly, they staggered to the river, laughing and fragrant with sex, whirled in a cloud of butterflies. They waded in together, arm in arm, and swam in the placid water. Three man-sized otters raised their heads across the river with amused and mustached faces, watching them without a word. A white hawk soared against the tumbled afternoon sky.

When they came dripping from the water, she knew she could not ignore her fear. She ravaged Twi with her mouth, bit him and sucked and pumped mercilessly with her hand until he was hard, until he was thick and curved and black like Twi —*like Twi's cock!*—then jerked him from her throat, jammed him into Munai's body, and kissed her in a frenzy as the three of them came. Relentless, she bit and tickled Twi until he was frantic and moaning once again and then took him into her from behind, slapping her buttocks against his belly. She wanted fear downriver, away from her. It seemed to her that Munai and Twi understood, though she still had not a single Wa'atani word for what roiled in her.

Twi rose and looked at Diana for a long time. He slipped into the forest and returned, not long later, with two bulbous ants pinched in his fingers. He knelt between Diana's legs, and as she watched, not daring to breathe, he coaxed them angry to bite her inner lips, once, twice, and then again. The pain seared through her like acid, and she screamed. Twi put himself inside that white heat, and rode her. She bellowed and came. Again. Again. Again.

As the pain receded and her mind cleared, Munai and Twi held her calmly, touching, saying nothing. Boston and fear waited still, but far off. If she looked, they would be out of sight. She cupped Twi's velvet sack in her hand and pressed her lips against the curve of Munai's breast.

After they rested and dreamt, tangled in the sun and brushed by butterflies, she rode Munai's thigh, kissing her until they both climaxed, and then she made mirror love with her, brown and white, each dancing the other exactly through their joy. Twi stroked and held them, constant and nurturing, laughing with their pleasure. Diana asked Munai to lick her as Twi glided in her from the side. They held trembling and let butterflies light over breasts and thighs and bright, spent cock. An emerald swallowtail pulsed its fragile wings and drank from Diana's clitoris while her lovers kissed her breasts. Diana and Twi floated Munai and her grand belly in the river and kissed her from head to foot, pink toes and brown nipples, laughing like village children. Boston, she thought, looking for the fear, but found only the river.

They floated together, buoyed by the current, a part of the river, trying to touch every inch of skin to every other inch. Butterflies came and crowned their heads.

They came to Wa'atani in the gathering night, to sit around the fire, pressed together, listening to the stories of old men and women. Until the day of her departure all she ever wore again was the sash that Munai had twined. That, and her own naked radiance. Day by day, the women came to put their hand over her heart. "*Wa'atani,*" they said, stretching up to kiss her face.

They slept in one hammock now all the nights that remained to them, and no one in the village said a word of it. Each night, they felt the child stirring in Munai's belly, hour after drowsy hour.

When it was time for her to go, it was too close to the baby's time for Munai to leave the village. Twi paddled Diana downriver to another village, and arranged there for a man to take her overland to one of the larger towns. A week later her plane rose above the squalor of Lima. The Pacific fell away westward. The Andes shone to the east, the towering tops of cumulus clouds signaling the forest and rivers that lay far beyond the peaks.

Diana laid her seat back and immersed herself in the steady thunder of the engines. She closed her eyes. Her breasts burned like beacons beneath her thin traveler's blouse. Joy pressed at her ribs. A tear made its way down one cheek. She rested her hands on her belly to feel for the tiny life, the not-yet-moving river she bore within her body. *Boy or girl?* she wondered, contentment flooding her. Her river, her butterfly river. Her life. Twi's. Munai's.

The plane thundered on, hurtling across unimaginable distances toward Boston, yet Diana had no feeling that anything was left behind.

She laced her hands back over her belly.

Naandu. She shaped the word voicelessly, with her lips alone.

Naandu.

Welcome.

Slut-faced, lips open, eyes

William Dean

She's standing at the corner:
slut-faced, lips open, eyes
the color of fuck-me-harder
tonight, right now, when you want;
standing at the corner of the kitchen
counter, dressed up in her ass-tilted
heels, thigh-stockings almost
framing her glassy, oiled slit.
She pirouettes, balletic, humming,
slapping her belly on the flat wood,
arching her ass high, perched on toes,
looking over her shoulder, looking
for the raw, hard thrust of cock
to burn her dinner to.
Later, sprawled, one foot flatted
on the arm of the chair, eyes half-closed,
two fingers opening her pink lips,
thumb welded to clit, she wiggles it
waiting for tongue tip glissando
to lullaby her dreams alive.
"Master, Daddy, baby," she whispers
and the crash of a mind comes out
of my throat.

Chapter and Perverse

Chris Bridges

I would like to go on record as saying that I am completely and totally against all manners and categories of sexual perversity and I hereby call upon all of our upstanding citizens to . . .

What? Oh, no, you can still do *that* if you want. That too. There? Yes, I don't mind if you want to stick it in there, as long as he doesn't. Excuse me? Oh, sure, whip the hell out of her, consensually, if you please. No, no, I think we have our terms confused.

perversity (per-vûr-sî-tê) noun 1. The quality or state of being perverse, deliberately acting against others. 2. An instance of being perverse, obstinately persisting in an error or a fault; wrongly self-willed or stubborn.

I don't care what you do with your bodies, or even your partner(s)'s body/ies, provided everything is consensual all around. But it's those damn little sexual perversities that get me riled. And don't tell me that these are just coincidences. Ha! That's what they *want* you to believe! Look, here's some examples:

- Cats and small dogs are oddly attracted to thrashing humans and always always always pick the precise wrong time to suddenly lick your face. Also, as a rule: dogs are fantastically interested in sudden new smells while cats are drawn to play with dangly things. Be warned.

• Small children always break in and try to interfere. ("You're killing mommy!")

• Older children will come home while you're helplessly pushing the dinner table centerpiece around with your head. And they'll bring their friends unexpectedly.

• When you most need it to be up, it won't be. Begging doesn't help. Neither does screaming, crying, thinking about Drew Barrymore or even having one more beer, "to take the edge off."

• When you most need it to be down, it won't be. There is absolutely no polite way to explain or adjust a recalcitrant erection during, say, a christening.

• Most small car shock absorbers can't absorb as many shocks as you'd think.

• Condoms can sense ovulation and become correspondingly weaker. Condoms never break under rigorous testing procedures but let them sniff one egg and pop goes the weasel.

• When your rhythm is perfect, when you're both rushing towards the end, when you're slamming your parts together frantically, harder and harder, that will be when it slips out and tries to make a new entrance with varying degrees of success.

• If you're giving a blowjob and you pull away to say something, you'll get it in the eye. Scientific fact, it's been proven in one laboratory test after another.

• Pockets of gas that would have waited for nature to take its course during any other time are remarkably insistent during intimate moments.

• No matter what the duration of the encounter may be, your fingers/tongue/jaw will always cramp and wear out at the exact instant that your lover was about to go over the edge.

• It doesn't matter how well you hide your vibrator, it will always make a surprise appearance at the most critically important moment possible such as your mom visiting or your new boyfriend coming over. If your boss is over and your vibrator appears, it will still be wet, and possibly still running.

• You will never be able to get out of the knots as fast as you thought you could, and now your priest will never visit your house again.

• Mosquitos are especially cruel to outdoor lovers—they'll let you almost finish before they swarm.

• Your ex-lover will always get a better next lover than you will.

• If you were to duck into the bathroom just as sexual contact was about to commence, you would be able to see the brand new pimples still forming on your previously smooth lower regions.

• The day you meet your "love-at-first-sight" dream mate is also the day you figured no one would notice if you wore the ratty grey underwear with the ragged holes and the mysterious jelly stain.

• Don't ever call out names, even if your memory is perfect. You're just asking for trouble.

• You're watching a porn movie, you've reached the perfect, save-it-for-last scene and you're about to pop. Guaranteed you'll lose it just as the scene switches to either a fake male orgasmic reaction or a house exterior establishing shot.

• You won't when he wants to, he'll be asleep when you do.

• UPS, RPS and Federal Express delivery people are specially trained to wait until they hear bedsprings before ringing your bell.

• The phone will always ring 35 seconds before climax, unless there are extenuating circumstances:

• If it's a salesperson or survey, it'll come just as everyone involved in the sex act is completely in the mood.

• If it's a friend calling, it'll happen right in the middle so you have to make a snap decision to either hang up politely and try to keep going, give it up and finish the conversation, or keep going while you're talking and hope that they are somehow oblivious to your obvious state.

- If it's your lover calling while you're with someone else, everything freezes. Everything.
- If it's your mom, it'll happen .05 seconds before climax. Sorry.

hiking south

Heather Corinna

There is
the longest stretch of skinsoft road
on the path your lips start to traverse
between my own,
and the soft cradled canyon between my hips.
I could get lost
in your kisses,
if I did not know as your hands curled around my waist,
your destination has no haste.

As your mouth seeks my neck
beneath
my trembling chin,
and then to seek
the long flat length of skin
along my collarbone before
the swell of breast, pink nipples sore
that ache when tickled by your cheek,
that burn when pulled within the deep
warm cavern on your mouth,
then cooled by chilly air;
your lips a one-way traveler, heading south.

A pull, a draw, from strings unseen
that brings my hips to curl and seek
the delicate soft tracery
your mouth sketches along the seam
already drawn between my ribs,
over the small swell of my stomach,
your pointed chin that moves across
the down disguising your destination.

I do these things before their time:
a sigh, a cry, an arching climb
of tone and voice, a curling of toe,
a trembling of lip
because I know
where you will reach before you arrive;
before my mind is twisted, tangled, tied
in mingled threads of tongue and skin
in losing thought to let touch in.

Before this twisted knot has bound me up
in tightly wound tremors and trembling thought
a heat swells coursing through my skin.
I do not know if I am breathing,
out or in, I cannot say
what I was thinking, feeling, dreaming, scheming
before your mouth slow-suckled round
the pulsing swell of my hidden skin;
Before I breathe you out,
you drink me in.

The Symbol for Intensity

Allison Lonsdale

"But if you never cut anything with it," said Lord Bontriomphe, "then why sharpen it at all? Wouldn't it work as well if its edges were as dull as, say, a letter opener?"

Master Sean gave the London investigator a rather pained look. "My lord," he said with infinite patience, "this is a symbol of a sharp knife. I also have a slightly different one with blunt edges; it is a symbol of a dull knife. Your lordship should realize that, for many purposes, the best symbol for a thing is the thing itself."

—Too Many Magicians, Randall Garrett

I long ago came to understand that the disturbing elements of force that run through my sexual fantasies are not there because I want to be forced.

Force is a symbol for intensity.

When the fifteen bikers (all of whom just happen to have recently bathed and brushed their teeth—in my heart of hearts I am hopelessly bourgeois when it comes to hygiene) play their games with the virginal Catholic schoolgirl in my head, I am neither ravisher nor ravished, but somewhere in the interstices between longing and the object of desire. And the greater the disparity there, the greater the tension. There is a tension like that between the spoken and the meant when you call me "whore" while your eyes are saying "goddess," and you know what that does to me. Blasphemy is a kind of tension, too; the story you told me, about wanting to break into a church and fuck my face before the altar, was very hot.

Tension is a symbol for intensity.

Fisting is a hell of a powerful symbol, though for years after I discovered it in the real world, it didn't become a part of my fantasy life. Not until the night you told me about wanting to use your fist inside me to lift my body halfway off the bed and slam it back down, until you growled "I'm going to split you open, tear out your heart, and eat it," did it become a strong enough symbol for intensity to start showing up in my fantasies. And then I made you fist me that hard for real, and I can still feel my nipples burn as I remember the look on your face when you realized just how much I could take. "Say it," I growled, and through a palpable haze—*this is sick and wrong to tell a rape survivor*—I pulled the words out of you: "I'm going to split you open, tear out your heart, and eat it." Right then, I was a vast wave of light and heat, and could easily imagine giving up a piece of this soft carbon vessel to make a beautiful gesture.

Because when other people talk about power, they mean control. But when I talk about power, I mean energy. How could I be "giving up power" by taking your fist inside my cunt when it wakes the heart of a small sun in my belly? All I'm giving up is control, and that's easy. Trying to maintain control over that much power would blow my head off. I just let it move through me while I go to the place where time, space and ego don't exist. Who needs mescaline when I've got your hand?

Loss of control is a symbol for intensity.

But the biggest symbol for intensity in the smoky pit of my fantasies has got to be assfucking. In my mind, it is the shorthand for *do something to me so intense I can't stand it and have to keep going, so intense I beg for mercy and more in the same breath.* Which is why I shivered the first time I heard you use the words, balls deep in your ass, and I made you say it again so I could feel your voice moving inside me. Which is why, when you're telling me nasty stories on the phone while I furiously rub my clit, I always ask you to talk about fucking my ass when I get close to coming.

And that's why I got so hot when you first made it clear to me that you wanted me to fuck yours. "I feel female tonight," you said, and later you used words like *bottoming* and *subspace*, but those things are meaningless to me. I don't process the concepts the way other people do. I can't. What I had to become to go sane after my rapes—roles are not my friends. Control games are not my friends. Fuck gender, fuck top and bottom, fuck dom and sub. I am what I am, and that demands that I contextualize some things in alien ways to keep from erupting in rage.

But I could listen past your words to something I understood perfectly: the hunger for intensity. And I felt that pull like a surge of molten metal in my groin. So when you said you were lying face-down on the bed with your legs apart, I wedged the phone between my cheek and shoulder so I could reach down and start stroking my swollen clit, and I told you what I was going to do to you: the trail of bites up the back of each thigh, the nails raked over the cheeks of your ass, my tongue working over your balls and then up the crack of your ass and inside you. And when you whimpered and started begging me to fuck you, I told you about the strap-on I was wearing and how I was going to impale you on it and hammer it into you until you screamed. You made yourself come while I told you, and I listened to you go over the edge, feeling it in my clit as you cried out. God, that made me wet.

Fuck gender. You actually thought, back then at the beginning, you had to explain to me that just because you wanted to be fucked up the ass it didn't mean you were gay—look, gender is an illusion; gender is a joke; gender is

Silly Putty. I'm a faggot with a cunt, you're a dyke with a dick, it doesn't matter. It's a game. I play it the way I want to play it. I play it hard as hell and I don't take it seriously for a second.

All I take seriously is desire. Desire and intensity.

And that's why I'm doing what I'm doing tonight. The message you left on my voicemail at work: "I'll be waiting for you face-down on the bed when you get home." Going into the women's room to slide one end of the L-shaped silicon toy up into my wet cunt. Through the harness ring, straps and buckles in place. My hard cock pressed uncomfortably up against my belly by the jeans, its root inside me grinding back towards my spine. Walking out to my car, I see each person I pass box me in a role: buzz-cut, no makeup, bulge in her jeans—must be a dyke on her way to fuck her girlfriend. Yeah, buddy, what's waiting for me has long hair, and on weekends at the club he's in face paint and velvet, but he's about as femme as a .45 automatic. And twice as much fun.

I catch myself watching the ass of a little Asian woman walking ahead of me. Black hair down to her waist, wiry little frame, fine-boned, skin color somewhere between peanut butter and bronze. The alien aesthetic calls to me, and for a second I imagine her impaled on what I'm packing, riding me. A pretty study in contrasts. Then the head turns and I see his moustache. I laugh to myself. Fuck gender!

Getting home through evening traffic is much more interesting when I'm sitting on seven inches of silicon, with the other half caught between my clit and the crotch seam of my jeans. By the time I hit the driveway I've soaked through the denim. I know you're grinding your hard cock into the mattress when you hear me unlock the door. I put on a Cocteau Twins CD and head down the hall.

The door is open and I can see your hips moving against the bed. I leave my boots and shirt on the floor outside the bedroom. I walk in, barefoot, in jeans, my black sports bra, and the harness and cock. I see your fingers dig into the pillow at the sound of my steps. Your face is hidden in the sweep of your hair. I know you have your eyes closed. I open the toy drawer and that's when I realize what I'm going to do to you tonight.

The noises are part of the foreplay. That's why the music is on soft enough not to interfere. The rasp of my zipper sends a barely visible tremor through you. The rustle of latex: you expect me to wear a glove if I'm going to warm you up with my fingers. Short as I keep my nails, they're still nails, and nails are evil there. But the wet noises that are causing you to move harder against the mattress aren't what you think. I'm not lubing up my cock for you.

I'm lubing my gloved hand, clear up to the wrist.

You feel my weight settle onto the mattress, feel me straddling one of your legs. My bare hand traces up the back of your thigh and settles on your ass. Can you feel the wet heat at my crotch? I know you can feel the firm curve of the silicon where it comes out of me and, caught in the ring of the harness, arches out through the fly of my jeans. I grind the base of it against the back of your leg as I dig my nails into your flesh. You moan softly, spreading your legs a little further. I trace a wet finger from my gloved hand along the crack of your ass and you open up, pushing your hips back, begging with your body. I start a slow circle against your anus with one finger as you growl deep in your throat, your hips pushing back like you're trying to capture my finger. Two fingers now, stroking back and forth over the hot flesh. I'd like to keep teasing you until you actually start begging, but you have made sure I know exactly how infuriating that is. By the time you gasp "please" I have already begun pushing a finger inside you. The ring of muscle grips my slick finger tightly, and the heat inside you is dizzying. I swear, as soon as wet nanotechnology gets good enough, I'm going to get myself an actual penis. Just to test-drive it in your ass. Fuck gender. I keep moving my finger inside you, curling it down to stroke the aching knot of your prostate, as you groan and pump against the mattress.

Two fingers. The noises you make as I flutter them back and forth, the joints popping past each other, are intoxicating. I pull out, teasing your anus with just the fingertips, then slide back in, twisting as I push. The mixed hunger and pleasure in your voice when you groan "more" makes my nipples tighten until they ache.

Three fingers. You are bucking back against my hand, your cock sliding over the slick spot you've leaked onto the bedsheet. I am driving rhythmically in and out, angling to press against the root of your cock on the inside. You growl as you writhe under me, the back of your leg pushing into the base of the dildo and driving it deeper into me. I know it's deliberate; you're doing it so hard I'm getting sparks at the edge of my field of vision.

Four fingers. You are clawing at the mattress. Your spine arches and your head lifts, throwing your hair back. "Fuck me, damn you," you snarl. I say softly, "I will give you what you want, but not the way you expect it." I tuck my thumb into the center of my hand and start a slow, steady push. Then you realize what I am doing, and the shock of it sends you suddenly, ferociously over the edge. Your face drives back down into the pillows and you give a muffled roar that seems to come from somewhere deep under the house. I feel your ass clamping down on my fingers as the spasms wrack you; I stop pushing and hold steady as you clench so hard my knuckles are grinding together. My clit is burning, my cunt flexing in sympathetic spasms around the pole buried inside me as I imagine what your climax must feel like. I taste blood where I am biting my lip.

Finally the waves ease, and your body goes limp under me. But I know you'll be getting aftershocks for minutes. I debate briefly: too dangerous to make you take more when another spasm may hit? I give a tiny push. The noise you make goes straight to my clit: a whimper of surrender and disbelief. Then another wave of orgasm bursts through you and your ass tightens again. I am in almost up to the knuckles, and your cry is more than half pain. I start to ease out of you and your immediate gasp stops me. "Please," you hiss. "More." I am not going to argue with that tone of desperation. I keep pushing, very slowly but without pause.

A minute ago your hands were white where you gripped the mattress and I could feel the strain in your legs; now you feel boneless under me, limp as an unconscious body. You're either willing yourself to relax so this impossible thing I'm doing doesn't tear you, or you've hit the place where your motor nerves are fused into a lump of radioactive glass and your bones all turn to jelly. I only know you're still conscious because of the noise, a long, low, keening sob. It sounds hauntingly familiar. I've made that sound myself a time or two.

The heat and pressure on my hand would hurt if my pain threshold hadn't been jacked up into the stratosphere by arousal. I assume yours is in orbit, or you'd never be able to take this. It should take hours for me to work this much of my hand inside you. The rules for everything change around you. I keep pushing, slowly, mercilessly. Watching more of my hand disappear inside you. Feeling the heat in your ass that matches the heat in my cunt right now.

My knuckles hit the stretched ring of your anus and move into you, exquisitely slowly. A wave of trembling starts at your shoulders and moves down your body. The CD finished some time ago; now the house is silent except for your ragged breathing and the almost imperceptible wet sound of my hand penetrating you. I am forgetting to breathe, my pulse thundering in my ears. I continue to push. Past the knuckles, down the length of the palm. You're split open by the widest part of my hand when I feel a tiny preliminary shiver inside you—and I drop into adrenaline-fueled clarity as I realize that the thing I am afraid of is happening now. Another aftershock is going to hit while you're stretched this wide, and if I don't do something *now* it's going to tear you. My brain spits out lightning-fast estimates of risk while time slows down around me. There is no way I can pull enough of my hand out of you fast enough without causing you some serious pain, maybe damage; my only option is to get you to the nearest narrow spot. My wrist.

Hope you'll forgive me for this.

I grit my teeth and shove.

You start to scream.

The wave hits partway through the motion, and the rest of my hand is literally pulled into you as your ass clamps down around it. Your hot flesh spasms around my wrist as my hand closes into a fist inside you. The scream draws out, muffled in the pillow, and your entire body tenses beneath me, shaking. I endure one second of absolute hell, thinking I've torn you up inside, and then I realize that you're coming again. Each contraction of your ass around my hand, I can feel in my clit. It goes on and on. I start gently rocking my fist against your prostate, and the scream changes timbre. I add very slight clenching and relaxing to the rocking motion. God, I'll be lucky if I get out of this without burns on my hand, you're so hot inside. You've emptied your lungs and now you're breathing in ragged sobs, rocking under me, the sensory overload pulling you up to dizzying heights where the air is very thin.

The symbol for a sharp knife is a sharp knife. The symbol for intensity is intensity.

The spasms ease, fade out into aftershocks. I stop rocking but continue clenching and relaxing my hand inside you. Slow and steady. Looking down at my wrist disappearing into your ass, I feel a wave of heat roll over me and settle at my throat and my groin. This is incredibly erotic. I'm inside you, in a way I can actually feel, and you trust me completely, and oh *fuck* the grip of your ass around my hand is good. I never quite realized how many nerve endings were in my hand. And they are all very sensitive to temperature and pressure, oh yes. You're whimpering, in a way that almost says pain, but I can tell from the tone that if I try to stop it will be a lot worse on you than if I keep going.

I keep going.

Slowly you start to move your hips again. I realize you want me to go back to rocking it inside you as well as clenching and relaxing. When I do, you move against the fist splitting you open so it presses harder into your insides than I was moving it. Not much harder. But a little. I keep going, gently, mercilessly. I lose track of time. The universe contracts: your noises, the heat in my groin, the heat gripping my hand. Your rocking is gradually getting faster, and I move to match it. Your noises are gradually getting more desperate and louder. Seized by a wicked impulse, I lean forward, resting my free arm on your shoulders to support my weight, and I snarl into your ear, "I'm going to split you open, tear out your heart, and eat it." You've let me as far into your mind as you have into your body, and I can tell by the way you cry out and tremble under me that I hit the right spot. I hiss, "I am going to keep doing this until it kills you, and then I'm going to bring you back from the dead and do it some more. I won't stop when *you think* you can't take it. I won't stop until *I know* you can't take it. I am going to tear you in half. I am going to turn you inside out. Even when this stops, part of you will always be right here, right now, with me inside you." Every word is a blow, a caress. You are shaking uncontrollably now, with a fold of the pillow caught between your teeth, and I keep whispering cruel and impossible things to you and moving my hand within you until your body arches, every muscle contracting, and your head snaps back and a long note of perfect clarity tears out of your throat, a frozen vapor trail in the stratosphere.

This isn't orgasm. This is something from the other side of orgasm.

Am I a top? I am working hard to pleasure you, what does

that make me? Are you a bottom? You are filling with infinite power, what does that make you? Fuck roles. Fuck gender.

Fuck your sweet ass with my hand until your whole body fills with fire.

Then it's over and you're back from that strange realm, gasping, "too much," and I'm pulling out of you with infinitely careful slowness, wincing as you flinch and shudder, biting back a useless apology for hurting you, yet still aroused by the wet sucking noise as my hand comes back out of your body. I peel off the glove, discard it, stretch out beside you and take you in my arms. You roll into the embrace faster than I would have believed you could move after all that, holding me so tight my ribs creak. My strap-on slides between your thighs and the end inside me moves so I can't help but whimper.

You bury your sweat-stained face in the side of my neck and the sobs start wracking you, coming from somewhere so deep it seems like there's no end to them. I hold you while the waves move through you for a long time, until you've wept yourself empty against my shoulder, clinging to me like I'm the only thing left floating after the storm.

"I got to the light," you say finally, voice raw and cracking.

I raise an eyebrow. "Thought the place you go was dark, the perfect void," I say.

"Usually. This wasn't."

You've seen where I get my poetry from, the luminous reality on the other side of matter. "What did you find there?" I ask, curious.

"Somebody had written on the light."

"Written in what?"

"Light."

I snort. Of course. "What did it say?"

Your grip on me had eased when the sobs faded; now you hold tight again, like I'm the only solid thing keeping you from blowing away in the storm winds. I grip back, tears easing from

under my own closed lids.
    "Your name," you whisper.

Jitterbug

Souvie

The man turned on the lights when he entered the hotel room. He put a brown paper bag down on a small, battered table beside the bed, and took out an old mason jar. Inside were dozens of bugs, all shapes and kinds, crawling all over each other, looking for a way of escape. He rubbed his hands together and smiled. He still had a few minutes until Vanda was due to arrive.

Alfie felt like screaming. In fact he did, as a rather large grasshopper stepped on his head. "Stupid morons," he mumbled. "We've been shut in here for hours and no one has found a way out yet. It's not likely to happen anytime soon, either, I tell you."

As usual, he was ignored. Actually, he probably couldn't be heard above the din. Other bugs were shouting, calling for help, plus there was the scraping of legs against bodies as the ones who hadn't already resigned themselves to whatever fate awaited them, scrambled to find a way out.

Suddenly the panic level in the jar subsided, as eyes turned toward what was happening outside the jar.

The man scrambled off the bed at the first knock. "Vanda, love," he said, kissing the raincoat-clad woman full on the lips as she stepped into the room. She tossed off her coat, revealing a black leather corset, garter belt with matching stockings, and impossibly high heels.

"Do you got the music?" she asked, her accented voice omitting some of the words.

He clicked on a portable CD player; nothing was more sexy than the tango. He got comfortable on the bed, opening his trousers and taking out his limp cock. He ran his hand over the head, and licked his lips. Showtime.

Alfie held on for dear life as the lid was wrenched off and the jar upended, bugs falling out upon the floor.

Alfie gave in to his panic and screamed.

The woman started dancing in time to the music, her heels beating out a sharp staccato, smashing the bugs on the floor into gooey little smears.

The man's cock was at full mast now, his hand pumping in time with the tempo.

The keening of the remaining bugs reached an all-time high. Alfie wished for ear plugs. Then he wished for ears.

The man was just on the verge of orgasm, and Alfie was already counting his katydid days over, when in through the window came the largest swarm of dragonflies that Alfie, or the two humans, had ever seen.

The woman started screaming hysterically. The man was torn between finishing his orgasm, or pulling up his pants and getting the hell out of there.

Alfie was caught in the pandemonium (hard to jump when you're at the bottom of a dogpile of beetles). He'd managed to push his way through when he looked up and saw a size 11 shoe headed his way. He froze.

"Alfie!"

One minute he was facing impending doom, the next he was clutched in the grasp of a soaring dragonfly. He looked up. "Harold?"

"You looked like you could use some help," his iridescent-winged rescuer replied.

"What in the heck is going on?"

"Hell, we all heard the largest damn dragonfly orgy going on in here, and wanted to get in on the action. Since I don't see any lady dragonflies, I guess it was something else we heard."

Alfie felt like laughing, crying, and praying all at the same time. He breathed in the fresh air as Harold headed through the window, out into the night. "Where do you want me to let you off?"

"Anywhere," Alfie hollered, to be heard over the rushing wind. "You know that field over by the new Wal-Mart?"

"Yeah, you want off there?"

"Yeah."

SPLAT!

Any reply Harold would have made was gone forever, just as Harold was. He'd not been paying close attention to the area around them, trying to remember where the new Wal-Mart was, and got nailed by a car. A car traveling at 65 miles per hour, and a dragonfly moseying on along, add up to one dead dragonfly.

Alfie screamed in horror as his friend and savior was obliterated, and he fell with a jolt to the hood of the car. Actually he was wedged in between the windshield and the hood of the car, down near the wipers.

As luck would have it, the driver turned the wipers on. "*Oh shiiiiiiiiiitttttt!*" Alfie called into the night as he went flying off the car.

Alfie crawled into his little house just as the sun was peeking over the horizon. He tried not to wake up his wife.

"Just where have you been, mister?"

Alfie cringed at the shrill voice. He hadn't been quiet enough.

"I've had a bad night, Gladys, all I want is to get some sleep."

"You've been hanging around that dumpster, haven't you? Sipping that fermented dumpster wine. Laughing with your buddies about how you left the old ball and chain back at home. Well I'll tell you, mister . . ."

She got close enough to smell him.

"What's that? Is that perfume? And . . . dragonfly? You've been down at Marty's Cross-Species Cantina haven't you, seeing one of his women? You've . . . you've had your wings rubbed by someone else!" She broke down into tears, wailing about how it would scar the children for life if they ever found out, and wondering why she wasn't good enough for him.

Alfie sighed and covered his head with a leaf.

Grady's Bar & Grille

Aria Braverman

Hushing my mind at Grady's Bar & Grille on a Friday afternoon, 3 p.m.—white wine, cheese fries, no phones, the repeated search for truth. Old Uncle Eddie owns the Grille, and I wonder—does he know that every man here still wants from me what he stole so long ago?

Maggie, he says, *you're looking beautiful as always*. I only want to look wise, talented, brilliant, safe. He liked me a lot when I was thirteen—ripe, pure, giggly at his hands under my short skirt; his kisses; his prick up against my ass, my body pressed so hard against the wine rack that I thought if I breathed every single bottle would tumble down and shatter, bringing each customer back to peer at the cheap little girl who couldn't keep men's heat off of her.

So I laughed and spread my legs and I let him. *I let him.* I let him breathe his cabernet-soaked breath hot onto my chest and stick his big fingers high up inside me and I heard him say over and over again—*mi amore, mi amore, mi amore*, as he let his sticky outburst come and dry down my strong young legs, like the sauce that oozes over the pasta on every single old oak table at Grady's Bar & Grille..

More wine, Mags? he asks me now, and I drink. I drink to forget, or to remember; to remember how to laugh when a man pretends to know me and then tells me to spread my legs; *spread your legs little girl so I can reach you better; just behave and nobody will hear you, nobody will come; you know deep in that sweet little heart that you love my hand deep inside of you; you wouldn't look the way you do if you didn't need to lie down and get fucked.*

At fourteen we moved from hands and fingers to spoons and spatulas, in me and on me, *spanking the way your own worthless father never would*, he said, and when I bent over his knee with my little skirt raised I knew it must be true.

At fifteen he stripped my panties after I came through the door to work; *bend over Mags, now,* he would say back behind the big black freezer and I would, I would bend over and hold my ankles and let him take me hard. It was a game, our game, and I was a good sport and never made him stop.

But he took me to the doctor, the dentist, the Catholic church. He taught me to pretend, to play, to behave. He was all I had, Uncle Eddie, godfather of my two children now; both boys, thank God. Today he is old, I am free, we are friends, no stories are told—he is my family.

At seventeen I stopped coming to Grady's Bar & Grille, stopped seeking whatever it was he gave me—the attention, the brand new feeling deep in my soul, the craving for the smell of cabernet and the scratch of grown-man whiskers. I lived my life and he lived his and he never asked me why.

Each night when I drive across the bridge toward home, I cry. I wonder what it means, that I can't feel love, can't keep warm, even in the heat, and that all I can do is fall right in when anyone touches me just so, keep spreading my legs and opening wide for every man who offers hope, and try not to wonder why I never said ***no.***

How Not To Have Sex

Emily Nagoski

I got the idea from some clients—a very sweet couple married thirty years. They had not so much as held hands for a year and a half; the wife resisted *any* physical contact for fear that mere cuddling would inevitably escalate into sex. In an earnest effort to help her feel more comfortable with her sexual boundaries, we (the husband, the wife, and I) set a rule:

Hand-holding only. No sex allowed.

With this rule, the wife could feel safe initiating the physical intimacy she desired without pressure to go further. The husband nodded vigorously, yes he was willing to try anything to help his wife feel comfortable, he said.

When they returned the following week, the wife reported that she had begun kissing her husband when he left for work, though she knew it was "against the rules."

Astonished, I asked her what brought on this change. All she said was that it "felt right."

After I whipped them soundly for being bad clients and not obeying my rule (kidding!), we made a new one: hugging and kissing only.

Of course the next week, the wife reported that they had spooned extensively, and she had asked her husband to kiss her breasts. She had even wanted more than that, but was reserving intercourse for their anniversary, ten days away!

Thus, in a matter of weeks, this sexually jaded middle-aged couple went from a completely stagnant, virtually non-existent sex life to the hot, lusty necking of high schoolers in the back of Daddy's Caddy.

All because they decided not to have sex.

It makes sense, right? Think back to those lascivious days making out in the backseat of the car—the lust triggered when his hand first sneaked up your shirt—second base! The thrill of defying authority, breaking rules, going where you swore to your friends you would never go.

So I tried it too.

I said to my man, "Man, no more sex."

He didn't quite know what to say at first. He thought I was angry and pulling the old "you don't get any pussy 'til I get my apology" trick.

I explained the plan, and he agreed to it on the condition that he be allowed to masturbate. (Well, duh honey, you could masturbate anyway. We're dating, not dead.)

The first night was fairly ordinary—a kiss goodnight and then off to sleep. After a few nights though . . . well you can't keep a good man down, as they say . . .

It was incredible. Because we weren't having intercourse, we were forced to be creative. Over the course of the experiment I believe he sprayed come on every part of my body other than my cunt. I found parts of my body I didn't know existed, I licked parts of him I'd never licked before.

At one point I started to feel guilty. Surely we were opportunistically using our psychic scars of shaming social conditioning that had taught us that sex is naughty and dirty; how dare we capitalize on such negative messages? How dare we further the taboo? But ya know what? Fuck it. It felt good.

And yes, okay, sometimes we did have sex. We couldn't help it, we were grinding and groping and parts were so slick and sometimes it would just sneak in. Oh! those surprise moments when suddenly lock slides effortlessly into key and all your sweating and clawing suddenly halts so you can fully experience this glorious fit, motionless, electrifying. We would hold each other, still and silent except for our laboring breath and racing heartbeats, feeling the union of our bodies.

Sometimes we just wanted it too badly to see the value in resisting. One night when I was particularly aggressive, sucking my man for all I was worth and finger-fucking myself, my hips flailing madly in the air, I planted my hips over him and swallowed his cock into my pussy before he knew what hit him. The lovely boy—God bless him —whispered hoarsely (hot breath in my ear, the smell of pussy on his breath), "You are such a bad girl, breaking your own rule. You know you shouldn't be doing this. Squeeze your cunt muscles around my cock. Oh, bad girl!"

Yeah, I came like a rocket.

So what are you waiting for? Try it at home! You too can enjoy sex-free bliss. Just follow this one simple step:

Don't have sex.

There is lots of flexibility in the rules you can make—no mouth, no hands, no genitals, no nudity, no whatever. You can do it the official way, following the rules of the Masters and Johnson "Sensate Focus Program." Or you can just say "No Intercourse," like my cheeky monkey and I did.

Establish a rule, any rule, for yourself and your partner. Really mean it. Try to stick to it. You will be gloriously shocked at how slowing down sensual experience brings it to life.

Since I wouldn't dream of leaving you high and wet without means of sensual experience, here is a list of things to try instead of having sex (feel free to add your own ideas):

• Kiss. For hours. Kiss your partner and enjoy kissing, just kissing, without expectation of more, because more is not allowed. Experience the kiss as an end in itself, savor it, taste every curve of your lover's lips. Lust after your lover's lips, dream about them, write poetry, draw pictures . . . soft, pink, delicious lips parting to accommodate your curious tongue. Kiss until your lips are numb and tingling. Then run an ice cube over your lover's mouth. Maybe your partner will let the cold clinging drops of water run from her lips to yours. Maybe he'll let you suck the droplets from his lips. Maybe he doesn't have a choice, and you'll pin him down and lick the water off with just the tip of your tongue running in a slow straight line over his swollen lips.

• Pet your lover. Stroke your partner's arms and legs and feet and those other oft-neglected body parts too frequently overlooked in favor of "erogenous zones"—as though every body part isn't erogenous. Massage your lover's scalp, brush their hair—on their head *and* on their genitals. Touch and love every body part. If your lover has a part he or she particularly dislikes, cherish and worship that part. (Mine is my belly—nothing beats a boy who can kiss and stroke and love my belly without the least hint that he wished it were flat, instead of soft and round.)

• Play Sherlock Holmes. Search for new and different sensitive spots. Suck the tender flesh between your lover's fingers. Tickle the wrist with your tongue. Find out how your partner really feels about having freshly showered toes suckled and caressed. Let your beloved remind you of forgotten trick spots you took delight in discovering so long ago. Breathe on her neck, trace your finger along his collar bone so lightly that he's not even sure you're touching him.

• Use your nose. By now everyone must know how fundamental olfaction is in sexual arousal. Smell your partner everywhere, armpits, genitals, breasts, hair, feet. As you sniff, let the tip of your nose caress the sensitive skin in each of these places—that little tip brushing on your lover can feel astonishingly like a tiny little hard penis . . . (the nostrils do contain erectile tissue, after all).

• Leave your clothes on. Touch and fondle and caress through layers of fabric. Suck wet rings into sweaters, blow tea-heated breath through jeans, follow seams with eager fingers. Threaten to tear the fabric off your beloved's swaddled body, but don't. Want to shred that expensive silk shirt, those favorite pants from your vacation in the tropics. But don't. Then get in the shower, fully clothed. Suck water out of sopping cotton, trace the lines of underwear under translucent fabrics.

And let your partner do it all to you.

Finally, a couple of things to remember as you play with your partner, while not having sex:

• This is not "just foreplay," a precursor to sex. It is the sum total of the sex you're getting in that session or scene.

• You (or your partner) may not have an orgasm every time. That's pretty much the point, actually—to suspend satisfaction, deny gratification. This is about pleasure and exploration, not about orgasm.

In America, you can get anything you want, anytime you want, pretty much exactly the way you want it.

Deny yourself satisfaction. Waiting can be a lot of fun.

Trilogy

David Steinberg

1. Python

Waking in the middle of the night, out of God knows what dream, holding onto you and something dark and purple beginning. Holding onto you and you holding me so richly, and some kind of tearless crying, moans that were connected to nothing, some feeling without a name. And then some kind of transformation, so that I was dropping down down down into a thick deep pool of viscous, syrupy squeezing and pulling and pressing—a new daimon rising out of the depths, bearing some resemblance to the earlier one, the panther creature, but also quite different—slower, heavier, larger, stronger, not so sharp or frantic, a statement not of fire but of something thickly liquid, something absolutely inevitable. The energy focusing in my hands and arms rather than my mouth or teeth, the energy huge and unstoppable, the sheer size and force of it demanding and compelling, broad and wide, so that I found myself pressing into you not with my fingers but with my arms, my elbows, my knees, broadbrush energy, so that when I did finally bring my mouth to your cunt it was not a matter of licking you here and there, but of taking the whole of your cunt into my mouth, as I might more familiarly do with your breast, sucking all of you deep into the cavernous suction, my mouth open so wide—or of surrounding parts of your body with everything of me in the vicinity, enclosing you in all of me and then tightening myself around you, squeezing, compressing. Call me latex; call me bondage bag; call me, I suppose, python—wrapping myself slowly and quietly around you and then tightening the enclosure with slow, continuous determination.

If the other was panther, then this was python: slow, slithering, sinuous, insidious, continuous, gradual, inevitable. It was absolutely intoxicating, to be pulling you, pressing you, opening you, compressing you, stretching you, pushing into you with such complete and undiluted determination. And then all of that multiplied by feeling your immense surprise, your amazement, your fascination, the edges of your fear and your resistance yielding to the willingness to be washed, to be transported, wanting to be taken in this way. And so we were both gone, obliterated, transformed, churned with the ocean of it, the power, the undertow, pulling us both far far out to sea.

And then, as mysteriously as this force had come up out of the shadows, it turned and subsided into the depths, with one last almost comic promise to return, and I was restored to being a simple human again, wrapped into your body, the two of us panting, amazed, amused, bewildered. Which somehow then evolved into you sucking and licking and rubbing my cock into what has to be the most perfectly shaped orgasm I have ever known, the wash of it fitting my form so precisely that afterwards there was not even the slightest trace of incompleteness, every millimeter of me touched, opened, emptied, satisfied, so that I didn't want to move a single muscle to disturb the feeling of utter, total peace.

Say what you want: these are the realms of the gods, no two ways about it. These are places of being inhabited by the primal forces and energies of which the universe is built. There is sex that comes from physical need, and sex that comes from emotion, and sex that comes—deeper—from earlier needs and emotions, cravings that have been cured and aged, gathering power and intensity and soul along the way. And now there is also sex that comes from something beyond, or so it seems, beyond personhood, beyond self, beyond the specifics of me and you and here and now. You turn yourself over to me, and I also turn myself over, to whoever/whatever this is that comes to find me, to call me, to dare me to yield, to give over my body in the service of the particular force that is making itself manifest.

At these times, literally no one is in charge, only the primacy itself, and it is only by trusting the sanctity of these energies that I can yield to them without fear or resistance. Or maybe it is only when I can trust them and be ready to yield to them that these energies arise at all. These are the forces the Christians call devils, the forces they demonize (not just the Christians, of course), the forces that can take us over in the middle of the night when all is darkness and shadows, and the defenses grow soft. The wisdom which is my body can only kneel, offer honor and thanks, and murmur *blessed be*.

2. Chains

This is about Sunday. About taking out the toy bag and the bag of chains. About showing you the screw eyes in the corners of the bed and watching your eyes go wide with delight. About the inspiration, the sudden knowing of what was right, of wanting to give you a taste, an anticipation to carry into next week. The moment when the wandering ceases, where direction emerges, undeniable. When I put on the robe, make the transformation, become the Other One.

All at once I know exactly what is to be done. I tell you to sit on the floor at the foot of the bed. You know immediately that we have changed worlds and you give yourself over without so much as an instant's hesitation, flames licking your eyes even before your mind catches up and gives its blessing. You sit at the foot of the bed and I get out the chains and the cat collar cuffs and everything is going sacred and you are already radiant with delight and expectation, your excitement mixing with my own so infectiously that I have to take a minute to breathe, to center, to honor what I am beginning, to inhabit the responsibility along with the giddy delight.

"Just a taste," I say, acknowledging the constraint of our limited time together. The lengths of smooth chain, the carabiners, the smooth black collars around your minuscule wrist. Giving you the feel of cold metal against your skin. The story of the man at the pet store when I bought the four cat collars, of the man who bought a crop though he had no horse, of the old man at the hardware store asking what we wanted the chains for. The smooth black encirclement of your wrist, your eyes sparkling, taking in everything. The chain hitched to the eyebolt in the bed, then to the band around your wrist. The look of your face against the heavy wooden beam of the bed, your arm up and to the side, the silver gleaming. You holding on to it already, playing with the feel of it, the first tug of restraint. Then the second wrist, second chain, second arm held up and out. The look of you racing to catch up with the experience of it and not quite making it, of you watching me, watching my face for clues. Letting myself like the look of you there, helpless and not helpless, the complexity of your face, allowing me this with you, excitement and just a little uncertainty, amazement, wonder, the willingness to be uncertain, trusting what you know of me to not need to be certain of anything.

I pull your body out from the bed. The chains are awkward and uneven but it doesn't matter. This is just a sample, just a taste of magic. Already you are wriggling, reaching your pelvis high in the air, for the stretch of it. You cannot touch yourself there, have no way to guarantee yourself any kind of satisfaction, any kind of release. I stretch you out on the floor, hold your ankles apart and down to the floor to show you what it would be like to be spread-eagled on the bed, where even the ability to arch yourself would be largely taken away. You light up at being held down this way, testing the strength of your legs against my hands. I hold your ankles still, pin them to the floor, give you this to pull against as hard as you want. I unzip your jeans and pull them and your underwear down around your knees, exposing your newly naked cunt and your much-worshipped ass, but letting the tightness of the jeans restrict your legs, binding them together. I press your ankles down toward your face, luxuriating in the picture of your naked cuntlips pouting from between your thighs, and the perfectly smooth curve of your ass that comes rising up from the floor every time I press down on your ankles.

Do I start playing with your cunt then, or later, pressing your puffy lips and swelling clit between my fingers, pressing down around them deep into the flesh of you? The string of your tampon dangling incongruously against your skin. The tip of my finger working itself just inside you, playing, moving, making you squirm, then moving into you more deeply, sharing the cave of you with the cotton swab, stirring you, heating you. Slapping your pouting cunt lightly with my hand, licking you briefly—outside, around your clit—when you ask me to.

I take out one of the latex strips, wrap it several times around both your ankles, and tie the ends through the two screw eyes, lifting your legs and raising them up over your head. You can pull against the straps, and they stretch so that you can bring your legs all the way down to the floor, but when you relax they pull you up again. Stepping back to enjoy the sight of you, twisting on the floor, all awkward in the tangle of silver chain, the stretched black lines of latex framing you, your face a wonderful mix of tension and pleasure, determination and helplessness. Later I take out the camera and shoot several pictures, the first I have taken of you, wanting to preserve this icon. If they come out they will be superb. You will get to see you in that state.

Time is a jumble, as usual. I remember playing inside you on and on, remember you straining, reaching, taut with the impossibility of using your hands for relief, stretching further, and finally coming. I remember, later, with you excited again, releasing one of your hands so you could finally have that specific release. I remember taking out other toys, fixing the nipple clips to you, and pulling the chain, tugging both your nipples at once, while you moaned with delight. Taking down my pants and offering my cock to your hungry mouth, your head stretching as high as it could reach to get me, to take me in. Moving my cock in your mouth while I pulled the chain to your nipples. Pushing my cock deeper into your mouth, moving into you and then away, giving myself to your heat and holding myself back, and eventually coming all over your chest while you watched.

The next day you will tell me that you were awake all night, playing with the possibilities. I cannot tell you how delightful it is to do this with you, how delightful you are to initiate. You are so present, so alive, so willing to travel, such an incredible mix of vulnerability and strength. I know it is a rare honor to be allowed so deep inside you, and I know too that it is and will be more a deep healing for you to open these doors. These are all the things I want most from this world —to be so completely received, to open new worlds, to heal the deep wounds. To receive all of this from you is such a profound holiness for me—my own confirmation and healing. You lick me nineteen times, wound after wound after wound.

3. Orgasm

There is so much of you flying in my head, demanding to be remembered, clamoring for the attention of memory, that I cannot focus on any one bit for more than a few seconds before the others rise up and take over my consciousness.

From today there is the power of your legs locked around my wrist, my wrist that still smells a little of you, the hot fury of your mouth devouring my cock, your head bobbing up and down in such total concentration and desire while I stretch out, reaching for you, reaching for the obliterating heat of you, for the wet slipperiness you bring to me, for the sound of the wetness, the sound that throws civilized propriety, image, self-consciousness aside, the wild animal of you calling me out from under decades of good boy, the crazed look on your face when you are staring inches away from my swollen, aching cock, when you say "Look at you!" And I do. I look at me, at you, at you looking at me, at the intensity that streams from your eyes, from the taut muscles in my back, from the glistening, leaking, pulsing, purpling head of my cock, from the feel of your hair thick in my fingers, curling, locking, twisting tight to hold onto you, pulling against you, toward you, toward me, toward whatever it is down in the center of me—twisting, turning, screaming to be set free, aching, waiting, wanting, begging, resisting, refusing, yielding, breaking, tearing, falling, crying, screaming, shattering, screaming, washing, washing, washing away.

The river of it, the sounds that come from me as if from someone else, and from you. The delight of you with my heat, with your power, with your power to dismember me, to take me beyond myself, to reduce me to the quivering, aching bursting, to the spasms in my back, my throat, my cock, my neck, my head snapping side to side beyond control, and then the collapsing, the falling, the way it all implodes, the movie of it rewinding, accelerating, swallowing itself as it goes down, down, down, the entire tower of energy collapsing to rubble, to mud, while I hold onto you for my life, dear life, for the dear life of this, for the dear life of you, for the dear life I take from you with unrestrained gluttony, give to you with all my soul—holding on to you to find myself so thoroughly and deeply shaken, needing to know that you are right there with me, right there where you are, shaken in your own way, "soaked" you say, companion to the yet again miracle of it.

How to write about these things? This is what I want to learn, yet another part of what I want to learn. To open myself this way to the sky and to be able to tell about it in some way that is true to the experience and that also can be heard by another, by you who were there, by an outsider who will have only the words for guidance. The urge to take the most personal, inexplicable heart of the matter and make it known, make it public, make it visible, the ultimate act of exhibitionism, of intimacy with all the world, or at least with those who are able to bear witness. The deep, deep urge to be seen, utterly naked, in this very particular way.

Phone Sex: A Hot Way to Ring your Lover's Bells

Isabelle Carruthers

Preparing myself for an evening of *l'amour*, I enjoy a long hot bath, emerging from fragrant waters to garb myself in sexy faded jeans (he loves zippers) and a sheer lace blouse that can be easily unbuttoned with one hand. I open a bottle of chilled white zinfandel and carry it to the bedroom, where I light a single candle and put on some music. Something soft and romantic. Miles Davis will do nicely.

I climb into bed and slide my fingers, now tingling with lust, across the sheet, reaching for the hard, smooth perfection of . . . my telephone. And then I wait for it to ring. And wait some more. Adam is running late tonight.

Such is the fate of long-distance lovers. Mine is a thousand miles away, and some nights it feels like a million. A minor inconvenience, we tell each other; and truthfully, we probably get along much better with a thousand miles between us than we would if we lived together. With one glaring exception: *we can't fuck!*

We tried the cybersex thing—which I prefer to call "e-fuck" because I like the way it sounds—but it lacked that personal touch. Seeing him type "your cunt" didn't do a thing for mine. And I was handicapped, too, because when I'm really turned on my fingers go numb, and so my efforts to type steamy things to get him hard ended up hopelessly garbled *" . . . mmm I want to slidf my moth onto your cofk"* did not achieve the desired effect. We also tried writing erotica for each other, but that just wasn't interactive enough. We had almost given up any hope of sharing ourselves sexually when, one fateful night, we stumbled onto The Joys of Phone Sex.

"What 'ya doing tonite?"

"Nothing. Missing you. Thinking about that night we spent at The Monteleon." (sigh)

"Yeah, I was thinking about that today too . . . making love to you all night." (sigh)

"Just thinking about it, I miss you more. I'm laying here, wet and wanting you. It's torture." (deeper sigh signifying pent-up lust)

"Mmm. You're wet? (combination groan & laugh) What are you wearing anyway?"

(In sexiest voice I can manage) "Cut-offs and a tank top . . how does that sound?" (slightly breathless laugh)

"It sounds like you're overdressed. (voice lowers to a hoarse whisper) Take them off."

You don't need to wonder how quickly I complied with this suggestion. As for what happened next, I'll let you use your imagination. No, it was better than that!

After that first experience, we laughed about it, and laughed at ourselves. Yes, we did feel a little goofy (who wouldn't?), but we also felt that same closeness that any two people feel after they make love and lie, exhausted and entwined, in each other's arms. The only difference was that we were entwined in our telephone cords.

The truly cool part of phone sex, at least when you're doing it with the same partner over the course of many months, is that you develop a kind of Pavlovian reflex, with your libido conditioned to the sound of your lover's voice. Sometimes I only have to say "hello" and it makes him become immediately erect. And it may sound implausible, but he could read the label on a soup can and make me want to fuck him. No matter how you get to that point, you can't deny it's pretty nifty.

The truth is, his voice has always done something to me. So warm, so rich. He's mystified by this, of course, because he doesn't think his voice is sexy. After all, it's the same voice he uses to order pizza and Chinese take-out. Maybe it was easy for us because we both tend to be verbal in bed. Not necessarily talking dirty, but plenty of moaning, groaning, sighing, and whispered endearments. Making the leap to phone sex wasn't too difficult, although it did require a period of adjustment, of becoming comfortable with the adjectives and nouns we didn't normally use in bed. I had to learn to talk about his cock, how it felt and tasted, and about my own anatomy, what I was touching—all the while describing how I felt. Like anything else, this takes a little practice; for me, a few dress rehearsals as well. Sometimes at night I'd lie in bed, imagining his voice through little copper wires, and whisper the things I would say if only he could hear. And when the next phone call came a week later, we were a little more open, a little more descriptive.

Over the course of a couple of years, when tele-sex was often our only means of "togetherness," we've become fairly proficient. It's not just panting into a receiver, after all. There are certain important things you need to know in order to achieve nirvana.

• Call-waiting is a *huge* distraction when you're trying to come, or trying to help your lover come. You'll definitely want to disable that. If you forget to do this, at least be sure not to accidentally depress the button thingy which makes you accept the call.

• Prepaid phone cards are great if you're trying to keep the record of the call from appearing on your telephone bill. But make sure you know how many minutes are left and keep track of them the best you can. It's worth the investment to spend $20 on a phone card that has something like 120 minutes available. You don't have to use it up all at once; but it's far better to run out of orgasms before you run out of minutes, and not the other way around.

- Make sure you won't get interrupted. If you doubt me, then you need only envision the look on the face of your roommate/parent/child/spouse upon finding you naked and writhing on the couch, with a phone stuck to your ear. Plus, any intrusion in the middle of an orgasm just sucks. One of those Excedrin moments they don't show on television.

- If you're having phone sex at your office, prepare to be extremely discreet. Maybe bring along a pillow to bite if you're a screamer; it's amazing what your neighbor in the next office can hear. I've been lucky, since my co-worker really does believe I'm clumsy enough to staple my finger at least once a week.

- Maybe this is just me being paranoid, but I wouldn't recommend doing this on a cordless telephone. Some people have police scanners and can pick up conversations occurring even a few blocks away. Consequently, any conversation that you wish to keep strictly confidential should be confined to a regular telephone.

Are you interested enough by now to try it for yourself? Of course, you and your partner will discover your own language of telephone love, as Adam and I have. But if you want some general advice to get you started, there are a number of resources available on the Internet. The sexuality.org Web site (www.sexuality.org/talk.html), offers reviews of some books on "erotic talking" and extremely useful excerpts.

In *Exhibitionism for the Shy,* Dr. Carol Queen makes these suggestions:

> "Even if you and your partner have never masturbated in each other's presence, you might want to try it over the phone. Touch yourself and describe what you're doing; ask him or her to direct you; direct him or her. You can pretend you're together making love, or you can pretend you're strangers. You can ask for things you're shy about when face-to-face; you can describe your ideal lovemaking to each other."

Queen also suggests paying attention to the voice that you use when you talk to your lover while you're masturbating. This is a good thing to do while you're rehearsing in the privacy of your boudoir. For this exercise, it doesn't matter what you say, necessarily; just imagine saying it to your lover, and listen to how you sound, trying out various erotic inflections. "You want to find elements of hot talk that make you hotter."

A more language-oriented exercise is featured in *Talk Sexy to the One You Love,* by Barbara Keesling. She's got some great practical advice to offer:

> "Lie down in bed, get very comfortable, and begin a genital caress. As you touch yourself, say whatever comes to your mind. Let it come out in a stream of consciousness.... Your stream might include moans, grunts, words, sentence fragments, random thoughts, descriptions of your body, descriptions of what you are doing, descriptions of what you are feeling, or descriptions of fantasies that are being triggered by your caresses."

She recommends that you keep this up for at least fifteen minutes, caressing yourself and continuing to talk the entire time, even if you're muttering nonsense. As she notes, "It doesn't matter if you are being silly, serious, outrageous, or incomprehensible. You don't need to make a single bit of sense.

All you need to do is let yourself go . . ."

While phone sex can still succeed even if all you can manage is moans and heavy breathing, many people do thrive on more explicit and erotic imagery. If you're blushing like a virgin at the very idea of putting your tongue to those words, Ms. Keesling recommends a little exercise that will help you get more comfortable with the kind of language you usually only read in bodice-ripper romance novels.

First, write down as many erotic adjectives you can think of, noting those that turn you on the most. Such a list might include: juicy, big, soft, wet, hot, lovely, aching, gorgeous, sweet, slippery, greedy, magnificent, nasty, tasty, hard, round, firm, wild, luscious, erect, tight, huge, naked, steamy, bare, throbbing, strong, swollen, stiff, gentle, raging, hungry. Practice saying these words, and pair them with appropriate nouns (I think you know which nouns I mean, right?) And finally, practice making compound sentences. For your final exam . . .

> "Call your partner and, in your sexiest voice...tell him how much you want him to have an orgasm before he goes to sleep, and that you'll "talk him through it" if he'll do the necessary work on his end. Tell him in the greatest of detail what you would be doing with him if he were in bed with you right now. Tell him what you're wearing (or not wearing). Tell him how you're touching yourself, and how that feels. Describe your body to him in detail. Talk to him about his body. Tell him how much it turns you on, and how you wish you were touching him."

Over time, you'll find your own rhythm together, discovering the words and images that evoke the best response. Once you're comfortable with the basic mechanics, go ahead and get a little experimental. Adam has discovered that, if he holds me back when I'm in mid-climb towards orgasm, when I do finally come it's much more intense. This requires, of course, that

I let him know when I'm about to come—and it also means that I have to be willing to let him guide me towards climax. Sometimes he does this to me three or four times until I'm almost begging him to let me go. While it does make for a longer telephone call, it's definitely worth that extra dime a minute!

To conclude, and at the risk of waxing rhapsodic, I'll just say that phone sex is much more fulfilling than you might think if you haven't yet tried it. It isn't better than the real thing, not by a long shot. But if you often find yourself unavoidably separated from your lover and wanting to bridge that distance, this might be just the remedy you need. And, perhaps more importantly, it's a wonderful way to open the door to a new level of intimate communication between you and your lover, to heighten your awareness of each other's desires. When the simple sound of your voice makes him want to toss you against something soft and ravish you for hours on end, that's an amazing power. And an amazing gift.

Zucchini

Raphaela Crown

I'll admit it . . . I don't always feel this sexy. Some days I just feel . . . big. But today I'm the Venus of Willendorf with clothes on, a walking fertility goddess: enormous balloon-like tits, huge handfuls of round ass, a broad expanse of luscious belly. Did I mention my tiny waist? Today men seem to be sniffing me from a block away; they look up as I pass, half admiring, half rueful. They know they don't stand a chance with the goddess. Is it because—despite the modest long skirt, there is nothing standing between the sidewalk and . . . me? Every step I take is breathing out a little pussy breath, breathing in the lustful glances of the street.

As I stroll by the fruit market, I blush to discover I'm sizing up the zucchini. That one is so thick, has such a nice curve. Or the cucumber—wonderfully smooth but perhaps not so big. I want it big. Today, I want it huge. But the nectarine—sliced in half, its juicy pit clit exposed, is looking pretty good too. I'm afraid I'll start to grab and suck—or worse, plunge that green monster right up underneath my skirt, so I say goodbye to this attractive produce only to find myself next door running my hands along the bowls and cups.

As the Venus walks in, the proprietor rises. He'd like to help me. "Feel this," he says, taking my hand and tracing the outlines of a vase. It's soft—yet hard. "Or this," he proposes, reaching up behind me to take down a truly magnificent tureen. I can feel his arousal without even touching him. He is emitting heat, but I want more, so I thrust out my ass so it will meet his front. I may be soft, but he is definitely hard. I shift just a little . . . ah, yes, we're in contact. I rustle my skirt slightly so he knows just how close I am. All he has to do is lift up my skirt and feed it to me. But he can't decide where to put his hands first—my full breasts, my dripping cunt, my hungry ass. Oh God, I want that big hard prick inside me, now. He solves the dilemma by reaching up under my skirt with one hand, reaching around the front with the other. My nipples are jumping through my blouse, as he rubs and pinches them and then, just as I think I can't stand it one more moment, he leans me over the table and thrusts himself inside me. "You are so wet," he murmurs, "I want to come all over you." We are fucking fast and furious, nothing can stop us . . . but then the bell rings, signifying a customer. We can't stop! But the ringing continues, so he pulls out, zips up, and leans me up against the table, leaving me wondering if somehow I can fuck an urn.

I am ready to kill this annoying customer, who dared come into a shop in the middle of the business day, but she is so cute—and so sexy. She quickly takes in the situation. "Can I play too?" she seems to ask, "I'm looking for something . . . round." Suddenly she has me pinned up against the wall, her hands under my skirt, rubbing my ass, licking my neck. She smells delicious, like lavender and cloves and mint. "You smell . . . like sex," she says, but my lips are already parting for her lithe, athletic tongue. I need her in me, but she keeps teasing, tickling, running her fingers along my thigh, circling the small of my back. Every time I try to meet her thigh, desperate for some relief, she manages to evade me. "Fuck me," I'm groaning, "fuck me!" "All in good time," she says, her hot breath sparking spasms far away, below. Just when I think I can't stand it a moment longer, she pushes me down onto the table, lifts up my skirt and plunges her tongue inside me. Now it's her tongue and fingers, God, I'm coming . . . but even though she is running the show so far, I notice her breath too is ragged. So I unzip her jeans, and reach my rings deep into her dripping pussy, then lick off her juice. Now it is my turn to tease, I keep approaching and pulling away, aided by the distraction of my own arousal. But finally we are grinding mons to mons, we can't help it, we must feel each other's skin, as much skin as possible, oh, we are coming together, in a hot wet wonderful gush. The pottery man—we can't forget him—can't resist us either. As I lie on top of her, he plunges into me, so that we are all sparking each other, his huge orgasm triggering mine, triggering hers. I have never been so satisfied—and so eager for more. Can this be? She maneuvers me into a storeroom and we stand there, simply kissing among the beautiful objects. "I have a huge bed and wonderfully crisp sheets," she whispers. I'm sure they smell of lavender and mint. As we turn to leave, the proprietor stops us. "I think I've found just what you were looking for," he says, handing me an exquisite porcelain . . . zucchini.

I Went Home Last Night With Stella

Pasquale Capocasa

We'll take my car,
she said, it'll be all right.

We moved across the common to the underground park
oblivious to the muggers snaking from tree to pole . . .

. . . and then, twenty-five minutes later
we pulled into a yard
that housed a large black dog
caught yellow-eyed
in the beam of the headlights,
and chained to a truck tire filled with cement.

He didn't bark;
he strained and glared,
and it was plain to me
he was schizoid.
That's Herbie, was all she said.

Later,
caught in the wonderful complexities
of limbs and mouths
with the colors simply brilliant
we heard from the open window:

bangbang!
bang! bang! bang!

Stella rolled to the floor
wth a practiced movement,
slicing at the lamp on the way down,
dragging me along with her.

Naked, and in the dark on the cool summer floor,
we heard two bursts of automatic fire:

rat tat tat tat-rat tat tat tat!
What the hell?
Shhhhhh, she said softly in my ear,
and then, astonishing me, bit it.
Yeah, well . . . what the hell, I whispered . . .

. . . much later, while drinking coffee
and reading about the shoot-out in Charlestown,
Juicy, the day bartender, said to me,
Stella lives down there,
she oughta move.
Yeah, I said,
mentally rearranging my apartment.

Dance Naked

Susannah Indigo

Baby it's cold outside . . . I live in the state of grace called Colorado, with 948 million aspen trees and an average 300 sunny days a year. But even here, the holiday season can be cold and somber for way too many people. There is too little joyous sex involved, and way too much false cheer and super-sized spending. I believe we need more displays of crazy reindeer and fewer visions of VISA cards floating through our night dreams in the month of December. And I believe our world would be a far better place if more people were wary of organizations that are divisive, from churches to political parties, and if more of us were energized by the simplicity of sex and kindness as a kind of religion.

Listen to the fireplace roar . . . Or sit quietly in front of the candlelight tonight. Today the light returns as the winter solstice arrives and the days grow longer once again. It is a time for a simple feast, for friends, for ringing bells, for dancing in a circle of love, whether it forms naturally around you or you have to create it for yourself. It is a time to meditate in the dark. Learn about *lovingkindness* meditation and give it a try—just sit comfortably and think kind thoughts, starting with yourself. *May I be happy. May I be safe. May I be peaceful. May I live with ease.* Then focus your power on another person, perhaps someone you've loved and lost. *May he be happy. May he be safe. May he be peaceful. May he live with ease.* Now is the time to slow your life down and learn when sunrise and sunset are and begin to observe them. I learned long ago that if I rise every morning and meditate through the sunrise, it helps keep me focused and makes me grounded in the now of the present moment.

Maybe just a half drink more (put some records on while I pour) . . . Drink something wonderful that warms you right down to your toes. Tia Maria on the rocks works for me tonight. Then dance naked. If you feel silly, drink a little more. Crank up the music. If you're alone, put on headphones to get the music all the way inside you. Try D'Angelo for pure sex. Dance by yourself, with a lover, with friends, with the cordless phone to your ear laughing with someone long-distance, with your cat, maybe even with those racy reindeer. Dance in a circle of love, in front of the mirror, in the glimmer of candlelight, in touch with your body the way it was meant to be.

I wish I knew how (your eyes are like starlight now) . . Now is the time to say *I love you.* It's free, and it's only made easier through practice. *I love you. You matter to me. Thank you for being in my life.* Those are the words everyone needs to hear, those are the real gifts of the season.

Gosh your lips are delicious . . . To kiss: the meaning of sex. To kiss the mouth, the neck, the heart, the soul. Kiss upside down, kiss early, kiss often, but kiss for a very long time when you can. Now is the time to forget the malls and the wrapping paper and just immerse ourselves in our own natural beauty and sexuality, kissing and holding and touching and making love through the night. Now is the time to envelop ourselves in more sex, more kindness, more dancing, and the next thing we know, the wild nights are calling and baby it's cold outside . . . no more.

34B

Annette Marie Hyder

Huge Mammoth Hooters
mine are not.
My cup does not *runneth over.*
But they're
full of personality
really outgoing.

Every time I
bend over low
they peek out at
the doctor's/salesman's/UPS guy's
face
to see him drop his
composure/stance/jaw.

I like to display these
brazen bas-reliefs
on pedestals
like works of art
unveil them slowly
theatrically.

What could be better
than cherries
on top of ice-cream sundaes?

I have brought down
Goliaths
with these small missiles.
And while it's true
that I have used them,
I've always only used them
for good.

A Wonderbra?
That would be like
giving firecrackers
a pep talk
like asking helium
to rise.

Carmen Who Lives at the Lake

David Surface

The first true story John heard about sex was about someone he knew, a wild, beautiful boy, diabetic since childhood, whose parents supplied him with sports cars he kept wrapping around trees and walking away from, unharmed. In this story, a group of kids are drinking quarts of vodka around a bonfire near the railroad tracks when the boy and his girlfriend disappear into the woods. After a while, there's the thunder and scream of a train passing by, followed by another scream. A moment later, the boy comes staggering back into the firelight, his right hand dripping red, blood spattered all over his shirt and mouth. *Because she was on the rag!* The storytellers howled with laughter—John couldn't tell if it was with disgust or admiration or some third feeling he couldn't name. Their laughter felt dangerous to him; he imagined that if he tried to join in, they would hear the lie in his voice, then turn that hard laughter on him and cut him with it until he bled.

With girls, he felt safe. They would look him in the eye longer than any boy would, so he trusted them. And they trusted him. They would sit very close and tell him their troubles while the warm smell of their skin or the sudden curve of a breast caused a quick, stabbing pain that left him confused and irritable. That he had never touched anyone—at sixteen—was a small but real worry. Listening to some other boy brag about *getting some wool, some stinky,* John saw the boy's face burn red and thought that all boys are sad, frightened liars. He knew he didn't want to be one. He wanted to love a girl without having to be a boy.

John had grown up indoors, drawing pictures and making up stories, and had missed out on the usual boyhood rituals. The first time someone threw a basketball to him during gym class, he'd frozen like a squirrel before an oncoming car, then blindly threw the ball to a player on the other team. The other boys surrounded him and screamed in his face for what felt like an hour, calling him pussy until his mind went blank. What kept coming back to him later was not the names or angry voices, but that moment when he chose to throw the ball, how he'd betrayed himself by pretending to know what he was doing. The thought of the same thing happening in bed or in the back of a car with a girl was unbearable.

He thought for a while that the problem might be the town—driving up and down the by-pass with the same neon signs he'd known since birth scorching their letters deeper into his brain, he felt sure of it—the girl who would have him was not here. He would have to go out into the world to find her. Unless, somehow, she came to him first.

He saw her for the first time from a long way off, walking home from school with two other girls on the right side of the road. She was smaller than the other two and dressed in darker colors. She walked looking down, body curled forward slightly as if against a cold wind. It looked as though she was carrying some kind of heavy package in both arms; when she was closer he saw she was cradling her own breasts.

In a school where nothing ever seemed to happen, it was easy to find out about new people. Her name was Carmen, and she had just moved to town with her father, an architect who had come all the way from Massachusetts to build a new type of bridge over the interstate north of town. John had already driven under the skeleton of that bridge many times. It was needle-thin, straddled the highway like a giant spider, and only blocked out a few stars.

Carmen was a small girl with a plain, childish body and the full breasts of a grown woman that she did her best to conceal. Her black hair was cut short, with what there was of it pushed up by a dark hair-band. Under boyish black eyebrows, her wide eyes looked even wider with their pale, water-colored irises. There was a small, exploding sun of gold in her right eye that would show up whenever the real sun struck it, but never under electric light. Her eyes, together with her spiky crown of hair, gave her the appearance of being permanently startled, which made John want to stroke and calm her.

Like him, she preferred to keep quiet and take in what was going on around her, so it was a while before he heard her talk. When she did, it made him think of church bells underwater. The next time she spoke, he told her.

"I like your voice. Your accent, I mean."

She turned her startled look on him and said, "Why?" He thought it was an extraordinary thing to ask. *Because you're not from here. Because I don't feel like I'm from here either.*

"Because," he said, "It's pretty. It's different."

"Not to me," she smiled shyly. Then, before he could decide to feel hurt, "Thanks. I just never thought it was anything special, that's all." When he saw how uncomfortable he'd made her, he knew he'd have to do something quickly to take the attention off of her.

"What about me?" he asked, "Do I sound different to you?"

She looked up, considering. "Yes."

"Do I sound dumb?" he drawled, doing his very best southern hick voice. *Laugh,* he thought.

She laughed. "You do now."

"But you can understand me, right?"

"Sure. I can understand you."

One day between classes he found her pencil on the floor. He didn't know it was hers until he picked it up and put it in his pocket, intending to keep it, then smelled his fingers. It was her smell. Some kind of scent she wore, like nothing else he'd smelled before. He started to walk through the school, looking for her among all the other faces and bodies in the halls, reaching up to smell his fingers to reassure himself he wasn't mistaken. In a few minutes the bell would ring for the next class and it would be too late. The he saw her from behind, head down, making her way through the crowd. He ran up behind her and put one hand on her shoulder. She jumped a little, turned and stared at him, then laughed her good laugh. "You scared me!"

"Here," he said, still panting for breath, holding out her pencil. She stared at it like he'd just pulled a dove or a ball of fire out of his pocket. "It's yours."

She reached out for it cautiously like she thought it might disappear, then took it. "Yeah," she said, then, "How did you know it was mine?"

"I could smell you," he said without thinking, "It smells like you." He waited to see what she would do.

She looked at him for a moment, then smiled, "Thanks." *She didn't run away,* was what he kept thinking. That was all he needed.

She had two laughs. One was a kind of unhappy bark she reserved for something she could see coming. When she laughed that way, her face didn't change much, and her eyes looked large and disappointed. The other laugh was for things that took her by surprise; she'd screw up her face and shake, her eyes shrinking to two bright glints she'd turn on him like she couldn't believe she was really laughing this hard and needed him to confirm it.

He liked the easy way they became friends. It was the crossing-over part that was hard for him. He was too polite to make a move on any girl he wasn't already friends with. By the time he'd made friends with a girl there was something strange, almost indecent, about wanting to touch her, like wanting to touch his own sister or cousin.

It had been like that with Beth, the first and only girl he'd ever dated. For five months they'd done nothing more than kiss and hold hands. Beth, who was a year older and almost as shy as he was, started going to other boys who would do the things she wanted without making her ask. Once when he'd been going on about Beth, Carmen looked at him and said, "You know, Beth's not as perfect as you think she is." Her eyes were bright with a kind of anger he'd never seen in them before; it helped hold off the pain of what she was telling him and from that moment on, this was the way he would picture her loving him—catching him in a screw-up, rescuing him from one wrong idea after another.

Carmen lived in a house her father had built at the edge of the lake north of town. He had designed it himself according to a personal interior logic that was new to John. John's house, where he lived with his parents, seemed to have been born the way it was, with all the objects in it created at once. Carmen's house felt random, chaotic and warm. Its walls and angles confused and excited him.

On one of the last warm days in September, she invited him out for a swim. A few trees had already started to turn, and except for the distant hum of a motorboat on the opposite shore, they were the only two people in sight. John had the feeling they were closing down the lake for the winter, that it was already past time, and the two of them were breaking some kind of curfew.

John was glad the day was a little cold so he could keep his shirt on. He was ashamed of his thin chest and kept it covered all summer, even when he went into the water. What was hardest about this was the memory of being five or six in his grandparents' garden and taking off his shirt to run, how he'd loved the way his skin warmed and tightened over his stomach and chest, the buzzing feeling the wind made on his nipples. Over and over, he'd bare his chest to the hot sun and dangerous bees, knowing that this was what he liked, this was what he wanted to be forever. *I want to be a pirate . . .*

"You look like one," Carmen said. John looked up, startled. *How did she know?*

"What do you mean?"

"I don't know," she smiled her good smile, "You just kind of look like one today. Maybe it's your hair."

He saw her eyes travel down the front of his body and the blood in him surged so fast that it hurt. Then he saw she was laughing. "You're getting your shirt wet." John looked down at the blue denim darkening around his waist and suddenly felt stupid. Quickly, he unbuttoned his shirt, his hands working underwater to reach the last few buttons, and threw it back on shore.

As the sun began to bury itself in the trees, their voices started to echo as if they were under a giant glass bowl someone was slowly lowering over their heads. When they noticed that the air had turned cooler than the water, they gathered their things and walked back to the house.

Since Carmen's parents were away, no one had turned on the lights and Carmen went around flicking switches that popped like gunshots in the empty house. The small fear that John had felt down at the lake had grown to a definite ache in the back of his throat, and he was grateful when Carmen brought them two mugs of tea from the kitchen. They sat drinking their tea while the light faded from the windows and the spaces between their talk grew wider and wider. When John felt he couldn't make it through the next silence, he put his hand behind Carmen's neck and drew her toward him. She didn't pull away, but set the muscles in her back and gave him something to pull against until she was all the way there. Her kisses were tentative and serious. Despite the warm shock of her mouth moving on his, it felt strangely familiar, as if this was something they'd practiced together many times. The first time her warm tongue slipped into his mouth he felt an electric shock go through him. They stayed this way for a long time, sitting upright, touching only with their mouths. When they finally lay down together, he was shaking so hard he had to stop and let her hold him. She held him lightly, touching only his shoulder and hip; he wished she would hold him tighter to help make the shaking stop.

The first time he reached up and cupped her full, warm breast in his hand, she drew away from him and sat up and he thought it was over, he'd gone too far—until he saw her lift the striped knit shirt over her head and pull it off, her bra glowing ghostly white in the dark. When they started again, it was like walking through a series of doors into a hugeness that almost frightened him. To hold on, he focused on the small particulars —the brown freckles between her neck and shoulder, the tiny, tarnished metal clasp at the front of her bra, the worn Navaho patterns of the sofa cushions behind her head.

He reached behind her back and fumbled blindly at her bra, looking for a clasp. "Wait," she whispered, "Let me do it." In amazement, he watched her reach between her breasts and undo the tiny clasp and let the twin cups fall away. Her breasts were larger than he'd dreamed, full and round with impossibly soft, milky skin. Her nipples were like smooth brown pebbles, so small they looked lost. He wanted to put his mouth on them. He cupped her breasts in his hands and gently lifted them, wondering at their warmth and heaviness. Slowly, he brought his mouth to her left nipple and felt it tighten between his lips. "Is this alright?" he asked. He didn't know what he'd do if she said No. He was beyond stopping.

At first he thought she hadn't heard him. Then he heard her answer, "Yes," her voice sounding small and tight in her throat. He took her breast back into his mouth and started to suck while she cradled his head in her arms. He could taste a little salt from her sweat, and a trace of another, sharper flavor he couldn't name, like sweet onion grass. The harder he sucked, the tighter she pressed his head to her breast until it was flattened against her ribs. He rose up for a moment and looked down at her body he'd waited so long to see, her left breast glistening wet where his mouth had been, her right breast dry and neglected-looking. He wanted to get both of them into his mouth at the same time. He pushed her breasts together as close as he could and went from one to the other, taking huge, hungry bites. She arched her back silently like an animal stretching, then slid her thigh up between his legs and pressed it against his cock that was aching and straining hard against his jeans. He knew if he didn't come soon, he would die.

When her hand reached down for the first time, his heart stopped. He listened for his heartbeat but couldn't find it, only the unbelievable music of his belt buckle clinking under fingers that were not his own. He rolled over onto his back and felt the cool air hit his cock as she released it into the open, then her small, warm fingers stroking and pulling with patience and insistence. The feeling was like a sun growing bigger and bigger inside, blinding him. The small part of him that still couldn't believe this was really happening, spoke.

"Wait . . ."

Her hand stopped moving. He could hear her breathing close to his ear. "You don't want to come?" she asked, sounding surprised—at the sound of the word from her lips he knew it was too late. He dug his head backward into the pillow and groaned as the first spasm took him. Carmen made a breathless, startled sound and started pumping harder and faster to keep time with his spurts, each one filling his brain with white-hot light that made him go blind for a moment.

When he could finally open his eyes again, the room was full of the warm, salty sea-smell of his own come. He saw her familiar face looking down at him, her eyes wide like she'd surprised herself. He didn't realize he'd made so much noise until she asked, "Are you alright?" and he folded her into his arms and laughed like she'd just told him the best joke he'd ever heard.

After that, they made love regularly, or as often as they could living at their parents' houses. Late at night, red-eyed and weary from waiting for everyone else to go to bed. They always started out the same way, talking until they'd run out of things to say, then him slipping his hand behind her neck and bending her toward him, pulling against her muscles' slight straining in the opposite direction. Every time, it took exactly the same amount of effort, no more and no less. He believed that this would change in time.

He loved her house in the woods, the colored glass windows, narrow like a church's, throwing light out over the leaves. He loved the long walk to her door, how he could use that time to think of who he was and where he was going and what he was going there for. This house, their house, seemed so holy to him that sometimes it was enough all by itself. He'd stand outside in the leaves and watch her family moving around inside and feel a kind of love for all of them. Sometimes when he was watching, a light would go on in a house across the street or someone would pull into the driveway next door; he'd wonder how he must look and thought of what would happen if some well-meaning neighbor called the police. It made him smile just to think about it, how the policemen would walk him up to the door, how they'd open the door and smile, *Oh yes, we know him.* He could picture this scene and feel warmer, even with the cold eating into his feet and hands.

When they made love in his car it was always in the front seat. There was more room in the back, but somehow they never ended up back there, partly because he felt stupid asking her to go to the back seat with him, so he imagined it was how she would feel too. And because once they'd started kissing he was afraid of having to stop and start over. Somehow they made it work. The steering wheel, the rearview mirror, the automatic gearshift all made room for them. He liked it best with her on top because he could keep from coming longer. On winter nights the windows would be white with steam, blotting out the outside world except for a few abstract smudges of light. He loved the way the cold air felt on his cock when she rose up, then the heat of her pussy swallowing him again when she moved down; then the cold, then the heat. He thought of a lighthouse beacon making the sea safe for sailors at night, and that was the word he heard inside every time she moved down on him. *Safe. Safe.*

He knew what he wanted but didn't know how to ask. All the words he knew for it seemed wrong, either too ugly or too silly but he said them anyway because he felt he could now. "Will you eat me?" The words came out strange and clumsy in the dark. He hoped she'd laugh out loud, not stay silent and make him suffer. Finally she gave a quick burst of a giggle and he laughed with her in relief and gratitude. After a moment she answered.

"I don't think I want to." She said it carefully, tentatively, as if she was asking a question instead of answering one.

"Sure," he said too quickly, then, "Why not?" He was curious; he thought the reason would be simple and have to do with the two of them. But when he saw her look down, gathering her words, he realized with a cold feeling in the pit of his stomach that he was about to get a story about someone else.

"A long time ago," she began, and he thought that this must be how all lovers begin stories about other lovers, a long time ago, "Someone asked me to do that. I said I didn't want to. And he called me a bitch." Here she laughed her short, unhappy laugh. "So I don't have very good feelings about doing that. I guess that's not very fair, is it?"

"No. I mean, it's all right. Don't worry about it." He'd listened to her story with a feeling like something in his head was about to explode. But by the time she was through he felt better, even stronger, knowing he was better than that, knowing he would never do that to her; he hoped she knew. If she didn't, he would show her; he would never ask again.

He was still self-conscious of his body around her, of his thin chest and the hips that were too wide for the rest of him, so when he turned out the light before they took off their clothes, it was more for his sake than for hers. He thought that this would change in time, and it did, a little, though whenever he had to cross the room naked and pass through a shaft of light, he felt the pale flesh hanging from his bones and it burned him, knowing she was watching.

Her body, to him, was a private miracle. Small as a child, there was so much of her, so much to learn, he knew he'd never be able to know all of it. Even if he kept going for the rest of his life, there would still be more.

"What do you call it?" he asked, because he thought he could now.

"What?"

"What do you call yourself—here?" he asked, cupping her, holding her between her legs.

"Nothing," she said after a while.

"What do you mean?" he looked up, smiling, and saw that she expected him to believe this. Nothing. No name for what she had. He wanted to say the name, but he wanted it to be the one she used. He was sure she had a name for it and that it would be beautiful. Even if it was one of the names he already knew, she would say it in her voice and make it beautiful. He'd thought they would share it. Now she was telling him they would not. Even though they both had no clothes on, he felt like he was the one who was naked.

"Nothing," he said, "That's a funny name," but what he wanted to say was, *Don't do this. Don't leave me here.*

Christmas Eve, and they'd been kissing naked on the big couch in her parents' living room for an hour before John felt brave enough to start moving down the front of her body, kissing his way down. When he slid his hands under her hips he could feel her go tense with what he hoped was her own pleasure. He waited for his mind to get used to this new way of seeing her and himself. Her hair, her scent, were amazing and almost blinded him to what he was looking for; he couldn't believe how hard it was to find at first. He pushed his tongue around in the bristly, chestnut colored pubic hair until he found the soft lips and slipped the tip of his tongue between them. What he tasted went straight to his brain and cancelled out every other thought, except the memory of being five or six and pushing his tongue out underwater toward the aluminum ladder, the hard, bright taste of metal pulsing through the water to his tongue in electric waves.

Carmen jerked and a sharp laugh came out of her. "Sorry," her voice drifted down from somewhere above. When he went back to what he was doing, she laughed harder and rolled away.

"What's the matter?" It was difficult for him to speak.

"It tickles."

"It tickles?" He felt like he was trying to push the words through from the other side of a deep and vivid sleep.

"Yeah," she said, pushing herself up and out of his reach on her elbows. "Okay?" It was not really a question.

John suddenly felt the cold light falling across his naked legs and ass, the ridiculous posture he was in. He felt a door close in his face. *This is all I will ever have of this. No one I love and who loves me will ever look down at me from up there and say my name.*

She had a dog—her father's, really—that lived under the house and ran out snarling whenever he drove up. A beautiful black and white mongrel, part shepherd and part collie, it could run faster than he could drive and literally ran circles around his car whenever he drove down her street. The dog, whose name was Travis, would escort him from his car to the front porch, running a wide circle around him through the fallen leaves, then shoot up the stairs ahead of him to be waiting at the door. He'd ring the bell and at that signal, together with Carmen's footsteps, her unlocking and opening the door, Travis would become ferocious for five seconds until Carmen shouted his name, so that her first greeting to John always came together with this ritual anger.

Inside, Travis would watch John from the far side of the room until John sat on the floor and let his hands hang loose over his knees toward the dog. Then, the cautious approach, the preliminary sniffing, the inevitable walk into his open hands. It was a perfect little drama that played itself over and over again and he loved it. Sometimes he would stay on the floor for hours, rubbing rough circles in the animal's warm neck, thinking, *This is what I do best. This is what I love.*

He wanted her to like it again. That was all. But when he tried to touch her now, there was something in the way. And that something had nothing to do with him—that was what she told him. As if that would be a comfort to him. What stopped him cold was how beyond it all she seemed. Not in any snobbish, superior way, but with a deep sadness, a weary despair at what they were doing—at what he wanted her to do. It had become that, so soon—something he wanted her to do.

Like TB victims, he thought sunlight and fresh air could cure whatever was killing them. He took her to mountaintops (such as they had around there), ruined cabins, hidden rivers that flowed out of hillsides and back underground. Once when they were lying side by side on the ground, not touching, she started crumbling dry leaves in her hand, holding them up against the sun and watching the flakes sift down between her fingers. "Look," she said, "It's so great." It was the first time he'd heard pleasure in her voice in a long time. He picked up a leaf and crumbled it himself, let the pieces pepper down onto her creamy arm, then reached over to brush them away softly with his fingers. Instantly, she jerked her arm away and stood up.

"What?" he asked.

"I was doing it because it was beautiful," she said. "You were doing it just to get on me."

He watched her walk back toward the car, stood in a numb haze to follow her and realized she was right, that he was now making up ploys to touch her.

There was a hill in the center of town where the hospital and water tower were. This was where young couples had gone to park for decades, except in winter when the roads could be too steep and slick for any car to climb, but that was when he took her, shifting down to second gear, then third, ignoring her questions, *Where are we going?* They were going to do this, he thought, climb the hill and do this like before, although they'd never made love here—he was relying on the history, the spirit of the place, all the people who had been here before to rise up and help him. And the fact that she didn't want to be here started a little fire of anger down low in his body, and it hit him that this was what he needed to get through his fear of her.

When they reached the top of the hill he was surprised to see that other cars had made it here ahead of them and were parked along the lip of the hill overlooking the town, some of them at crazy angles as if their drivers couldn't wait to start what they'd come here for. Carmen had been silent for a while; now he felt her silence deepen. He turned off the engine and immediately the cold crept in, reaching through the windows to touch the side of his face.

They sat for a minute looking at the lights of town scattered over the dark hillside below, and it struck him how small it all looked. He thought this was something she might like to hear coming from him.

"It looks a lot smaller than I thought. From up here, I mean."

"Really?" she spoke, her voice sounding strange and small to him, "It looks bigger than I thought." He heard her making quiet laughing noises, then realized with a stabbing feeling in his chest that she was crying.

"What?" he asked, touching her shoulder, all thoughts of what he'd come here for gone. "What is it?"

"I'm just glad you're my friend," she sobbed, then folded herself into his side, her sobbing shaking his whole body. His eyes searched the lights outside the car as if he could find among them the thing she'd seen that made her cry. He didn't ask why she was crying; he didn't even feel the sting of what she'd called him *(my friend)* because he was too busy feeling the warmth of her body against his for the first time in weeks, rejoicing in her need of him, though it was not the kind of need he'd hoped for. *I can do this,* he thought, holding her tighter and stroking her hair. But soon he couldn't help thinking that he could make her feel even better. If she let him.

The biggest shame was this—how could he still want it when she didn't? If the reason she didn't want it was because she was in some kind of pain, how could he still want it? Didn't that mean he was bad, like all men? Wasn't that all the proof she needed? She was better than him, that much was clear. He would dry up and blow away needing her, while she would stay the same forever.

Another Christmas Eve, and they sat in the little room under the stairs to her mother's bedroom with one light on behind her head and her face in shadow, the torn paper and the gifts they'd given each other forgotten on the floor at their feet. It was at Christmas, many years ago, that he'd first felt the wall come down. Standing in front of the tree he'd just helped his mother and father put up, he'd waited for the lights and the pine smell and the music drifting in from the stereo in the next room to do their familiar work on him, but nothing happened and the feeling was like being inside a glass jar; the good things that got through before could not reach him and he felt suddenly afraid that this would last and that he would feel this way forever. He wondered (but could not ask) if it was like that for her now, whether this was something she made happen or something that happened to her the way it had happened to him.

He was waiting for her to say something. This was happening more and more; she would stop speaking and after a few attempts to ask her what she was thinking, what was wrong, he would give up and wait for her. Tonight he'd been waiting for nearly an hour before she spoke.

"No one really does anything for anyone else." She said it without looking at him, staring straight ahead, her eyes full of that hard and distant look that frightened him.

"What do you mean?"

"I mean no one ever does anything for anyone else unless they get something out of it. It's all for yourself. It's always for yourself."

He sat with his hands folded in front of him, giving his very best impression of patience and understanding, leaning forward slightly like a priest in a confessional, hating himself for not knowing what to say to help her, wishing she would just let him touch her. What they did for each other with their bodies was real—what she was talking about now was not real—if she would just let him touch her, she would see that. This thing that got inside her would go away and they would be all right again.

"I don't know," he spoke carefully. "Maybe some people just like to help other people. Maybe they get something out of it, like it makes them feel good. But if it helps the other person, what's wrong with that?"

She kept staring straight ahead for a moment, then turned her face toward him in the lamplight. "You know," she said, "You think you're always going to feel the way you do now, but you're not. You're going to be just as fucked up as everyone else."

Later, driving home past all the houses with their Christmas lights he decided; he would prove her wrong. He would do nothing for himself; it would all be for her from now on. Because he loved her it would be simple and right. It would make him happy to do it. Unless, of course, that meant he was getting something out of it for himself, which would make her right again. He thought about it like this until his head felt like it was going to explode, but in the end he knew he was going to stay with it. He wanted to defeat her by making her happy.

But by the time he turned off his headlights and ignition and rolled silently into his parents' driveway, he was taking the same words he'd used on her and turning them around on himself. *And what difference does it make if I don't love you anymore, as long as I do all the things I'm supposed to do and say all the things I'm supposed to say, what difference does it make?* He knew he'd never ask this question out loud when he realized he didn't know how to answer it—he thought it was the kind of question only terrible people couldn't answer.

There were many foreign students in John's English Lit class. He'd already made friends with several of them, including a group of Iranian men and a tiny girl from Thailand whose best friend was a Japanese girl named Keiko. The Thai girl talked and laughed constantly while Keiko said almost nothing and would glide silently by her friend's side, head bent patiently to catch whatever the smaller girl was saying.

Keiko sat two desks in front of him. Though they had only smiled politely and had never spoken, he loved watching her. She was somewhat larger than other Japanese women he'd seen, but she moved her strong hands and solid arms with such delicate control that she seemed much smaller than she was. Her face was a big, calm moon that would appear from time to time out of a curtain of black hair.

The teacher was a harmless charmer who considered it his mission to open young people's minds. "Go out," he said one afternoon, "And do something you've never done before."

John took Keiko to see a performance at the university theater, a company of Flamenco dancers—not the pretty kind, no sequins or bright colors; it was wild, sweaty and frightening. The women stamped and fumed. One man threw himself to the edge of the stage on his knees and started wailing a song about the five bulls of his senses, about the five gates that would swing open inside him.

Later, the shock of a new mouth moving against his, new breath coming into his mouth. He was surprised at the smallness of her tongue; her scent, which was like some kind of wonderful sourdough bread, seemed to emanate from there. He loved the way her long black hair covered them both like a curtain when she was on top of him. On the couch at his parents' house, she pushed her crotch against his so hard that it hurt. He realized he'd never seen another woman come—he wanted to see what Keiko looked like when she came.

He reached down and unbuckled the big turquoise and leather belt she wore, unsnapped her jeans and slid his hand down into the humid warmth between her legs. She grabbed his wrist and started to pull his hand out until he found her lips beneath her warm, bristly hair and started rubbing them in slow, lazy circles. She held on to his wrist, but didn't move it away. He kept rubbing and watched her big face grow smooth and still like she was looking for something inside herself. She had stopped kissing him and pressed her lips together tighter and tighter until she finally opened them and took six or seven sharp, knife-like breaths and said a word he didn't understand—for a moment he thought it might be somebody's name.

When they were through and a violent thunderstorm was

lashing at the windows, he tried to make her tell stories about her childhood because that was what he felt like hearing now. To help her get started, he told her one of his own about the Shabby Man, the ancient, blind bum who steals bad children out of their beds at night. He asked her what kind of stories her parents told her when she was bad. "Who did they say would come and get you if you were bad?"

She smiled, her great face so close. "The wind."

"The wind?" he teased her, "That's not scary."

"Yes it is! It *is* scary. The wind is very scary because he lives in a cave in the ocean, all alone, and when he comes for you, you do not see him."

Earlier John had wondered if he would think of Carmen, maybe even see her face at certain key moments the way people in movies sometimes do, but he didn't. Afterwards he felt surprised to realize that he hadn't thought of Carmen once.

John and Keiko never fucked, partly out of some strange kind of loyalty to Carmen, but also because he could do things with Keiko that he'd never been able to do with Carmen, so that fucking seemed like a waste of precious time. With Keiko, he didn't put a name on the things he wanted for fear she wouldn't understand, so he'd start slowly, showing her what he wanted by doing it.

One night he was getting up from the couch when his hard cock accidentally brushed the side of her face, grazing her cheek. "Sorry," he laughed.

"Don't worry," she smiled, looking up at him, "Is all right."

He looked down at her beautiful moon-face looking up at him in the dark and felt new miles of permission opening between them. "It is?" he said.

"Yes," she whispered, her smile turning a little wicked and

dreamy. Feeling brave, he took his cock in his hand and rubbed it gently against her cheek. He'd spent hours exploring the more secret places of her body, but this was the softest, warmest thing he'd ever felt.

"Is this all right?" he whispered.

"Yes," she said. Like a cat, she closed her eyes and rubbed her cheek affectionately against his cock in a way that made his brain catch fire.

Feeling like he was standing outside of himself, watching, he slowly traced the outline of her jaw, carefully avoiding her mouth. He traced the shape of her closed eyelids, feeling her eyelashes brush against the soft skin on head of his cock. "Is this all right?" he whispered again. This time she didn't speak, but nodded her head slowly. He hated it when Carmen held completely still, but this was different.

When he took his cock away from Keiko's face he saw a thread of come stretch between her cheek and the tip of his cock, then break. He reached down and rubbed the tiny wet spot into her cheek with his thumb. She took his thumb into her mouth and sucked it for a moment, looked up at him and said, "Is all right?" Before John could answer, Keiko cupped his ass in her hands, drew him toward her and rubbed her face back and forth against his cock, brushing her nose and lips against it without taking him into her mouth.When he saw what she was doing, John felt his mind start to tear loose from his body. Keiko lifted her face for a moment, looked up at him and smiled, "Is alright?" This time it was John who couldn't answer.

No matter how much he enjoyed what they did together, he thought of Keiko as something he was going to have to pay for later. He kept waiting for his punishment but it never came. The fact that it never came just reinforced his feeling that it was out there waiting for him, gathering strength every time he went from Carmen to Keiko and back again.

While he was seeing Keiko he could not touch Carmen, though the cause was not obvious since he and Carmen had reached that point in their relationship where it was not unusual for a whole series of evenings to pass without their touching or kissing. She made him tea in her kitchen. No matter what else had changed, no matter how far either one of them went into their anger or silence, there was always the kettle and the brown mugs and the tea bags all the way from England. Life could not be that bad, he sometimes thought, if we can still do this.

Still, he hoped for more. Not to go back to what was, as it was dawning on him that what was hadn't been as good as what could have been, but to break through into something new. He still believed that was possible. Not now, though. There was still too much of the old, dead love around them. To feel the way he wanted to feel with her, they would have to become new people. He remembered something he'd heard in school, that human beings undergo a complete change of cells every seven years. That meant they still had two more years to go. He didn't know if he could wait that long. He'd have to find something to help speed up the process.

Carmen's room was at the top of a long narrow flight of stairs. Climbing those stairs in the dark lit by colored flashes from the TV above, John's heart would beat faster because he knew that Carmen and one of her friends would be smoking pot, which John had never smoked and was afraid of. Whenever Carmen brought out the red bong and the little lacquer tray of pot, John would turn away and keep his eyes on the TV while behind him he'd hear the flick of the lighter, the gurgling sound of water, then the long rush of released breath and the sweet, charred smell that made him think of Halloween. Tonight when Carmen's friend Eva routinely offered the bong, John took it, put his finger over the tiny hole the way he'd seen them do, set the flame to the thimble-sized bowl and drew in.

He watched the white smoke curling up inside the red plastic tube like a genie taking shape, then shut his eyes and let the hot cloud roll into his chest. When he let go, things were already different. Carmen joined them, and he watched her bend over and take the white smoke into her mouth while the little flame lit up her forehead.

When Eva left, John and Carmen stayed on the huge bed, watching TV. He felt larger inside, more wise and generous, like there was room for everything inside him.

"So," Carmen said, "I didn't know you had a thing for Asian women." Part of John felt stunned, trapped, but then that feeling dissolved when he remembered that there was no need for that anymore. They were new people now, he told himself.

"Oh yeah," he smiled, "That. That was a while ago." He heard what she was saying and it stung him a little to realize he was still not past lying to her. Then, one more hit and he decided that it didn't matter.

They were laying on the far side of the bed from each other, and the space between them felt dangerous and electric to him. Carmen was laying on her side, leaning on one elbow with her head propped up in her hand, looking at him with a strange mix of amusement and curiosity, like she was seeing something different in him. He felt the same way. "You know," she grinned, speaking slowly as if she was surprised by what she was saying, "I really feel like making love to you now."

John felt his blood surge inside, flooding his body with warmth. "You do?"

"Yeah. Do you?"

"Yeah," he returned her smile. "I do."

She reached over and kissed him once. Her kiss seemed to stay on his mouth for a long time, even after she stood up to leave. "Excuse me," she smiled, "I'll be right back." John watched her go, then took off his clothes and pulled the covers up to his waist. It crossed his mind for a moment that this might be some kind of joke, that she was not coming back and that the next person through the door would be her brother or her Dad. Then, that thought dissolved in the taste of her kiss still in his mouth, and he relaxed and lay there alone, watching the TV throw its changing colors on the ceiling, his whole body humming in anticipation of what was going to happen.

The ease. That was what stunned him. The ease of it.

Soon she was back, wearing a black kimono-like robe with white flowers. "That's nice," he said, genuinely surprised and pleased. He'd never seen her wear anything like this before.

"Thanks," she said, crawling up from the foot of the bed on her hands and knees until she was poised over him. Through the split in her robe he could see the beginning of her heavy white breasts hanging down and the deep black shadow between them. "Well . . ." she smiled self-consciously, then giggled. He put his hand behind her neck and pulled her mouth down to his the same way he had the first time they kissed. The familiar taste of her tongue was a welcome jolt to his brain as they gently explored each other's mouths with the familiarity of animals. He reached up with his hands and parted her robe like curtains and looked at the creamy softness of her naked body, the fullness of her breasts swaying above him. The covers were still on him, and he struggled to get them off.

"What?" she asked, "What's the matter?"

"I want to feel you," he said. She helped him pull the covers away and climbed on top of him again, their warm legs sliding in and out between each other, her soft pubic hair brushing against his thigh, the warm weight of her breasts on his bare chest. It was almost too much for him. "Wait, wait," he said, biting his lip and squeezing his eyes shut tight against the white hot light rising fast inside him.

"It's okay," she said. "It's okay."

"No," he gritted his teeth, "I don't want to come. Not yet."

"It's all right," she said again, "Really."

"No," he said, opening his eyes again and looking at her, "Not yet," he struggled for a way to say what he wanted to say. "I want to stay. Like this. I want to stay like this a really, really long time." And saying that made him suddenly feel like he could.

They lay there together for a minute without moving, her head nestled into the crook of his neck, the familiar smell of her hair in his face. He ran his fingertips over and over down the length of her body, from her shoulders down the curve of her back and over the cheeks of her ass until he felt her quiver. She rose up on her arms and looked down at him with a dazed, serious look in her eyes. Then, still looking into his eyes, she reached down and took his cock in her hand and gently placed the head at the mouth of her pussy. John groaned and tried to push up deeper inside her, but she drew away. "No," she said, "Like this. Lie still."

He did what she asked and watched her slowly moving herself back and forth over him. She rode him so the tip of his cock pushed just inside her lips, then out again, no deeper, but she seemed to like it because he began to hear wet kissing sounds from down there and her face took on that sleepy, feverish look she always got right before she came. He wanted to grab the warm cheeks of her ass and pull her down on him, push his cock all the way up inside her, but he made himself lay still the way she asked because he wanted to give her what she wanted. When she came, she bowed her head and started puffing hard breaths through her nose ("like a little freight train," he used to say), then she bent her head back and opened her mouth, her lips moving silently like there was a word she was trying to say.

When she was through, she lay quiet for a minute while he stroked her ass, feeling the last little quivers run through her muscles. After a while, she looked up and smiled, "Do you want to come?"

"Will you do something for me?" John asked.

"What?"

"Will you rub me? With your breasts?"

Carmen closed her eyes like she was picturing it, then, smiling sleepily, crawled over John on her hands and knees and lowered her heavy breasts down onto his belly, then slowly leaned forward on her knees, dragging her breasts up John's stomach to his chest. He bent his head forward to watch. She didn't look into his eyes but kept looking down at her own breasts and what she was doing to him—it was her sleepy, serious smile that drove him crazy. John watched until he couldn't stand it anymore. "Here," he said in a choked voice, "Come here." Carmen understood and brought her breasts over John's face. He took her left breast into his mouth and sucked hard, rubbing his tongue back and forth across her nipple until it felt pebble-hard, loving her faint salty taste. Suddenly, she rose up on her arms and pulled her breast out of his mouth with a wet, popping sound. "Hey," John groaned, "Come back . . ."

"Sorry," Carmen grinned, reveling in her power the way John had never seen her do before. She slowly lowered her breasts back onto his face and John began sucking again. Then he thought of the way her face had looked when she was touching him with her breasts, and he knew what he wanted.

"Will you do something else for me?" John asked. He felt like he could ask her for anything.

"What?"

"Rub my cock. With your breasts." Carmen looked at him, and for a moment he was afraid she was going to refuse. He saw her sleepy, wicked smile come back, then watched her move back down and lean over his hips, her full breasts swaying over him. Then she lowered them down and brushed them back and forth. John felt her hard nipples graze the underside of his cock and thought he was going to faint.

Then she took her breasts away, and before he realized what was happening, he felt Carmen take his cock into her mouth for the first time. His whole body jumped like she'd touched him with a branding-iron. Stunned, he felt her tongue rubbing insistently against him like a living thing, the frightening graze of her teeth, the hot white light being drawn up from deep inside him. When he finally dug his head back into the bed with a loud cry, she pulled her mouth away and pumped him with her hand as he came harder than he ever had before, until the hot white light had left him and there was nothing more inside.

A moment later, she was back up with him again, curling into his side.

"That's the first time you've ever done that, isn't it?" he said after a while, talking softly into her hair. In her silence he felt the blood rushing to his brain to get there first and stop the blow he knew was coming.

"No. It's not."

In an instant she was leaning over him. "I'm sorry," she said in a frightened voice, "I just didn't want to lie to you." She held him closer like he was freezing to death and she was trying to save him. "It's just that you asked and I didn't want to lie to you. Don't you understand that?"

She wasn't crying, but he held her as if she was. "It doesn't matter," he said because he knew he should, then because he started to feel something. "It doesn't matter, it's all right, it doesn't matter," he kept saying it over and over. Grateful, amazed, and a little afraid that it felt true.

It was the red shirt that told him, finally. The red flannel shirt he'd never seen Keiko wearing before, two sizes too big and rolled up comically at the sleeves. He liked the lost child-like way she looked in it and asked where she got it without thinking of the kind of answer he might get. The look she gave him and the long difficult silence that followed told him all he needed to know, but she told him more, how it belonged to the guy she'd been seeing for two years, a graduate assistant in anthropology, how he'd asked her to go to South America with him next semester. She didn't have to explain that she'd said yes.

While she was talking he looked at the shirt and tried to picture the sleeves rolled down to their full length, the broad shoulders and chest filling it out, the untrimmed beard and pony tail, probably. He tried to hate what he was imagining, but before he could call that feeling up, the picture dissolved and there was only her, looking at him to see what he would do.

He took her out to a field where he used to run with his friends when they were boys. It was the first place he'd ever drunk beer and laid down under the stars. He'd been meaning to bring her to this place for a while, to explain what it meant to him and help her feel it too. But that didn't seem important anymore, and he was moving with a silent deliberation that felt new to him. Branches reached down and clawed their faces but he went on ahead, pulling her along behind him by the hand.

Under the harsh, blinding moonlight, he pulled her to her knees in the cold wet grass. "Not here," she kept saying, "Not here," even while he was rolling the red flannel shirt up above her breasts and pushing up her bra. When he took one of her breasts into his mouth, she stopped talking. With his mouth still on her, he opened his eyes and saw her allowing this, staring off at some distant point on the horizon. She was looking toward whatever was coming next for her.

There was a light on the horizon, a single streetlight shining through a row of black trees—this was what she was looking at. He closed his eyes again and saw that light travel all the way across the field into her eyes, then down through her body into his mouth, filling him slowly. As it filled him, he was realizing that they could stay here like this until dawn and no one was going to come and take him away, lightning would not strike him, wild dogs would not tear him apart. Everything he thought he'd had was gone, but that was not how this felt. He felt the beginning of something inside his body; the longer he sucked, the clearer it grew like writing on a sign still too far down the road to read. He wanted to know what it said.

2 AM

Dorianne Laux

When I came with you that first time
on the floor of your office, the dirty carpet
under my back, the heel of one foot
propped on your shoulder, I went ahead
and screamed, full-throated, as loud
and as long as my body demanded,
because somewhere, in the back of my mind,
packed in the smallest neurons still capable
of thought, I remembered
we were in a warehouse district
and that no sentient being resided for miles.
Afterwards, when I could unclench
my hands and open my eyes, I looked up.
You were on your knees, your arms
stranded at your sides, so still—
the light from the crooknecked lamp
sculpting each lift and delicate twist,
the lax muscles, the smallest veins
on the backs of your hands. I saw
the ridge of each rib, the blue hollow
pulsing at your throat, all the colors
in your long blunt cut hair which hung
over your face like a raffia curtain
in some south sea island hut.

And as each bright synapse unfurled
and followed its path, I recalled
a story I'd read that explained why women
cry out when they come—that it's
the call of the conqueror, a siren howl
of possession. So I looked again
and it felt true, your whole body
seemed defeated, owned, having taken on
the aspect of a slave in shackles, the wrists
loosely bound with invisible rope.
And when you finally spoke you didn't
lift your head but simply moaned the word god
on an exhalation of breath—I knew then
I must be merciful, benevolent,
impossibly kind.

The Vulva: A Guided Tour For a Rainy Afternoon

Jaie Helier

It's wet—the weather, that is. Striding over heather-covered mountains would be stupid; tennis is out of the question. You're bored. Your lover is with you—she would like to be entertained. Indulge her. Coax her gently to lie down, naked. Sit beside her. Kiss her for a long time. Caress her and make her warm. Take off your rings and bracelets so you don't hurt her with them. She needs to feel willing and comfortable. You're going to take her on a wonderful journey—around her vulva and deep inside.

Begin at the top—the mound of Venus. This is the fleshy area, often partly covered in hair, that protects the pubic bone. Venus is the Roman goddess of love and this area is full of sensitivity. Its fleshiness cushions the impact of sexual intercourse when it gets fast and furious but that's not today. Today it's for playing around on with your fingertips. Touching just the hairs at first, no more, but then tickling the sides of the mound and searching the skin on it and nearby, like an anteater searches an anthill. Press down on her; discover the shape of that arching bone that is the cathedral roof of her sexual sanctum.

Immediately beneath it are the labia majora, thick protective folds of flesh that are closed like lips over her inner vulva. Enjoy these, because every moment spent caressing them is making her more ready, more wet and more likely to want you to touch further inside her. Every part of her outer labia may give her pleasure—from the very soft smooth skin at the tops of her thighs; down to the perineum, that marvelous no-person's-land between her vulva and her anus (avoid her anus for today, as touching both of these areas in one session brings a danger of infection); and right across the length and breadth of the labia themselves. Touch them softly. Kiss them, which may tickle the hell out of her at first but will still probably be pleasurable. Press and massage them. Some women have labia that cover completely and meet in the middle. In others, the labia minora or inner pussy lips show through. Either way, be in no hurry to make her more open or to touch the upper area around the clitoris. The rain's not going to stop—you've got all afternoon.

Opening her pussy further is best done from near the perineum. If moisture hasn't already seeped between her outer labia then it is most likely to be found at this lowest point (assuming she is lying on her back), furthest away from the clitoris. The moisture is supplied by what are named Bartholin's glands, on either side of the vaginal opening. Let your finger bathe in her moisture and then gently spread it upward, over the delicate inner surfaces including her labia minora. If she moans and writhes at this, then softly smack her leg. She's to lie still and behave with decorum. Explore her inner labia, their shape and slippery texture. Kiss her, lick her there a little. Let the taste of her spread over your lips too. Let your finger stray upward around the area of her clitoris to see if it's awake yet. It may not be, so don't touch it directly. Stroke and kiss these delightful inner lips until she pleads with you to enter her. When she does, then stroke and kiss her some more, just to show her who's leading this expedition.

Between the inner lips of her vulva is the entrance to her vagina. Press gently around the mouth of it and quite firmly beneath her pubic bone. When you feel her urging you through, press in the middle of her vaginal opening and let her draw you in. Be gentle in your exploration; be gradual in the way you introduce your finger further into her. Stroke her clit softly with your thumb at the same time and let her body's reactions be your guide. She will move encouragingly in spite of your stern instructions—well, you never thought she'd obey, did you? Open her, stretch her a little at a time. Push your finger in as far as it can go. You may find that it goes all the way to the cervix, or womb entrance, so be careful there—it can be a sensitive area. A penis, of course, is generally longer than a finger but, to accommodate that, the cervix has a clever knack of lifting out of the way, so that the vagina can take as much length as your lover wishes to accept. Withdraw your finger again, pressing and stretching her. When you are sure she's ready, introduce a second finger.

Around an inch and a half inside her vagina, pressing with two fingers firmly towards the front of her body, you will discover whether she has any great sensitivity in the area of her G-spot. She may not, or it may just make her feel she needs to pee, but it may be that she is one of the fifty percent of women who would enjoy enormously what you are doing at this point. The existence or otherwise of the G-spot has been the subject of contention since Grafenberg suggested it. Even to the believers, however, there remains the question of whether G-spot orgasms are better than clitoral orgasms. Interestingly, they may turn out to be the same thing.

Recently, some research by an Australian surgeon named Helen O'Connell of the Royal Melbourne Hospital, revealed that the clitoris, far from being just the tiny point of joy that everyone thought it was, is actually quite a large mass of nerves and tissue that extends back and is more or less wrapped around the urethra, at about that point where the G-spot is supposed to be. The tissue is erectile; it swells during arousal, which may have the function of shutting off the urethra during intercourse to prevent infection in the bladder. It may also be that it holds the vaginal wall firm during penetration. The as-yet-unproven, implication of this is that when you press on that spongy area of ducts and glands (known as Skene's glands), which we refer to as the G-spot, you may actually be pressing on the back part of the clitoris. Such technical details may seem irrelevant to a column about gently exploring your lover's vulva on a rainy afternoon, but knowledge gives confidence. If you are confident, she is more likely to have confidence in you.

If she is truly relaxed and wants to go further, it is possible to introduce three or four fingers into her vagina without damaging her in any way. This part of the process can be endlessly pleasurable to her so take lots of time, and lots of, preferably pre-warmed, lubricant for this. It is possible to manage with her moisture up to a point, but the more you stretch her vagina, the riskier it becomes. When putting your fingers in her vagina, especially several at once, make sure that your nails are clean and short, and that your fingers and wrists are free of jewelry. For her maximal protection, you should wear latex gloves. If you take time, her vaginal opening can stretch a lot. Anyone who has ever seen a baby being born would understand that. It may be that she wants that feeling of being stretched, and gets huge pleasure from it, but the further you go, the more important it is to listen to and be guided by her. Stop and carefully retreat a hundred times if she asks you to. Don't do anything she doesn't want.

If you have four fingers squidging around inside her, awash with water-based lubricant, there may come a point at which she would like to feel your whole hand inside her. At this point, make an arrow by putting your four fingers and your thumb together and press gently at her stretched vaginal opening. By this time, her vaginal muscles may be working in ways that neither of you would have expected. There may come a moment in which you actually feel as if she is drawing your hand into her. Wait for that, then keeping your hand as narrow as possible, twist it and let it slip inside. Carefully, once that inward motion is completed, you can fold your fingers together to make a fist. Again, make sure this is comfortable for her.

The feeling of having such a large object inside her will probably be quite overwhelming. Communication and patience are of the utmost importance. Don't hurry anything, but gradually you may be able to move your fist inside her vagina, drawing it in and out and perhaps twisting and turning it a little. Do it slowly, especially at first. Your fist will stimulate all of her vagina and the feeling could be very strong and emotional for her, especially if this is the first time she has done this. It could also be extremely uncomfortable for you.

If you start this, you must understand that vaginal muscles are very powerful and, at some point in this procedure, they will probably begin to contract. It could be quite painful for you—your hand will probably feel as if it is being crushed. Stay calm if that happens and realize there is nothing she can do about it and that both you, and she, can get in worse trouble if you try suddenly to withdraw. Keep going for her until she asks you to stop. She will love you for it. When she is ready for you to withdraw your hand, let her muscles push you out in their own time. An orgasm reached in this way can be very long and very full—something special, not easily forgotten. It could also leave her feeling quite emotionally and physically tender. Take good care of her afterwards. Keep her warm and hold her. Give her lots of time—and maybe some red wine in front of the log fire.

There—wasn't that a delightful afternoon?

Blue in Cuba

Patrick Linney

Come to me, my Blue, my writer cunt:

There must come a time soon when visiting me one day a week won't be enough to satisfy your needs—or my own. You'll recognise the moment by an image of yourself, flashing repeatedly before your eyes. I don't know precisely what the image will be, but it will betoken a desire for a greater test of your service to me, a test that would be the portal to a more lasting servitude. Maybe you'll be screaming, or craven, or just imploring, in the image: I don't know.

When the moment comes you are to telephone me and say simply, "Yes sir, I wish to go to Cuba."

Yes: Cuba. The taboo place. You'll know when you're ready. Here is a narrative of what might transpire. I await your call.

You'll fly down to Mexico. In Cancun they'll give you a visa, no questions asked, no stamp on your passport. Only in the washroom at the airport are you to strip, and open the blue body paint, and mark yourself, on your arms and legs and belly and breasts and buttocks and sides, YANQUI, in big bold lettering, concealed, but with the edges of letters almost revealing themselves when you dress again, in your long-sleeved cream blouse and your long blue dirndl skirt.

Imagine. You'll sit on the plane, once it's airborne, about to break the taboo against Cuba, imagining the Cubans deciding to search you on the way in, discovering your body covered with the word YANQUI. Imagine.

It'll be evening. Maybe you were expecting hassles, but it was easier to get into Cuba than into your own country, and the next thing you know I'm hugging you, and leading you to where I've parked the rented jeep. I put you in the back. I pull your arms behind you roughly, and handcuff your wrists together.

Soon I'm driving us through the thin traffic towards downtown Havana, and I'm telling you to spread your legs. "The visit has a story to it, Blue," I say, quite loudly against the rattle of the roof, "I want you to start telling it to me now, extempore. It's a dimestore torture story. Maybe a man once showed it to you under a table somewhere. It may even be translated from the Spanish. You're a beautiful American agent. The Cubans are going to imprison you and torture you for the secrets you hold."

"She stares out at the dimly-lit streets," you say straight away, my writer cunt . . . mmm . . . how I want you, "the metal of the handcuffs chafing her wrists, the fear of what may happen to her pounding against her heart . . ."

In the Hotel Inglaterra a woman will be playing lounge piano in the bar. I'll have sent your bags upstairs, and draped my white linen jacket over you, so that you can sit with a mojito cocktail in front of you, your handcuffed wrists hidden beneath my jacket. You suck at the straw, smiling at the zing of the rum in your veins. Then your lips go to my right ear as the woman plays an extravagant version of *Love is a Many Splendored Thing*: "She waits and waits for her interrogation to begin," you whisper, "wondering if the sinister Englishman is the one who will really hurt her, and as she waits, she tries to tell herself that she isn't getting wetter and wetter at the very thought of his torture . . ."

You'll come for me almost as soon as we're in the hotel room. You'll be on all fours, just inside the door, my right hand at your cunt, my lips now over your left ear: "At last he clamps the electrodes to her cunt-lips. At last the electricity surges through her. At last his voice demands her secrets. At last the pain, the game begins, as he says to her, between shocks: cunt, confess, cunt, cunt, confess, cunt, cunt . . ."

I wake you at three in the morning. You're naked on the cold tiled floor, bound by your left ankle to my right wrist with the nightdress you perhaps imagined you'd wear. I wake you by forcing a rubber dildo into you. "They don't let her sleep," I say to you, "just when she sinks into merciful slumber a truncheon penetrates her most private places, and then their slaps and kicks . . ."

"Their terrible blows," you respond, to my surprise, in the darkness, as if out of the dream you must have been having, "hit and hurt and fuel her hatred and yet, again, despite her efforts to deny them, nevertheless her clitoris begins to throb with every slap and kick . . ."

Oh, but we can be simple tourists too. The next few days we can walk through the streets of Old Havana and Viedado, and the beach to the east and the villa where Hemingway lived and wrote standing up at his typewriter, and we can eat in the restaurants where they only take dollars and strangers might mistake us for simple tourists: an Englishman and an American woman in love, holding hands a good deal, whispering in each other's ears a lot, smiling at the men offering bargain cigars on every street-corner.

The strangers wouldn't know, of course, of our secrets. That I have washed you clean each morning, and required you to come in the shower, and then hand-painted your body with the word YANQUI, over and over again. That we are murmuring to each other, not loving imprecations, but an escalating tale of torture inspired by our surroundings: "In the courtyard of the old palace," you might be saying to me, "she hangs by her spreadeagled ankles, as her torturers begin to whip her between her legs and the Englishman watches as they lash and lash and . . . please Master may I cum, may I find a bathroom and cum, please Master, please . . ."

On the fifth day I wake you early. "To disorient and exhaust the American woman, her cruel captors keep waking her in the night," I murmur to you when you can hardly understand what's happening to you, nude on the floor of the hotel room. My fingers penetrate your vagina; my thumb rests on your clitoris. "But there comes a night when the Englishman himself wakes her. And his hands are invading her. And he's telling her that at the end of today she will be fucked and hurt by many men . . ."

Your eyes widen in the darkness. The loud horn of an early bus on the street outside makes you jump. My hands move on you and in you. Just for once you seem bereft of storyline, unable to tell me what happens next. So I continue: "He tells her that she must live through the day knowing that, once night descends, she will suffer terrible pain and humiliation. And there is nothing she can do to prevent it."

At my instruction, you wear a bikini to breakfast. Everyone looks at you. Your body glistens with the lotion I have applied, after your shower. In three places your skin bears the name

YANQUI: circling each of your nipples, and on your mons: three places hidden by the skimpy two-piece blue swimsuit.

At my instruction, you do not feed yourself at breakfast. I feed you pieces of mango, grapefruit, pineapple. I hold your head and tip coffee to your lips. I kiss you with fragments of boiled egg.

It's not at my instruction, but you seem incapable of participating in our story today. Perhaps you are genuinely frightened. Certainly, your senses seem electric. When I take your hand and lead you back to our room, and place my hand within the lower half of your bikini, you kneel straight away, and make animal noises I've never heard you make before as you come for me . . .

I drive the jeep south, you in the back, still in your blue bikini, your hands behind you, each touching the opposite elbow. "They drive her through the countryside," I say to you, "past mile upon mile of sugar cane, and all she can think of is that at the end of the day . . ."

"I am yours, Sir," you say, and I see you're weeping, and I go on with the story:

"And as they drive her, they talk in Spanish, and then, occasionally, remind her of what is to happen to her tonight . . ."

We have checked in at a hotel complex on the beach. Each room is a bungalow separate from the others. By the entrance to the complex is the Bay of Pigs Museum. I have guided you, in your bikini, round the photographs of the failed, farcical invasion while the Cuban woman guide looks you up and down and shows her contempt for all things American. Yanqui.

And now it's dark and we're on the patio outside our bungalow and you are nude, on all fours, your skin glistening with lotion, and sweat. Stillness. The sound of the sea.

I place a blindfold on you. I place a collar round your neck. I attach a chain to the collar. I crouch beside you. "As night falls," I murmur to you, "they strip her, and make her squat on all fours, and fasten a collar and chain around her neck. Soon they will tell her to make noises like a pig. Soon they will lead her to the beach. Soon she will be fucked and hurt by many men . . ."

You follow blindly, tugged by your chain, over the sand, snorting, yes, like a pig. And you hear the hiss of a lighter, and feel the first pain—wax on your right shoulder, as I hold you still, wax dripping and dripping and dripping on to the same place as I say to you: "The first Cuban drips his hot cum on to the shoulder of the blind, naked, helpless American. And then a second man's sperm cascades on to her left buttock," as wax drips on to your left buttock, and drips, and drips, and drips. And I worry that you won't understand, that I've driven you too far, as you fumble for me, on all fours, and cling to my legs, and try to press your mouth to my cock through my shorts.

I push you away with my leg. You fall back spreadeagled on the sand, on your back. To my amazement, as I light another candle, a sort of smile ripples across your lips. And I drip wax on your left breast, and on your right hip, simultaneously, and I say, "And then a third and a fourth Cuban join in the punishment of the American woman, spreadeagled on the sand, dripping their cum on her, and she lies there helpless, alternately . . ."

And you grunt like a pig, and then you say, "Yes, Master, yes please."

" . . . alternately grunting like a pig, and then pleading with her tormentors to hurt her more, to invade her more, and more, and more . . ."

And as I drip the wax I kneel beside you, and sit one candle in the sand for a moment, and lift your head by your hair, unzipping my shorts, my cock to your mouth, and you lick, and try to suck, until I throw your head back to the sand and pick up the candle again . . .

Come to me, my dear Blue, my writer cunt, when you are ready for this. For a story such as this. For pain, and humiliation, and pleasure such as this. Come to impossible Cuba to be with me. Later I will hold you close, and tell you how much you mean to me. But this is what I want, what I need, Blue. The days of tales and torment; the final scene on the beach. That out of the stories in my melancholy heart, interwoven with the stories in yours, we may find a perverse pleasure, aesthetic and erotic; that we may reach for joy; that we may achieve a kind of redemption for all the sadness and self-doubt our stories have caused us over the years, before our stories met, and began to mingle, and grow, and to climax, sometimes, in two people embracing, after coming, in a place beyond dreams, a beach in impossible Cuba perhaps, on a hot night, finally naked together . . .

sloppy seconds

Gwydion McCarthy

he loves you.
i know by
this heat,
this wet,
this salt,
this scent

drowning in
this warm flood,
surrounded

i close my eyes,
i love you
you are God
man and woman
together, blended

this is heaven,
taking him,
taking me

when i come
i know
i love him too

Sexcapades: The Whoopee Report

Gary Meyer

Get in the Habit

The Catholic League for Religious and Civil Rights was not amused by the San Francisco Sisters of Perpetual Indulgence, a group of gay men who turn out in nun's habits, elaborate makeup, wimples ("ear brassieres"), and wigs for their annual Easter Sunday anniversary bash. Their street party in the Castro includes a "Hunky Jesus" contest. Founded in 1979, the Sisters (www.thesisters.org) vow to "promulgate universal joy and expiate stigmatic guilt." Raising funds for San Francisco Sex Information, AIDS victims, and gay rights groups, they take their ministry seriously: "We are not making fun of nuns; we *are* nuns."

Auntie Domme Whips Brazil into Shape

Brazil's hottest turn-of-the-century sex symbol and TV star was masked dominatrix/quiz-show hostess "Tiazinha" ("Auntie" in Portuguese). Bedecked in the traditional stilettos, garter belt, and corset, and brandishing a riding crop, she waxed teenaged male contestants and ripped out patches of leg hair to penalize wrong answers. An anthropologist observed, "Maybe it's the economic crisis. Brazil has chosen a sex goddess who demands a little sacrifice."

Ooh, Baby, Yes, Yes—Look Out for that Truck!

A naked, coupled couple were pulled over on an Israeli coastal highway for zigzagging along at 25 mph. Ticketed for reckless driving, the driver confessed an irresistible urge toward the hitchhiker he had just picked up: "She was a pretty girl and I forgot myself."

OK, Ma'am, Put Down the Vibrator and Come Out with Your Hands Up

Alabama was successfully taken to court by the ACLU and Sheri Williams, proprietor of Loving Enterprises, Inc., over a statute banning the sale of vibrators and other sex toys. It remained legal for Alabama physicians to prescribe Viagra for men, but devices designed solely to stimulate the genitals were outlawed.

Brewhaha over Rutting Rhinos

Harlem residents were offended by an ad campaign for Steel Reserve High Gravity Lager that featured the slogan "Research Says Sex Sells Beer" accompanied by tasteful illustrations of giant turtles and rhinoceri doing the rumpy-pumpy. Reverend Calvin Butts said, "You don't see this in store windows on Park Avenue. You see them in poor neighborhoods." The ads were removed from New York but continued elsewhere.

It's Not Just Tinky Winky

Doctor David Reuben published an updated edition of his

best-selling, sixties pop guide, *Everything You Always Wanted to Know About Sex, But Were Afraid To Ask,* in which he blows the lid off the media conspiracy to indoctrinate children into S&M through the Saturday morning cartoons. "Look at the dog being blown to bits by a stick of dynamite! Then watch the terrified statement of the tots in the audience as they are being prepared to enjoy Sado-Masochist good times."

Something Naked This Way Comes

Protesting an anti-nudity law in Seminole County, Florida, three dancers at adult-entertainment venue Club Juana took advantage of a loophole and performed a portion of Macbeth in the buff. Seems that "bona fide performances" are permitted to let it all hang out, and the Three Witches never had so much hanging out before. Investigative Bureau Lt. Sammy Gibson critiqued, ". . . they were not professional theater-type performers."

See, Porn Does Lead to Violence

In order to ascertain whether a gay Web site called Chisel.com was violating the Canadian Obscenity Act, which bans explicit sex involving violence or degrading, dehumanizing treatment, police officers carrying machine guns broke down the Vancouver company's doors with a battering ram. Chisel webcasts live gay sex shows. No charges were filed.

Pentagon Requests $100 Billion for Anti-Bra Defense System

As part of the Canadian Defence Department's Clothe the Soldier program, Captain Frank Delanghe (known to his staff as "Delangherie") is studying the feasibility of supporting the troops with the world's first Combat Bra. Amid worries about a typical military approach (one size fits all?), the country's 2,500 female soldiers were surveyed to obtain their requirements for a brassiere comfortable enough for long term wear and durable enough for "violent, physical activity." Why not just test it on dates?

What Do You Say to a Naked Woman with a Razor?

You say, "A little off the top, please," if you're getting your hair cut in Moscow's Maksimych salon, where the uniform of the day for ten young, female barbers is high heels, period. The tariff is $50-$130 and owner Maksim Lyadov, a journalism graduate, also offers naked billiard opponents and masseuses au natural. Flirting is permitted, but remember she's got the scissors. Seems to be a trend here. A Moscow TV station boasts about how little gets covered when Svetlana Pissotskaya does her daily nudecasts.

Officer, Do Your Duty

Kenyan women from 24 Catholic church groups shut down the town of Kandara, north of Nairobi, when they stormed the police station there. They demanded that the police chief either order his men to make love to them or close the illegal bars where their husbands were getting too drunk to fuck. "Our men have turned to vegetables," lamented one of the wives.

Hello, Sailor!

Eleven crew-women of a Dutch naval frigate got their commander in hot water when they stripped to the waist to flash passing NATO vessels in the Mediterranean Sea. They ended up on the front page of Amsterdam's largest daily, De Telegraaf, as well as on the Internet, when an Italian sailor snapped the action. Naval officials reacted sternly, "This is shameful, dishonorable and unprofessional. Can we see the picture again?"

Hello, Trucker!

49-year-old William Rees, who lives with his parents in Tarbolton, Ayrshire, couldn't wait for a passing lorry driver to photograph his naked dance of greeting, so he set up a video camera and taped himself whenever he sprang out of the bushes to welcome eighteen-wheel jockeys with a wave and a jiggle. The cops, alerted by a critic who was not amused by Rees's pieces, demanded to see the instant replay. Despite his explanation that he flashed trucks exclusively, since they wouldn't be carrying women and children, Rees was fined 500 pounds and sentenced to 18 months probation.

Bobbies Called Over Lady Godiva Barbie

A lifetime Barbie fan, 54-year-old Marcelle Bremmer, used an empty shop window below her flat for a doll display. A neighbor in Moniaive, Dumfriesshire, complained to the cops that some of the Barbies were showing too much leg and one was entirely naked, riding a horse bareback. No action was taken by the police. Everybody knows that Lady Godiva rode nude through the streets of Coventry in 1040 on a dare from her Lord, who promised in return to repeal some cruel taxes. (Yes, that's where Form 1040 comes from.) According to legend, all the townsfolk averted their eyes, except for a lone tailor who was struck blind, the original Peeping Tom. According to Hollywood, Lady G had really long hair.

Take a Letter, Vagina

What's an ex-KGB agent to do? Well, if she has 12 years

experience in the harem of an Arab sheik, she joins the faculty of the School for Geishas in (where else?) Moscow and teaches the pubococcygeus (PC) muscle control she allegedly learned in the Middle East. The PC muscle is part of the pelvic floor in both sexes. To find yours, attempt to halt the flow when you urinate. The PC muscle contracts during orgasm and helps a man pump out semen from his prostate. In a woman, it tightens the love tunnel, enabling her to hold a pen there and write notes, a talent that the School of Geishas' mysterious Eastern Woman promises to impart in a mere three months. Before men book airline tickets to go explore other applications for this rare ability, note that the School for Geishas is strictly hands off and dicks to yourself. But you can always send your girlfriend.

Police Publish Guide to Getting Stoned and Getting Laid

No, not the NYPD. Amsterdam's English-language "Police Red Light Guide" was designed to help summer tourists obtain sex and drugs safely. Written by Wim Schild, who's walked a Fun Zone beat for 12 years, the guide advises visitors to avoid street dealers and always purchase their pot and hash at city-regulated coffee shops. (Somebody should pitch this concept to Starbucks.) Space Cake snackers are advised to drink plenty of sweet liquids, and prostitution patrons are warned that what you think you see isn't always what you get; that charming gal in the window may turn out to be a guy.

George Washington's Boner Crossing the Delaware

If you look closely at Emanuel Leutze's classic painting of GW being rowed by his troops across an icy river, you may notice something suggestive in the vicinity of George's groin. If you have a dirty mind, a very vague sense of anatomy, and total suspension of disbelief, you may just interpret a sliver of white background framed by an oar and the hem of GW's cloak as a crudely rendered, rampant dingus. At least that's what Guy Sims, the Superintendent of Schools in Muscogee County, Georgia, saw in a fifth-grade textbook reproduction. Heroically working against time, he and a brave squad of teacher aides spent two weeks painting out the offending area in 2,300 textbooks. Hey, any guy who can get it up while crossing a river in an open boat in the dead of winter deserves to be known as "The Father of his Country."

Mary for Breakfast

Jamie Joy Gatto

The kitchen was incredibly warm, since all the gas burners had been going at once. Mary slipped off her thick, terry cloth robe to feel cooler, more comfortable. It had been years since she'd cooked in the nude, and frankly, it just felt right. For a moment, as Mary turned the sausages in their sizzling pan, she was worried about the grease popping her bare flesh, maybe even scorching a jiggling breast. The thought made her giggle to herself. Her nakedness made her feel silly. Playing with huge sausages, naked in her kitchen, suddenly made her laugh aloud. Jim didn't seem to notice.

"Mary, pass the milk, please," Jim said, not looking up from his morning paper. He poured a white cloud into his coffee.

Mary stirred the strawberry sauce so it wouldn't stick, then turned off the heat to let it cool. The red berries sparkled under their ruby glaze, inviting her to taste their sweet-tartness. As she lifted a gooey finger from the pot, plop! A dollop landed on her white breast. Warm and smooth, it dripped from her nipple and onto her rounded belly. Mary laughed aloud again, dabbing strawberries from herself, licking sticky fingers clean. Her good mood, combined with her nakedness and the warm sauce on her skin gave her a great idea—*Mary for breakfast.* Jim was in for a real treat.

Carefully, she selected the two roundest, fluffiest pancakes from the stack. She dabbed a bit of strawberry sauce on her breasts, then fashioned a homemade pancake bra for herself. She crowned each pancake breast with a succulent red nipple of strawberry. Next, Mary chose the longest sausage from the pan and carefully patted it dry with a paper towel. She took the sausage into her mouth, licking and sucking at it as if it were an erect cock. She savored the warm, juicy spices that oozed into her mouth. Boldly, she bit off one end, and relished the tender flesh between her teeth, chewing with delight. As she ate and sucked the morsel, she decided to put it where it would please her in a different way. Mary eased the length of sausage between her pussy lips, wickedly stroking her clit with the hot meat, then pushing into herself, still savoring the flavor on her greasy lips. She sighed. Pancakes slipped from her tits and onto her belly, creating a red trail of strawberry delight.

Looking up from his paper at last, Jim found his wife masturbating with their breakfast. At first he looked confused, but Mary's big smile and dazed look of desire made him think twice. She called him over to the stove with a wave of her hand and Jim stood up, laughing. Apparently, he couldn't believe his eyes or this strange scene in his kitchen. It must have made him crazily horny, for when he removed his boxers, his cock was hard and almost as big as his rival sausage.

Jim's lips were tender upon Mary's skin, lapping delicious berry treats from her tits, her slender waist and her womanly belly. With a sigh of pleasure, Mary offered Jim a taste of the sausage from her pussy. It was covered in Mary's sweet juices; he ate it ravenously.

Jim entered her easily, her walls lubricated by the sausage-cock. As Jim pounded away at her on the kitchen floor, Mary floated in warmth and happiness, opening her legs wider, beckoning him deeper. Jim scooped a fingerful of pancakes and berries into her mouth just as she started to come. Her mouth watered. Her eyes sparkled. And as she savored her breakfast, she felt like she exploded into a million stars.

I Sexualize Everything

Jonah Raskin

I sexualize everything and everybody,
I sexualize me and you.
I sexualize sleeping, skiing, skin-diving, skinny dipping.
I make every symbol into a sexual symbol:
Roots & Flowers
Cigars & Caves.
I sexualize my penis, balls, semen, lips & hips.
I even sexualize sex.
And I think about sex constantly, invariably, uncontrollably.
I find everything about you sexy—
The way you floss,
The way you put your finger inside you and inside me.
The way you reach down inside my pants and touch me.
I sexualize going to the movies, and eating eggplant
sandwiches.
I sexualize reading:
Opening a book is always an erotic experience,
The greatest of aphrodisiacs.
The act of reading stirs up memories of my penis inside you,
And you around me.

Okay, you're thinking
I get the fucking point.
But I'm not sure you do,
Because I haven't said it all yet.
Haven't explained that I don't find
Victoria's Secret sexy.
And if you're wearing a teddy or a camisole
I'll ask you to take it off and throw it away, or burn it
Because it turns me off,
Makes it impossible for me to get an erection,
Or even think about sex.
And I think that maybe there's something wrong with me.
Driving a car isn't sexual for me either.
All cars are asexual, nonsexual, though some guys
Insist there's a connection between the car you drive and
how often you get laid.
But I don't believe them, never have, never will.
And death doesn't turn me on either.
I've never fucked in a cemetery, or on a grave.
And dead women don't excite me.
And holding power isn't a substitute
For taking your breast in my mouth,
Or going down on you or having you kiss my neck.
And I don't want to be turned into a sex slave
Though I tried that.
But I want to sleep sex, eat sex, be sex,
Have sex in secret, in the dark,
Without mirrors or satin sheets,
Just skin.
Your skin, my skin.
Skin to skin.
Sexy, sexy, skin.

A Day in the Life of a Kinky Couple: Fantasy vs. the Reality

Jane Duvall

A little introduction to this is probably in order. I've been fantasizing about bondage and BDSM for as long as I can remember having sexual thoughts, and several years ago I decided to actually look for a relationship in real life that fulfilled those needs. I was online, reading everything I could find, hanging out in BDSM-oriented chatrooms and the like. I was also reading fiction, like *Story of O*, the *Beauty* trilogy by Anne Rice, and others. I know I had a totally unrealistic expectation of what things would be like, and I know I'm not the only one who went through a period of adjustment—realizing there is no way fantasy could become reality—so I thought this might help.

Fantasy: I wake up in the nude, bound spread eagle on the bed. I learned to sleep this way because as a "proper" submissive, it's my duty to do all I can to please my Top.

Reality: I wake up cranky, my arm stiff from being in one position because I slept with one hand cuffed to the bed. I like feeling like a "slavegirl," but my arm fell asleep this way and it's starting to tingle as the blood gets back where it belongs.

Fantasy: My Top is awake, he's been watching me sleep,

tenderly watching over me. He is, of course, ready to play with me already. When he sees I'm awake, he's already reaching for toys—a gag, a vibrator, a riding crop.

Reality: The children are yelling upstairs—they have school in 45 minutes, and I'd better drag myself out of bed soon to get them ready. My Top is snoring away beside me, dead to the world. I nudge him impatiently, needing him to get the key to my cuff.

Fantasy: We spend the next two hours in bed, flogging, fucking, my state of mind in that wonderful submissive place I love, the word "Sir" coming easily to my lips whenever I speak to him.

Reality: I spend the next two hours getting the kids off to school, answering e-mail, and gulping down large quantities of coffee. Jim is at his computer now too, typing away.

Fantasy: Jim decides I should spend the day as his naked sex-toy slavegirl. He lets me up from the bed, but leaves me with just a collar and cuffs on. I wander upstairs to get him breakfast, and bring it down to serve him in bed. He has me lie on the bed, and rests his hot coffee mug on my properly toned and gorgeous tummy (hey, this is fantasy, right?) He eats the muffin I brought him, feeding me small bites. We fuck like crazed weasels again.

Reality: With the children gone, I go to Jim, sit by his feet watching him work. When he finally notices I'm there, I ask him nicely if he wants to play. He says yes, as soon as he gets this last little review done. I go back to my computer and start another project. Before I know it the afternoon is over, and it's time to pick up the kids.

Fantasy: There are no children—it's just me and Jim in our little fantasy world of D/S. He has me don the proper dressed slavegirl attire (short skirt, stockings, 7 inch monster heels, no panties of course—that's the golden slavegirl rule, "open and accessible") and we head off to a fabulous fetish party.

Reality: The next few hours are spent helping with homework, making dinner, arguing about who does more work around the house and whether our next spare money should go to a new computer or a new digital camera.

Fantasy: Arriving at the fabulous fetish party, we are of course surrounded by other gorgeous slavegirl creatures who want nothing more than to play with us. My Top is so incredibly naturally dominant, they all flock to him. And I, of course, am the perfect example of submissive beauty—obeying every command with a smile and without the slightest hesitation, even stuff I don't like. I live to serve.

Reality: After grouchily cleaning up from dinner (do I have to do everything around here?!) I get the children off to bed. Jim and I go into the office to work on our respective computers.

Fantasy: After several hours as the tied-up dungeon babe, we leave the party. Despite hours and hours of nonstop play, we're both still incredibly horny and energetic, so we fuck like crazed weasels when we return home.

Reality: We talk again about playing that evening. Then a TV show we like comes on, and by the time it's over I'm yawning. Jim tucks me into bed, and we promise each other again that the next day we'll actually set aside time together.

So what's the point? That even in the fantasy world of BDSM there is still a real life—and balancing that can be difficult at times. Raising children, running a business, and the day-to-day things that come up all eat into that time. Life just isn't one continuous Anne Rice novel. Still, though I'm now awake and living in the real world, I'm happier than I've ever been. There is time for play, and even after many years together, there is a wonderful undertone of D/S in most of our relationship. And honestly? I wouldn't have it any other way. Being a character in *Story of O* might sound like a good time, but I think that'd wear off after the first time my arms fell asleep from bondage.

The Valentine's Gift

Alex M. Quinlan

In a green as dark as navy blue, the velveteen dress sheathes her. A leather belt, wide as a large man's hand, dyed dark as the dress, laces her waist. It collects the velvet tightly around her, pulling it down so that her shoulders are bare and her breasts swell upwards almost out of her decolletage. Thin red lines, parallel across both breasts, only heighten the paleness of her skin. Her skirt spills around her as she kneels before the pagan altar, the black lace kick-panels blending against the green of her dress, invisible in the dim room except where she can see the floor through them.

Her long dark hair is collected up, spilling out of a net of silver chain studded with virginal white seed pearls and garnets the color of fresh arterial blood. A choker, green velveteen with a black lace frill, is tied around her neck. The velvet is narrow, just more than a half-inch in width, but the lace is as wide as her neck, coming up to her chin, and down past her collarbones. A simple silver chain around her neck bears an amber heart, encased in silver filigree. The pendant lies on her cleavage, too large to slip between breasts so closely compressed.

Her hands are clasped before her, not quite in her lap. The black lace frills attached to the wrists of her sleeves show glints of the polished black leather manacles that lock her wrists closely together. She holds a rattan cane, which matches the lines marking the white swells of her breasts. Her head bowed, she holds in her mouth a rose the color of the garnets in her hair, thorns thick along its length. A slight trickle of red traces from the corner of her mouth.

She hears him enter, and does not move—no motion to be stilled, for she was already still, waiting. Walking around her, he sees his orders followed—skirt flared out, wrists locked together, his gifts to her held without regard to self, that last having been enforced by some early reminding. His breathing changes, deepening, getting rougher and fuller. He starts to speak, and has to modulate his voice out of the growl that rises from his loins.

"Tonight. Tonight is the *Night of the Full Heart*—the end of that day of romance, of sun-drenched lovers gifting." He chuckles, deeply, brushing his hand feather-lightly across her confined hair. "What is it you would gift me with, oh my daring darling?"

Bending over unsteadily, she lays the rose at his feet. She briefly pauses to kiss each foot, careful that the blood from her mouth does not stain his wine-dark boots. Raising herself again, swaying, she swallows before she speaks. Her voice is hoarse, the deep rich texture of long misuse, or overuse, of the throat.

"You have the right to all of me, oh my Master, my Owner. I do not know what you may want that you have not taken. Yet there are things you have not taken, I know not why. I offer them to you tonight—clearly, explicitly." She breathes in deeply, glancing up to his face for a moment before looking down again. Slowly she exhales, and continues. "I offer you my heart—the deepest recesses, the most complete control. To you I would submit all my liaisons, for approval. Your word, your whim, your will—law to my heart as it is to my body. I offer you my blood, of which you have tasted the merest hint . . to feed your soul, your need, your control of me. I offer you the three tastings, of your blood in my mouth, so that I cannot get away even should I try. I offer you the binding of my body—literally, figuratively, virtually—that this," she lifts her hands, "is but the merest symbol of." She lifts her face to his now, candlelight glinting from the shining traces down her cheeks. "I offer you all of this, Master—but it only becomes a gift when it is accepted." She inhales sharply, her breath catching. Swallowing, she bows her head again. Bending over, she kisses his boots again, and retrieves the rose before resuming her position.

Standing before her, he reaches forward and twines his fingers into her hair. Just holding his hand there, he looks down at her, not keeping her from moving her head. Slowly, eventually, she looks up: past his well-formed legs in their tight black cotton; past his full crotch, visible only from her angle; past his beautiful red silk shirt, mid-thigh length when belted, that strokes across her welted skin so delightfully. Meeting his eyes, she swallows. He holds her gaze till he senses she is about to close her eyes, and says "You are mine." She whimpers, softly, her eyes getting wider, darker. "All of you is mine. That which you offer to me is mine already—just as supplies I have bought, and shelved, but not yet used, are mine. I . . . accept . . . that you have become ready to give me this fullness of you. And that is the gift that I will take—your readiness to give me so much."

Still holding her hair, he slowly kneels down before her. "And before this, our sacred space, I say to you that I do accept all you have given me—all the gifts you have offered. And I thank you for accepting all that I am capable of giving you." He takes the rose from her mouth, and pulls her to him, kissing her deeply, passionately, repeatedly licking the cuts in her mouth from the thorns.

How Do You Make a Screaming Orgasm?

Shanna Germain

If only it was my lover asking and not these pasty-faced
bar boys with their fake IDs, and their desire
to see me blush. I tell them about raspberry liquor,
pineapple juice, the clink of ice against the glass.
But I can tell it is not what they're looking for,
their eyes following the shift of legs, the curve of hip.

If only it was my lover asking, then I would say:
Start with an ounce of slow soft strokes.
Combine two pats of butt with a whisper
of tongue against teeth.
Add a touch of hand to the back of the neck,
a lick of earlobe, a pinch of nipple.
Stir until you reach the desired consistency.
Serve hot.

But to these boys with their expectant young eyes,
the excitement is still in the words:
screaming and orgasm fitting into their mouths
like an ancient language they cannot translate.
Someday, they will come
to understand and will drink it up,
smooth and rough like liquor upon the tongue.

Woman Being Tongued to Orgasm While Reciting the Names of North American Capital Cities

Mark Aster

She steps into view slowly, calmly, her face placid. Under the loose olive-green sweater the shape of her body is indefinite, but certainly female. Her skirt is short and tight, and before she sits down she unzips it and slips it down her legs. She has nothing on underneath. The hair over her sex is short and dark.

"Aguascalientes, Aguascalientes." It begins like an invocation. Her voice is smooth and low. "Montgomery, Alabama." She pauses after each name.

"Juneau, Alaska. Edmonton, Alberta." This is her normal speaking voice, her daily voice, and we savor the sweet ordinariness of it. Soft hands slide up her bare legs, gently caressing her skin, and she feels herself relaxing, opening up. Her heart is beating rapidly, but we can't see it.

"Phoenix, Arizona." Warm lips touch the tendon at the top of her right thigh in a long kiss. Her eyes close for a moment, but her voice stays level. "Little Rock, Arkansas. Mexicali, Baja California Norte. La Paz, Baja California Sur."

The finger-touches and lip-touches play gently over her skin. "Sacramento, California." She is smiling, her lips a charming curve. Is she looking forward to the loss of control?

"Campeche, Campeche. Tuxtla Gutierrez, Chiapas. Chihuahua, Chihuahua." Now the mouth withdraws, and the fingers move in, pressing the closed folds of her outer labia. "Saltillo, Coahuila. Colima, Colima. Denver, Colorado." The fingers begin to move, and warmth spreads out, warmth and pleasure, out into her hips and her stomach.

"Hartford, Connecticut." She sighs deeply, rocks her hips slightly forward. "Dover, Delaware." Her eyes close as the fingers move, the buried bud of her clitoris is nudged gently up and down. "Durango, Durango. Tallahassee, Florida." Now her mouth opens in a long ecstatic gasp, and her head goes back. She leans backward, her body supported on her arms. "Atlanta, Georgia." The sweater is tighter across her chest, and we can see her breathing. Her voice catches in quick soft gasps in the middle of each "Guanajuato." Her voice is softer now, breathier.

"Chilpancingo, ahhhh, Guerrero." Now the fingers on her labia are moving in complementary circles, gently opening her. For a few heartbeats she stops speaking. We are quite content with the quiet tension building in her breath. "Honolulu, Hawaii. Pachuca, Hidalgo. Boise, Idaho." She has found a rhythm, the syllables of geography flowing from her in time to the strokes between her legs. "Springfield, Illinois." She is singing, head back and eyes closed, at some plateau of pleasure. "Indianapolis, Indiana. Des Moines, Iowa." Her hips move to the same rhythm, but barely perceptibly.

"Guadalajara, Jalisco. Topeka, Kansas. Frankfort, Kentucky." The words come effortlessly; her voice is suffused with pleasure. The warmth between her thighs manifests itself, and she feels the juices starting to flow in the still-closed flower of her vulva. "Baton Rouge, Louisiana. Augusta, Maine." She could do this all night. She would love to do this all night. Her hair hangs down behind her, over her upper arms. "Winnipeg, Manitoba."

"Annapolis, Maryland. Ahh!" Her eyes fly open. Her face is startled, flushed. As the fingers stroke her, the lips have kissed her, open and wet, on that slope just below the navel, a place her skin is particularly sensitive. She feels herself opening, spreading, filling with blood. "Boston, Massachusetts," she moans.

"Toluca, Mexico. Lansing, Michigan." Her outer labia are slowly parted. She feels the skin moving back, the deeper parts of herself becoming exposed. "Morelia, Michoacan. Saint Paul, Minnesota." Her voice is breathless, distracted, all her concentration on the opening blossom between her legs, the touching fingers, the gentle wet mouth. "Jackson, Mississippi."

"Ooohhh . . ." Barely touching, the warm tongue has slid up between the folds of her vulva, stroking the outer edges of her most intimate cleft. "Jefferson City, Missouri." Like a prayer. "Helena, Montanaaaahhhh . . ." Now the tongue is setting up a rhythm, a deeper rhythm, long slow strokes that slowly slowly part her inner labia and come closer to her clitoris, hiding, blood-swollen, in its hood. "Cuernavaca, Morelos. Tepic, Nayarit. Lincoln, Nebraska!" She licks her lips with her blunt pink tongue. Her voice is not steady now, but she finds the rhythm, and again she is singing. "Carson City, Nevada. Fredericton, New Brunswick. Concord, New Hampshire." The song is faster, more strained. Is she pleading? The lips close on the hood of her clitoris, and the fingers continue the rhythm. "*AAAaaahhh . . .*"

"Trenton, New Jersey." Her eyes are open, but staring out into nothing. "Santa Fe, New Mexico *ooohhh* . . ." Her hips have stopped moving. She is motionless but for her mouth singing (her lips are perfect as they touch and part, touch and part, and I imagine I am kissing her), for the breath in her chest, and for the tiny motion imparted to her body by the hands and mouth busy between her legs. "Albany, New York. Saint John's, Newfoundland."

Her eyes open wide. "Raleigh, North Carolina *Uhhhh!*" One finger has parted the inner lips and slid barely inside her. "Bismark, North *DakOOOhhhta . . .*" It nudges her clitoris from below, and the tongue circles above. "Halifax, Nova Scotia. Monterrey, Nuevo Leon." Further inside her now, and her juices are rich and wet. "Oaxaca, Oaxaca. Columbus, Ohio." The heat flows out from her hips, down her legs, up into her chest. "Columbus, Ohio. Oklahoma City, Oklahoma."

She takes a deep breath, squeezes the muscles of her vulva around the penetrating finger, presses her hips forward. "Toronto, Ontario." It was in Toronto, Ontario that she first felt the warmth of lips between her legs, the tongue nudging inside her. "Salem, Oregon." The pleasure washes over her again, but she is back on earth for a moment. She is keenly aware of her breasts under the sweater, the cotton bra. Her nipples are stiff and tender.

"Harrisburg, Pennsylvania. *Oh, Uhhhh!*" Two fingers are in her now, slowly penetrating and withdrawing, and the tongue has teased her clitoris out to kiss. "Charlottetown, Prince Edward Island." Her body arches and her head goes further back as the fingers move insistently. "Puebla, Puebla *ah ahh AHH!*" Lips caress the stiff bud of her clitoris, and she gasps, moving outside of time again.

"Quebec, Quebec. Queretaro, Queretaro!" Her legs are spread wide apart. "Chetumal, Quinta Roo." She is panting now, her breasts heaving. "Providence, Rhode Island. San Luis Potosi, oooh San Luis Potosi. *oooh OOHH!* Regina, Saskatchewan!"

Regina, vagina. Her whole lower body is moving in time to the finger-thrusts deep inside her. Her open thighs glisten with saliva, and sweat, and the juices of her sex. "Culiacan, Sinaloa. *UHHH!*" Now she is grunting more than singing, finding a third rhythm, a deep, urgent beat in her loins. "HermiSIllo, SoNOra. ColUMbia, South CaroLINa. *Ah. Ah. AH!*" Her mouth is open wide. The fingers go farther into her and stop, holding her there pierced and open as the tongue thrums over her clitoris. Her hips rock.

"Pierre, South—South Dakota. Villa—a—ahermosa, Taba—asco." She is whispering now, between pants. "Ciu—oh—Cuidad Victoria, Tamaulipas. Nashville, ah, Tennessee." And suddenly the fingers move again. "*AHHHH!* Austin Texas!" They pull out, push deeply in, and the mouth closes on her clit again, and she screams. "Tlaxcala! Tlaxcala*AAHH!*" Her hips thrust eagerly back against the hands and the lips. "Salt Lake City—Utah! Jalapa, VeraCRUZ! *UH UHHH UHHNNN!*" She is coming.

Her breath is short and sharp and her mouth is wide open. She gasps out "MontpelierVermont!" . . . "RichmondVirginia!" in tumbled desparate syllables. She cries out again, a long wordless howl, and her body begins to spasm around the relentless fingers. *"Ah ah ah! OlymAhhHHpia Wahhh awshingon, CharlestonWeeeestVirginia, god god god Madison Wiscaaaaaahn-sin!"* Two final screams as she collapses back onto the cushions; the lovely orgasm-song versions of Cheyenne, Wyoming and Merida, Yucatan. She lies limp, the fingers still deep inside her, long motionless kiss resting on her mons. She groans long and loud and sated.

She twines her fingers in her lover's hair, and pulls the tousled head up, to kiss the lips that taste of her crux.

"Zacatecas," she moans, spent, "Zacatecas."

This Is How It Feels

Shailja Patel

when you go down on me
wind blows fragrant
through my garden
from your hungry lips
earthquake lifts my pelvis
chalice for your sips
your tongue a hot wet finger
separates my labia
as swimmer cleaves the water
as a seamstress slices silk
this is how it feels
when you go down

this is how it feels
when you awake
sleeping flushed-pink
clit child in her bed
you slide back
her fleshy hood
out she pops
all rosy plump
to sing
as you go down

your tongue now a silver fish
flashes up my narrow stream
your tongue now a matador
taunts rogue bull between my hips
and when your lips enfold my clit
grape so ripe she begs to split
her skin
a million vines flow burgundy
through every last capillary
my fingers rumba in your hair
living forest on my belly
you leave grape juice handprints
on my buttocks
as I birth your face
between my thighs

this is how it feels
when your tongue enters me
scarlet sacred blasphemy
sanctified profanity
woman's mouth
on woman's cunt woman's lips
in woman's labia woman's tongue
in woman's yoni girl
sings orchards into vineyards
into joy laughs joy
into another girl's
garden

here between my legs
eighteen wheeler trucks
turn cartwheels
skyscrapers fall to their knees
solar systems burn and shatter
pyramids give up their dead

Tell Me A Story

Susannah Indigo

"Take a deep breath, Rikki."

She smiles, inhales, and tries to relax.

"Now, slow down and tell me again," Alex says with a laugh.

"Oh, Alex, I won. I really won! I got the letter today, and I'm going to Italy. Thank you for all of your help."

He leans back in his chair behind the big mahogany desk and watches as she is barely able to sit still in her seat.

"Rikki, you look like sixteen when you're this excited."

She blushes. "I'm glad that I'm not. I never could have written that story without my years of experience. I can't believe it."

"Come here, Rikki. I haven't seen you in almost a month."

She looks up in slight surprise. Dr. Alex Russ has always been friendly to her, but he's never looked at her in quite this way before. She steps over toward his desk, still bouncing with excitement, unable to quite discern the look on his face, that handsome bearded face that has cajoled and laughed with her through so many of her writing struggles.

"Sit up here on my desk. Let's talk about what you wrote."

Rikki blushes again. A tale of sexual obsession was her choice of subject matter for the winning entry. The theme of the contest had been "The End of the World," and what would truly matter when that time came near. She had ditched her original ideas about survival and gone for what she knew.

"I'm pretty sure I was the only one to turn in an erotic story of domination and possession for my entry," she says. "But what else is there, when you strip away all of our pretenses?"

"Rikki, I have to tell you—talking about sexual obsession for those two months with a thirty-two year old woman who just dropped in to audit my class has been the highlight of my year."

Perched on his desk, she pulls the folds of her full forest green silk dress over her stockinged legs and crosses her ankles primly in front of him. "Well, you helped me a lot. Like we talked about, the only themes that really matter are sex, religion, death, and art."

"I've thought about you and your story day and night, and I have a secret to share with you."

Forgetting the writing contest for now, she begins to notice Alex's deep voice reaching her in strange ways.

"A secret? I love secrets," she says, trying to laugh it off.

"Look at me. I'm quite serious. I want to act out your story. With you."

"Oh my."

"Yes, exactly. It's all I thought of every time you left my office."

"I don't know, Alex, what are you saying?"

His eyes lock on hers, and she begins to feel the need for his hands on her, somewhere, anywhere.

"I want to feel it. I want to know if one person can truly possess another. Your writing is so clear, so erotic. We're going to take that journey together. Nothing else matters. We can think of it as the end of the world."

"Maybe it won't work in real life?" she asks, feeling the

wetness growing between her legs.

"Rikki, I can see it on your face. You want it as much as I do. Ask me to act out your story with you."

"We both have real lives elsewhere. And, we both know how it ends."

"It doesn't have to end that way. We can stop whenever we want to. We can create our own little secret world. Go close the drapes."

Alex lights a single candle, places it on the coffee table, opens a bottle of wine and pours two glasses.

"Do you like Coltrane, Rikki? You must."

"God, yes, I listen to him all the time when I write."

He starts one of her favorite CDs, "The Last Giant."

"Come sit on the floor with me, Rikki, and let's talk. You look nervous—tell me what you're thinking."

"Oh, you know. You know. I don't know if I can do it."

"Unbutton the top button of your dress."

She pauses.

"Do it."

She slowly reaches down and undoes the first button.

"That's not near enough. Undo another one."

She unbuttons the next pearl button on her dress, exposing the top of her cleavage.

"That's beautiful. Tell me you can do this."

She just smiles.

"You'll learn, every time you come into this office."

"Yes."

"Much better. Now, tell me what you're wearing beneath that lovely dress."

Rikki looks down shyly and says, "I'm wearing a white lace bra."

"Does it fasten in the front?"

"Yes, it does."

"Good. Never come to me again wearing any other kind of bra. Reach inside your dress and unfasten it."

She reaches down and unclasps the bra, freeing her breasts, feeling the hardness of her nipples against the silk of the dress.

"Beautiful. Now, what else are you wearing underneath?"

He still hasn't touched her. She tries to move over towards him, reaching for a more comfortable level of normal affection.

"No, Rikki, stay right where you are. I want your eyes on mine while we do this. I want you to be uncomfortable, to find an intimacy that's so easily bypassed by everyday sex."

She sits back down crosslegged, looking directly across the coffee table into his eyes. "Yes, Alex."

"Answer my question."

"I'm wearing thigh-high stockings, and panties that match the bra."

"Stand up."

Another pause.

"Do it."

Rikki rises and stands in front of him. She begins to sway to the music, to follow the rhythm as he talks.

"Lift your skirt up to your waist and hold it there."

He sits before her and watches as she gathers the full skirt up around her waist, exposing her ass.

"Take your panties off for me."

She reaches down and slips off her panties, dropping the dress from her waist.

"No. Lift it back up. And spread your legs."

Hesitating only for a moment, she follows his instruction.

Alex lays her panties aside. "Here are the rules, sweet Rikki." He finally touches her thigh, stroking gently up and down, never touching her pussy. "You will come to me twice a week, just as you did when we were working on your writing. But you will come in the evening, and you will plan on spending the night. You will bring nothing with you." Trembling, she stands before him, as he kneels, stroking and examining her.

"You will never wear panties. You will never wear jeans. You may wear any kind of skirt that you choose. When you enter my office, you will walk over and close the drapes, then come to me wherever I sit. You will lift your skirt, for inspection, without a word. Do you understand?"

"Yes, I do." The wetness begins to flow and she closes her eyes for the moment.

"If I call you and ask you to dress some other way, you will. You will tell me erotic stories when I ask. You will make them up on the spot if I so choose."

"Yes."

"We're going there, Rikki, we're going where the couple in your end of the world story went. We're going to where nothing else in the world matters but our desire for each other. No matter what it takes. And we will give each other everything."

His fingers are dipping into her slowly, withdrawing, coming to his lips as he tastes her wetness. He stands up next to her, holding her with one arm, and places one of his wet fingers deep into her mouth, running it around her tongue. "Taste, baby. Taste my finger." He opens her mouth wider with the force of his finger, running it across her teeth and down into her throat, fucking her mouth with his finger as though it were his cock. Her head drops back, lost in the intimacy of a single finger invading her mouth.

"Drop your skirt down, Rikki."

She opens her eyes in surprise as he withdraws his finger.

"That's all for today." He blows out the candle, walks away, and opens the drapes.

"I'm so proud of your winning that contest. I'll see you here on Tuesday at six sharp." He picks up her white lace panties from where they lay and tosses them in the wastebasket.

Rikki sits in her car and shakes, feeling her bare bottom touching the leather seat. *This is crazy—this is the craziest thing I have ever considered. We both have lives. It was just a story. Just fiction. I'll write him a note, that's what I'll do. I do have it in me to do this, but God, if I do, if I let go into this kind of sensuality, I'll never get back. I'm going to go home, get out my stationery with the roses on it, write him a note thanking him for everything, and then I'll never see him again. It was just a story.*

By Tuesday evening at 6:30, Alex is sure she's not coming. He's debating the virtues of calling her when he finally hears the knock on his door.

"Come in."

Rikki ambles in, obviously a bit tipsy. She dances over to him and poses on his desk, kicks off her shoes and places her feet in his lap.

"Hi, Alex."

"Rikki, aren't you forgetting some things?"

She wriggles her toes in his lap.

"Do as you were told."

With a flounce of her skirt, she hops down and heads for the drapes.

"And you're late.Where were you?" She pulls the drapes closed and turns to look at Alex. "Oh, you know, I just stopped down at the pub for a minute and had a glass of wine." She watches him from across the room, feeling rather like a pawn in a chess game, unsure of her next move.

"Come here."

She pauses, then joins him.

"What are you to do when you enter?"

"Close the drapes and then come to you."

"And then?"

Blushing, she reaches down to the hem of her black cotton skirt and lifts it up to her thighs.

"Not quite. Keep going, baby."

She sighs and lifts the soft skirt up around her waist.

The tops of her black stockings perfectly match the jet black color of her pussy hair. He reaches out to caress her soft hair and she moans.

"Yes, that's better. Now turn around."

She feels shy and slutty all at the same time. The two glasses of wine helped just enough to get her up to his door, but she suspects she needs the whole bottle to carry on much further.

He bends her over the desk. "Make yourself comfortable there, baby.." She looks back over her shoulder as he starts to caress her legs and her bare ass, talking to her the whole time. Her hands find the far edge of the desk and hold on.

"Was it hard to come here to me tonight?"

"Yes. I was scared. I almost wrote you to say I couldn't do this."

"But you didn't."

"No. No, I kept putting it off, and then I had a drink downstairs, and here I am."

Alex kneels down and starts to kiss her black stockinged legs from the ankles up, slowly. "I'm glad you were scared. It means you take this as seriously as I do."

He spreads her legs a little wider with each kiss rising up her thighs. "You're all I've thought about every minute of the day, baby. I've thought about what we're doing. About where we're going. About what I need to do to you."

Moaning and giving into his touch, she whispers, "It's all I've thought about too."

His hands slide up over her ass, slowly exploring every opening. "I have two surprises for you tonight," he says, with his fingers buried deep inside of her. "First, something for your body. Relax, this won't hurt at all."

She feels something hard and cold pressing against her pussy lips.

"It's just something to keep you warm inside for me while we take care of the second surprise. They're small silver balls, and they will gently roll around inside your pussy while we're out." He pushes the second ball in. "How does that feel, baby?"

"Oh, God. It feels very full and wonderful. Out where?"

Alex leans hard down on her back as she lies over the desk, pressing his stiff cock up against her ass. "You love it, don't you."

"Yes."

"Good. Then we're going out to dinner with a friend of mine. Let's get ready."

He helps her straighten up her skirt, keeping his hands on her ass while she catches her breath.

"I don't know if I can walk anywhere with these inside of me."

"Yes, you can. Let's go."

Walking down the street on his arm, Rikki realizes that although he hasn't even fucked her yet, she still feels completely possessed by him.

Waiting at the table in Sostanza's, Rikki says, "You know, Alex, there are things in my end of the world story that I don't want to do."

"Yes? Like what?"

"Some of the more dangerous things . . ."

She's cut off by the arrival of Alex's friend, Jonathan. After greetings and polite chatter, Alex brags about Rikki's prize-winning story.

"You wrote about sex at the end of the world?" Jonathan asks.

"Yes," she answers, "Sex and intimacy and stories and

passion." *Give me another drink,* she thinks, *and I'll even tell you the ending.*

"Rikki's a great storyteller," Alex says, "Some night we'll all have to get together and let her enchant us with her tales."

He leans over, whispers to her, "How do the balls feel deep inside of you?" and watches her blush.

They continue to talk of her story as though it were a scholarly work, dissecting what could truly happen and what couldn't. She listens in fascination while Alex keeps his hand high on her bare thigh.

"I was just telling Alex before you came," Rikki interjects, "that some of the things in that story are just fantasy, and people don't really do them."

"Like what?"

"Oh, just some of the more dangerous things, involving control and possession and physical harm."

"Rikki and I have been thinking about trying out some of them ourselves."

She looks quickly to see if perhaps she misheard. She didn't, he's smiling. She excuses herself and flees to the restroom.

Alex meets her there in the hallway five minutes later. "Jonathan's gone." He pins her up against the wall, kissing her deeply. "He's an open-minded guy, don't worry about him."

"How could you?"

"I could." He whispers fiercely into her ear, "I need to fuck you, baby, here."

"No, not here."

"Yes, here." He pulls her out into the dark alley behind the restaurant. "Lift your skirt and bend over."

"No."

"No? Let me help you." He does it for her. Pressing her fast up against the railing, he shoves her skirt aside and unzips his pants. "Tell me, Rikki. Tell me you want me to fuck you hard." He can feel her breathing fast, and reaches for the hardness of her nipples. "Tell me. Tell me how much you want it."

His cock is hard against her bare ass. "Oh God, yes. Yes. Yes. I want you." He spreads her legs and enters her pussy hard and fast, feeling the metal of the silver balls inside her against his cock. The heat builds until he's fucking her fast and furious and she no longer cares who can see or hear them. His arms are wrapped around her tight and they both come violently into the night.

As they begin to recover, they straighten each others clothes and laugh. "You make me feel like a teenager, Alex."

"You are, baby, in your heart. Let's go home. I need you to tell me a story."

Lying on the carpet in front of the single candle, Alex slowly removes all of Rikki's clothes, and then all of his own. He ties her wrists together with one of his red neckties, leaving her feeling vulnerable but not seriously bound.

She recognizes this as one of the scenes she has written, and is amazed at his attention to detail, right down to the color red and the single candle. She's also amazed that it feels exactly the way she thought it would, purely and wonderfully sensual.

"Tell me a story, baby."

She laughs. "Do you know where I got that whole thing from?" She's beginning to melt under the slow and gentle massage of his hands on her back.

"No, where?"

"It's a silly rhyme from my childhood—

Tell me a story and sing me your song
tend my heart gently to keep us both strong
make it a tale full of love and romance
or spin me the truth
and we'll each take a chance

"That's not silly, it's great." He pours lotion into his hands and starts in on her thighs.

"Now, baby. Tell me a story. Make it a true one."

She sighs with pleasure. "This is wonderful. OK, a story of my past."

His fingers press and probe gently as she begins to talk.

"This is the story of where all my tying up fantasies begin, I suppose. Once upon a time I had a boyfriend, when I was quite young and neither one of us knew much of anything about sensuality, who liked to play around with tying me up. He liked it, I liked it, it was pretty harmless. Mostly he'd just tie my wrists to the bedposts and fuck me. And he wanted me to do the same to him sometimes."

"How old were you?"

"Oh, probably twenty or so . . . oh my, that feels great. You are the sexiest man on earth."

He turns her over and places her tied hands behind her neck.

"So what happened?"

"It was fun, but not great, probably because we weren't that great together to start with. But then he got a little weird on me. He liked to tie me up and just leave me that way, all evening. He liked to sit me on a hardback chair with my wrists and ankles tied tight and just watch me. It was sexy in a way, but also scary and strange."

Alex straddles her waist and begins a serious massage of her nipples. She can feel his cock growing hard at her words.

"He would come by the chair and tease me every now and then, you know, touching me, caressing me, pinching my nipples. But he wouldn't say much, and we were so young we could hardly talk about what we were doing. It was like we knew what we liked, but we had no idea where to go from there."

"Not like now, where you can write stories that take you straight to the end of the world."

"Yes."

He slides up to her mouth and begins to stroke her face with his cock. "Tell me more. And keep your hands right where I put them behind your neck."

She squirms under the caress of his cock. "So, I often found myself sitting on this very uncomfortable chair, tied up for hours, just to please him. After the first hour or so like that, the stiffness of my body overcame any erotic feelings I might have had."

Alex slides the tip of his cock into her mouth, watching her close her eyes and run her tongue deliciously around it. "More story," he says, and withdraws.

"God, yes. Then, one night, he got kind of cruel about it. He not only tied me to the chair, he blindfolded me. Then I heard him leave the apartment. I was terrified. What if something happened? I think about it now, and I think it could have been sexy if we could have talked about it, if I had any idea what was going on."

His cock is hard in her mouth now, halting her words. She sucks him until he is ready to withdraw again and hear the rest.

"So, he left. And I admit, I was turned on in spite of it all. But I was angry too. It's dangerous to play too fast and loose in the realm of the senses like that. He came back hours later and I was exhausted from crying. But . . ."

Alex's cock is fucking her mouth hard now, stopping the story, his fist wrapped in her hair. "Finish," he says finally, withdrawing.

She takes a deep breath. "But . . . I admit we had the hottest sex we'd ever had that night. It was like he owned me. He left me blindfolded and held me on the ground and fucked me every way possible. I learned some amazing things about my body that night."

The story stops as he buries his cock deep in her throat, coming with force. "Yes, baby, yes."

She takes her time and licks her lips and swallows all of his come, and he leaves his cock near her lips so that she can lick him clean also. Untying her wrists, he holds her tight and begins to rock her toward sleep in his arms.

"That was a great story, Rikki."

"But you never heard the end. I left him the next week. It was all too much."

"You will never leave me, baby. You are the bridge to my darkest desires."

"But what happened to stopping whenever we wanted to?"

He holds her close. "We can. But you will never leave me. Never."

Tuesday and Thursday nights come and go in the fog of sensuality. Rikki starts showing up on time without the previously-required glass of wine. Some evenings she even shows up early. They experiment with schoolgirl clothes, with candle wax, and with spanking. Meetings stay as planned, but the phone calls begin—two, sometimes three times a day.

"Rikki, I want you to wear your prettiest dance clothes tomorrow night," Alex tells her one day on the phone.

She shows up in a deep purple chiffon skirt and black leotard, long black hair down and flowing, with no idea where they're going. She enters, closes the drapes, and comes to him for inspection. Lifting the swirling skirt and hopping up on his desk, she spreads her legs wide and tucks her toes around his waist.

"Hi."

He thinks perhaps he could die right here, watching this lovely woman be so free and open and sexual with him, so far into their intimacy that she no longer has any hesitations.

"I love you, Rikki."

"Oh, Alex." She's speechless beyond that. This is not exactly in the story they are supposed to be acting out. "Where are we going dancing?"

He runs his hands up over her legs, stroking her pussy through the leotard. "I don't even mind that you're not quite accessible in this, you look so beautiful."

She slides down onto his lap, holding him close, feeling the hardness of his cock beneath her.

"We're not going anywhere, Rikki. We're staying right here." He lifts her back up onto the desk and opens the bottle of champagne he has brought for them. "No glasses, we'll just share." He takes a long swig and then kisses her, delivering champagne directly to her mouth.

She laughs at the idea of being all dressed to go out and having only their own private dance. He lights the single red candle, they pick out music together and begin to dance slowly, wrapped around each other. He steps back from her.

"Dance for me, Rikki."

"A little more champagne, please."

More long kisses deliver the champagne.

Rikki begins to dance, swaying, swirling her skirt, trying to remember every move she's ever seen in strip shows. More kisses bring better moves, until she is standing right in front of him as he sits in the armchair. She removes her leotard completely, leaving only the long chiffon skirt and her black high heels. Her breasts move freely as she dances, over him, on him, for him, for her own sensuality, full of passion and power.

Alex strokes her breasts when she leans over him, then just lets her go. She dances over to the stereo and puts on Mickey Hart's "Planet Drums," and begins to dance and caress her body in the middle of the room as he watches.

"God, Alex, this music always makes me just want to lay down and be fucked hard."

"No. But you may touch yourself all you want while I watch."

He feeds her the rest of the champagne. She begins to perform a dance that involves fondling herself everywhere. She has no idea where this comes from, but she continues until she collapses in front of him and reaches an overwhelming orgasm while he watches.

"God, Alex."

"Yes."

They spend the rest of the night teaching each other every dance they know, from the tango to the Sugar Shack dance to an elegant waltz.

In the morning, Alex says, "Don't leave."

"I must."

"Never leave me."

"I won't."

Rikki calls him late that night at home at midnight.

"I need you."

"Meet me by the fountain in the Quad. Ten minutes."

She's there when he arrives, and he wraps her tight in his arms and holds her.

"Alex, this scares me. I need you so much."

"And I need you. We need to move forward. We need to complete our story."

The following Thursday Rikki calls him. "It's your turn tonight, Alex."

She enters promptly at six, wrapped in a long trench coat.

"You look rather like a secret agent, baby," he says, smiling.

"I have a surprise for you, Alex."

"I'm ready."

She closes the drapes and comes to him in ritual fashion. "You sure you're ready for this?" she asks.

"Yes, Rikki, I'm ready for everything."

She strips off her coat, and Alex sits back in surprise and admiration. She wears thigh high black suede boots, a red and black corset with matching garters and black stockings. The corset pushes her breasts high. She also wears a red and black lace collar.

"Rikki, you look like every man's midnight wet dream," he says, regaining his composure. "You actually drove here like that?"

"Yes." She's amazed how far she's going, how little she cares about anything in life but pleasing him.

He lifts her up and carries her across the room, laying her down in front of their candle.

"No, Alex, it's your turn."

He's fascinated by the tone in her voice.

Rikki undresses him slowly and guides him to lay down in front of her. She ties his hands above his head with one of her red silk scarves.

"How does that feel?"

"Rikki, I don't know about this."

"Just give into it, you'll love it like I do."

She stands over him in her high-heeled boots with her legs spread.

"Watch me."

He watches as she strokes herself, trying to reach up and touch.

"You need something more, I think. You're much less well-behaved than I am."

She ties the ends of the scarf to the leg of the coffee table. "Don't pull too hard or you'll tip the candle over and we'll be on fire."

He holds still.

"One more thing." She wraps another silk scarf around his eyes. "Do you like that?"

"I don't know, Rikki, it's strange."

"Yes, it is. When you're deprived of two of your senses like that, though, the seeing and the touching, everything else gets more intense. You've taught me that."

Rikki lowers herself until her bare pussy rests on his chest.

"Now, Alex, tell me a story."

"Oh man."

"Make it a true one."

"Alright." Alex breathes deeply and tries to relax.

"Let me help you relax." Rikki starts to stroke and kiss him starting from his toes.

"Yes, yes, I'll tell you about Paris."

"Paris?"

"Yes, Paris. I was there when I was in graduate school, just for a summer. There was a woman. She was pure sex. Pure abandonment. In fact, sometimes you remind me of her."

Rikki laughs. "I have nothing that exotic in me, I'm afraid. In fact, I'm only French in my kisses." She kisses him long and deep.

"God, Rikki, how can you ever tell stories and do this at the same time?"

"You've made me an expert."

"Anyway, I met her in a cafe one afternoon. She had dark short hair, she was very tiny, and not terribly pretty. But there was something about her that fascinated me."

"What was it?" Rikki moves down to his cock and begins to lick slowly.

"I didn't know when I met her, but I can tell you now. She lived in her senses. She was totally impractical. There was nothing she'd rather do in life than fuck."

"Yes," Rikki whispers, her face buried deep between his legs.

"And she wanted me. But she wasn't aggressive at all. She just let me know. It started out fairly normal, as young love affairs go. Lots of time in bed, lots of late nights. Then one night she told me what she really desired."

Rikki spreads his legs wider and starts exploring down the inside of his thighs.

"I need to see you while we do this, Rikki."

"No, you don't. Go on with the story. What did she want?"

"She wanted me to command her. To possess her, to own her. To tell her what to do. To use her, to abuse her. To completely dominate her."

"That sounds right up your alley," Rikki says with a kiss.

"It may be now, but I wasn't sure then. I loved it, but it felt bad. You know what I mean? The things she asked me to do shocked me. She was older, maybe thirty, and she'd had experience with this."

Rikki straddles him above his hard cock. "What did she want you to do?"

"She wanted to call me 'Sir' all the time. She wanted to serve me. She wanted to be on her knees for me. She wanted me to spank her. She wanted me to hurt her."

"And did you?"

"Yes."

"Tell me about it while I fuck you." She lowers herself down slightly, so that just the tip of his cock enters her pussy.

"I don't know if I can talk about it."

She slides down all the way, and holds him inside of her.

"Oh man, Rikki. That's wonderful."

"Tell me what you did. I want to know all the good and the dark things about you."

Alex tries to move his hips up to meet her, but she holds him still.

"OK. She would kiss my feet. At first because she wanted to do this. Then because I wanted her to. And finally because

I made her do it. You know *The Story of O?* It became very much like that."

"And you loved it."

"Loved, and hated."

Rikki slides slowly up on her knees until just the tip of his cock remains inside of her. "Tell me more," she says as she slides back down and leans over to kiss him deeply.

"I don't know, she just found something in me that I didn't know existed. The need to dominate. The need to be cruel. I often didn't want to even see her again, but I would. It only lasted a few months or so."

"What happened?"

Alex takes a deep breath as Rikki begins to ride him slowly to the rhythm of his words.

"It scared me to death."

"What happened? You can tell me."

"It just went too far."

Rikki leans over and unties his blindfold and his wrists. "God, I need your hands on me. . ."

He reaches for her breasts, then slides his hands down to her hips and raises her up. "Come with me, Rikki. Ride me hard. Come with me."

"God yes." Rikki reaches her climax at the same time that he explodes deep inside of her, and they collapse together on the floor.

Entwined together by the light of the melting candle, Rikki asks one more time. "Will you please tell me what happened?"

"No. I'd rather show you."

"What?"

"Next weekend we're going away. We're going to break all the rules."

"Where?"

"You don't need to know. I will take care of everything. And I will take care of you."

The following Thursday Alex calls Rikki in the early afternoon.

"Meet me tonight, on time, at El Chapultepec. Wear that red short dress with the black leather belt."

"Yes, I will."

She arrives to find Alex and his friend Jonathan in a back booth in the jazz bar, deep in conversation. Rikki begins to slide into the booth, but Alex stops her.

"Aren't you forgetting something?"

Rikki laughs. "What?—there are no drapes here."

Alex looks at her with that look that Rikki thinks he must practice in front of the mirror. It makes her melt every time—it's a look of absolute passion, yet absolute control.

"Lift your skirt."

"Alex!"

"Do it."

"Alex! Not here, not with him. . . ." She looks at Jonathan and blushes. He seems to just be sitting back relaxed, expecting this. "What can you be thinking of, Alex!"

"Look around you, Rikki. Not a soul is watching you. Except for us. Do it."

Options float through her mind like the jazz riff she hears in the background—*fright, fight, freedom, flight?* All seem like a dream, for she knows that this act is in her story and that she is caught hopelessly in the descending rhythm of her own writing.

"Yes, Alex."

Rikki looks one more time over her shoulder, avoids Jonathan's eyes, looks directly at Alex, and slowly slides the front of her red linen skirt up her thighs.

"Isn't she beautiful, Jonathan?"

"Yes."

Alex reaches out and touches her soft lips gently, making

her flinch. "You may lower your skirt, Rikki, and join us." Alex rises to let her slide in between them.

Rikki knows there isn't enough wine in this place to help her get through what she suspects is coming. She hopes perhaps he will alter her story and head in a different direction, as he has occasionally done in the past.

They chat about the blues singer in the spotlight, and Rikki tries to look at Jonathan and talk as though she hasn't just bared her pussy directly in front of him.

"I have a gift for you, Rikki," Alex says. He pulls a jewelry box out of his jacket pocket and presents her with it.

Rikki opens it slowly, and there it is. It is so close to what she described in her story that it brings tears to her eyes. "Oh, thank you, Alex." She lifts the choker up to examine its beauty, and finds her name inscribed elegantly in script across the golden underside of the heavy clasp.

Alex takes it from her and lifts it up toward her throat. The delicate filigree chains shimmer in the shadows and the candlelight.

"It's beautiful."

"It was designed just for you, Rikki. There's another piece that matches it, which you will receive this weekend."

Rikki kisses him with passion. "Thank you."

"Jonathan has read your story, Rikki."

"He has?"

"Yes, and he knows exactly what this means. When I place this on your lovely neck, there's no going back."

Alex pulls the intertwined chains snugly around her neck, and fastens the heavy gold clasp beneath her hair.

"You are mine, Rikki. You are never to take this off without my permission."

"God, yes, Alex, I do belong to you."

Rikki dances with Alex, and then she dances with Jonathan, losing herself in the music of the evening.

Sandwiched between the two men back at the table, she

feels warm and safe and loose and free, almost ready for anything. "It's time, Rikki. Jonathan's going to be so kind and lend us his cabin in the mountains for the weekend. I think we need to repay him for his generosity. Tell her about the cabin, Jonathan."

"It's pretty small, but comfortable," Jonathan responds, "and very, very isolated."

"It will be perfect for us," Alex says with a smile. "Now, Jonathan, what would you like her to do?"

"Only one thing. Tell me a story, Rikki. Tell me a story full of sex and romance. Oh, and just like in your writing, raise your skirt and let me watch you touch yourself while you tell it."

Rikki blushes until she's sure she'll die. "I can't."

"Let me help, Rikki," Alex says.

He turns her back toward his chest, so that she's looking directly at Jonathan. "Sit here, move in between my legs, that's it."

Alex slides her skirt up above the black stockings, just above the soft black curls of her pussy. "How is that Jonathan, do you have a perfect view?"

Rikki closes her eyes, pretends this isn't happening. Yet she feels herself on fire.

"Perfect. Tell me a story, Rikki."

By the end of the evening, Rikki's told several stories, always stroking herself to orgasm at the end of each one. She's told the story of the teenage finger-fucking episode in explicit detail, and the complete story of the three candles. Nestled safely in Alex's arms with her legs spread wide, yet discreetly, behind the table, she's made up a wild tale of a woman named Annie and her dancing and her Daddy. Jonathan's entranced, and Rikki imagines he wants her to go on through the night this way.

"Alex," she whispers, "I'm exhausted, and I need you. Can we go home?"

"Yes," he responds, stroking her hair softly.

They all leave together, and Jonathan hugs Rikki goodbye. "Thank you, Rikki, that was incredible. Take care of her, Alex."

"I will."

Rikki and Alex barely make it inside the door before they are tearing each other's clothes off, desperate to make love. They collapse on the floor in passion and wrap themselves tightly around each other and never let go.

They fall asleep immediately afterwards. Alex awakens her in the early morning with his tongue deep inside of her, letting her come to life slowly as he devours her.

"Oh God, it's late, Alex, I have to go," she whispers after recovering.

"Twelve hours, Rikki. In twelve hours we'll be leaving for the mountains. In twelve hours you will be completely mine in the wilderness for three days. Do you remember your instructions?"

"Yes, Alex. I will bring nothing with me. Nothing."

"Close your eyes tight," Alex tells Rikki as he guides her to the car.

"Why?"

"Close them."

She closes her eyes and lets him seat her in the passenger seat and fasten the seat belt for her. The aroma of flowers is overwhelming.

"Alex! What is that?"

"You may look."

Her eyes flutter open and the sight outdoes even the smell. "Look at all the roses! I've never seen so many roses together! How gorgeous, Alex, what a beautiful thing to do."

The back seat is full of roses. Huge bunches of yellow and

orange roses, piled high and wrapped several dozen at a time, all tied with pale orange and yellow ribbons.

"Those are my favorite color roses. But why so many?" She picks up one small bunch and inhales. "They're gorgeous."

"Because you deserve them. We'll figure out something to do with them all," he says with a smile.

"You are just too good to be true, Alex. I'm going to miss you."

"What do you mean?"

She puts the roses down. "Oh, you know my trip to Venice is next month." She realizes that this is the first time they've ever talked about the future.

"Are your plans all made?"

"Yes. I have a place rented for the month, and they have the conference all scheduled."

He's silent, and she peers at him through the dim light, trying to determine his feelings as they travel up the winding pass into the mountains. "We did say we could stop anytime."

Alex pulls the car to a stop at a visitor observation point. "Let's go for a walk, Rikki."

They climb up to the top of the deserted viewing platform. The lights of the city can be seen twinkling in the distance. The valley spans below them beyond the 500 foot drop-off. He guides her close to the edge, with his arms wrapped tightly around her waist.

"Take another step, baby."

"No, it's too scary."

"Do you trust me?"

"Yes." She steps forward.

"Another one. I've got you."

She trembles in his arms, but steps forward, wondering how far she'll go.

"I need you, baby. You have to trust me that I know what's right for us. I've reached the edge where I wanted to be. I can never let you go."

They stand together and watch the lights. Rikki has no words.

Driving miles down a private dirt road brings them to Jonathan's cabin.

"Wow," is all Rikki can say when she sees it. A small log cabin with a wraparound porch sits a hundred yards from a small lake that is only discernible by the shimmer of the mist reflected in their headlights. Small groves of aspen trees surround the cabin.

"Have you been here before, Alex?"

"Yes."

"This place looks like paradise."

"Wait until you see it in the daylight."

He guides her inside, where she gasps again. The ceiling soars to a peak of heavy logs, making the single room look huge. A narrow spiral staircase rises in the middle of the room to the loft bedroom above. One entire wall of the cabin ensconces a multi-colored stone fireplace. The far right side of the room holds an old-fashioned ten foot long pine dining table.

"Sit here at the table, Rikki, and put your feet up. I'll bring everything in."

"I can help. I'm a feminist, you know," she jokes, feeling rather helpless.

"So am I. Stay where you are."

Alex brings in the groceries and the one large suitcase. It takes him five trips to bring all the roses in and lay them before her across the table. He gets the fire going, lights the candles on the mantle, and puts some music on the CD player.

"The roses are not nearly as beautiful as you are, Rikki. Stand up."

She catches her reflection in the enormous picture window that has no drapes.

Alex turns her so she can watch herself in the glass. "Take

your skirt off."

She unbuttons the long straight denim skirt from the bottom, and lets it fall at her feet. She stands bare except for her shirt and sandals and the glimmer at her neck.

"Yes. Now the shirt and the shoes."

Rikki strips off the shirt and kicks away her shoes. Only the filigree chains remain at her neck.

"Yes, baby, yes. That's how I want you. That's how I want us here." He removes his clothes while she watches in the glass, and runs his hands down over her hips. "Civilization stripped away, all our pretenses gone. I want you to stay like this all weekend."

She's lost in his touch, in the glancing reflection in the window of him standing behind her stroking her, in the aroma of roses that are strewn across the table. She can hear Joni Mitchell singing about "dancing up a river in the dark" in the background.

"Come lay across the table for me. This table was made just for us." Alex clears a spot for her amidst the roses. "On your belly." Her breasts press down into the hard pine.

He climbs up next to her on the table and begins to unwrap the roses. "Close your eyes and just feel, baby." Roses run up and down her body, petals and thorns and then petals again. He caresses her everywhere, and she can only feel hands and softness and hardness and sharpness, until she cries out for him in need. He moves on top of her, hard cock pressing against her ass, entering her and fucking her hard, until nothing remains for either one of them but the fragrance of roses and love.

Hours later they are laughing and dancing around the kitchen area, trying to find enough glasses to put all the roses in. They line the glasses up down the middle of the table, finish putting the groceries away, and cuddle up together in front of the fireplace under a heavy blanket.

They tell each other stories, the silly and the serious, the important and the whimsical, until they fall asleep to the rhythm of their words.

In the morning Rikki wakes up shivering, and Alex gets up and finds her one of his big white cotton button-down shirts to wear while he cooks her breakfast. They relax in their closeness while gobbling down the scrambled eggs and toast. She tucks her bare feet up into his lap.

"This is the most breathtaking place I have ever seen, Alex. I want to set the next story I write here. Maybe I'll write about a couple with minimal clothing and an absolute obsession for each other. And lots of roses."

After breakfast, Alex finally takes her upstairs to show her around. There's just one room, with a big four poster pine bed with lovely old quilts on it. It's irresistible—they crawl under the soft quilts together and quietly make love one more time until they are momentarily satiated.

"Come with me, baby let's find out what it's like to be bathed in rose petals."

Warm water and bath oil, Alex's hands and a thousand rose petals seem perfect to Rikki. Afterward they sit on the bed for a long time, curled together, while he brushes and dries her long hair.

She starts to put his white shirt back on but he tells her not to. "I want you like we talked about last night, Rikki, with no clothing here. We'll keep the fire going all the time in case it gets cold. But we're not about to have any visitors here who can see us. You look just perfect the way you are, except for one thing."

Alex brings out a jewel box, and Rikki opens it to find another set of chains that match the ones around her neck. He kneels down in front of her to show her where it goes. He wraps the first section around her waist, and then runs the fragile chain down across her clit, teasing her and taking his time. The chain runs back up over her ass and fastens on the back of her waist.

"God, that's just gorgeous. Thank you so much."

She walks down the spiral staircase feeling completely open and vulnerable, shimmering in gold like an Egyptian princess.

In the afternoon it's perfectly sunny and they lounge on the porch in the soft chairs with no clothing and their feet kicked up, drinking lemonade. They talk and observe the crystal lake in front of their cabin, and finally read each other erotic stories from some books they find tucked away on a shelf.

"Jonathan must be kind of a kinky guy up here," Rikki says, looking at the stack of erotic books piled up next to her.

"He doesn't get to come up here much anymore. Rikki, I wish we could stay here forever." He makes her read some of his favorite dirty passages over and over. "You look tired, let's go back in."

He takes her back upstairs to the big bed. "Lie down and hold still for me."

She flops down on the bed, hearing the chains around her body clink together. Alex brings out the rope he brought in with the groceries and ties her wrists to each corner of the bed.

"You look so perfect there." He covers her with the turquoise quilt. "I'm going to go out for a walk, and I want you to just rest here for me like this.

"You're going to leave me like this?"

"Yes. Do you trust me?"

"Oh God . . . yes."

She hears the door close, and begins to drift off. She finds herself wondering dreamily about what they're doing.

Is this just meant to be? Is there any way to simply escape and live like this forever? Would it work if we did it all the time? What really happened to him in Paris that he's going to try and show me? Is he safe? Am I in love with him? Do I really trust him? She finds that just thinking about him like this starts to make her nipples get hard and the wetness flow between her thighs. Being aroused and alone and bound is frightening, and she pulls at the ropes in frustration. *What if he never comes back?*

A few minutes later she hears the door downstairs. "Oh God, I got scared after while, Alex. Please untie me."

"Yes, baby, but we both know what happens in your story after this, don't we. Do you think we can change the ending? Does being scared turn you on?"

She shivers. "Yes, oh yes it does."

"We have two more days here, Rikki, I want you to stay as you are, naked and bound in some way for me the rest of the time we're here."

"For two days?"

"Yes. Just let me take care of you."

He unties her briefly to let her get up, and then reties her hands behind her back. He helps her down the stairs and seats her comfortably on the bench at the table.

He feeds her dinner. "I feel like a child."

"Yes, but I may not always be so gentle here."

After dinner and wine, he takes her out for a walk on the patio with her arms still bound, slipping a jacket over her shoulders.

"It's so quiet here, Alex, it's like the end of the world."

They experiment that night with every possible way to use roses and their petals while making love. Rikki imagines she will smell these roses for the rest of her life. She's beginning to lose track of where she is and why she's here. He finally unties her for the night, and she feels lost.

Alex finds a way to help keep her comfortable and close and safe. He wraps her arms around his upper leg and reties her wrists, nestling her in between his legs to sleep. They both fall asleep with her head resting on his belly and her mouth gently on his cock. She awakens the next morning to find it's already noon. Alex's been up and gone out already. Rikki tries to stretch, only to find that he has quietly retied her hands above her head while she was sleeping.

He returns and brings her breakfast in bed.

"Alex, you're spoiling me rotten."

"I know." He feeds her.

As the day goes on, she notices his mood changes slightly.

"Baby, I want you to feel what it's like to be deprived of your senses, slowly but surely, until you are left with nothing but love and trust for me. I love you, Rikki. This is not just a story. We're going all the way. I know it scares you some. It scares me too. But I have to do it."

They go outside before the sun sets, and he reaches over and plays with her chains.

"I think we'll skip dinner tonight, and just dine on champagne. Take a good look at the beauty of the lake, baby."

She does, and then looks to him in trust. He brings out a black scarf and blindfolds her with it. Walking back in to the big leather couch, she gets a bit dizzy at the loss of both her hand movement and her sight. He lets her sit there comfortably on the couch, stretched out, feet up. "Tell me a story, Rikki. A truth. Tell me where you think we're going. How you feel about me."

She can't reach for him, or even see him. "I love you, Alex. I do." She pauses. "But I'm afraid we're going to consume each other and lose track of the line between what's real and what's not if we keep going."

He reassures her, and they talk for a long time. She notices that the apprehension over what they're doing often alternates between the two of them.

"One more sensation, Rikki. Are you ready?" Another

scarf. He wraps this one around her mouth, stopping her cry of surprise.

"That's beautiful, baby. You should see yourself, so helpless, so vulnerable, so trusting."

He doesn't touch her, just lets her spiral into the loss of movement and sight and speech. He sits down next to her and tells her his story.

"This is the kind of thing I did in Paris so long ago, but we did it all the time, and there was too much cruelty in it and not enough love. It was more like a contest to see who could go farther. To see who could be more evil. There wasn't enough trust, not like with you. You're soft and loving and imaginative and full of desire."

She struggles to say something.

"Just listen to me." Alex begins to play with the chain around her waist again. "The night you asked me about. She brought a knife out, and wanted me to use it on her body. It was the night it ended. I ended it. It went too far. I started to do what she wanted. I did. But I was afraid I would hurt her too much, and I was afraid I might like it. She knew what she liked. I wonder if she's still alive."

Rikki's getting slightly nervous at this story. She leans slightly away from him the best she can.

He holds her chain tight. "Don't ever pull away from me, baby. We're on the edge here, but we can stay there. I want to control you, I want to own you, but I will never cause you serious harm. Will you trust me?"

She nods slowly, struggling with the gag and the blindfold, scared, wet, excited, anxious.

"You just need to stay with me tonight, just let yourself go. Let yourself go for me, baby, there is no other world, there is only us and our passion. There is nothing more intimate in the world than giving yourself over completely to another human being. I want you to feel me tonight, I want you to know I am on you forever."

His words are becoming hypnotic to her.

"You've been bound since last night, but you've been able to move most of the time. Let me show you what control really is."

Alex lifts her off the couch and lays her down on the floor on her back. Spreading her legs wide, he ties each ankle to a leg of the couch. Her wrists are pulled over her head and tied across the carpeting to the armchair. She can only feel the warmth of the fireplace, and the smell of the roses that permeates the cabin. She's almost glad she can't speak, because there are no words for this feeling.

"Are you alright, baby? Just nod if you are." She nods. "Now, there is one last sense I can take from you."

Her body jerks involuntarily, with no idea what it could be.

"Before I do this, just know that you are nothing but the sensations of your body, and that you can trust me completely. I will always treat you like a precious object. And it will make us both strong."

Alex places tiny earplugs underneath the wrapping of the blindfold, and continues to talk to her, knowing she can no longer hear him. "I love you, Rikki. Good God, look at you. And now I am without a voice also. We are reduced to exactly where we should be. This may just kill both of us eventually."

As he begins to command her body, she gives herself over to him completely, feeling the pleasure, the ache, the withdrawal, the new sensations. Every opening and inch of her body is being explored and entered. There are strokes and there are slaps and she can barely tell them apart. Kisses begin to feel like bites and bites feel like sex. She hears stories in her head and they are like dreams, stories being told by someone else, someone who has total control over her and knows her from the inside out.

When Alex turns her over and reties her on her belly to

begin working his way up and down her back, she's lost in the dance on the line between pain and pleasure. With no sight, no sound, no control, no power, she finally gives into the absolute sensations of love and abandonment and her own wild hunger for passion and silently begs him for more, and then more, and then even more.

The return from the weekend had been very quiet between them. Alex calls her on Tuesday to say he needs to cancel that night, and wants to meet her for lunch the next day.

He holds her tight when she arrives at the restaurant. "Rikki, this is killing me. I wake up craving you. I think all day long of ways to hurt you and love you and own you. I forget to do important things, like pay bills. I can't get my work done. I can't find my way back across this bridge we've created."

She just listens. "We can stop whenever we want to."

"Rikki. Rikki. The weekend was incredible. I'm sorry. You were right, we're going to consume each other if we keep going. And I can't handle it."

"You loved it. And so did I."

He's near tears. "But I've lost the line. The line between fantasy and my own darkness. I'm falling apart, Rikki. If I stay with you it may kill me. It may kill you. We can't live in this secret dark world forever."

She watches him calmly, trying to figure out what to say. She's never felt stronger in her life.

"I have to stop, Rikki. God, I have to stop."

She rises to leave and drops her second airline ticket to Italy on the table in front of him. "I understand, Alex. It will be alright. But I have a surprise for you, just in case you change your mind. July first. Take care."

After three weeks away from him, Rikki's amazed at how strong and happy she still feels. She tries not to think too hard about why this is. She misses him. But their power shifted somewhere, and it satisfies her deeply. There are things that she wants and needs and now she knows how to get them.

Leaving for Venice, she writes him a short note on her rose stationery. She asks him only to take care of himself, to be well.

Sitting on the airplane gazing out the window, she fingers the filigree chains that she still wears tight around her neck. Shortly before take-off, Alex arrives, out of breath. He looks thinner, worried, a little older. She just smiles, reaches over, closes the windowshade, crosses her legs, lifts her white sundress up to her waist, and presents her bare pussy for his approval.

Alex watches her, surprised, enchanted. "You knew I'd be here?"

"Yes."

His hand is strong on her thigh as they take off. "Tell me a story, baby."

Contributors

MARK ASTER (www.asstr.org/~Mark_Aster) is the pen name of a part-time writer and fiction-junkie living on the east coast of North America. When not writing stories about people in the throes of orgasm, Mark likes to photograph ordinary household objects, and to lie in the sun with his eyes closed.

DEBORAH BACHARACH'S poems have appeared in *Paramour, Calyx, Switched-on Gutenberg,* and *Poet Lore,* among others. In the next year, she'd like to get her black belt in aikido and publish her poetry manuscript, *Welcome to America.* She lives in Seattle and teaches at Highline Community College.

JEFF BERESFORD-HOWE is a writer living in Oakland.

GARY BLANKENSHIP is a retired federal financial manager whose avocation is writing poetry. His work has appeared in several zines and countries. Since he resigned from several other Web positions in August, he can concentrate on editing the poetry page at Writer's Hood (www.writershood.com), his own work, and spoken word in the Puget Sound area.

ARIA BRAVERMAN is a poet and teacher living in Santa Fe, New Mexico.

CHRIS BRIDGES is the proprietor/host/bouncer of Hoot Island (hootisland.com), a Web site devoted to silly sex in all its forms. He is four-hundred-thousand yards long in his mortal guise, which he only assumes for special occasions or as an amusing party trick. His contribution to this anthology is negligible, although it is easily the most important bit of the whole shebang or, indeed, of erotic literature in this epoch. He has all of his fingers.

REBECCA BROOK and her husband have been involved in the leather community for the past decade. Rebecca moderates a Yahoo!Groups listserv called *Leatherchurch*, where kinky people of all faiths and orientations can discuss the intersection of sex with spirituality.

JANICE CALLISA lives in London and works in finance, passionately pursuing good music and exotic travel whenever possible.

PASQUALE CAPOCASA is the editor of *Poems Niederngasse* (www.niederngasse.com) and the poetry editor at *Clean Sheets.*

ISABELLE CARRUTHERS is a fiction editor with *Clean Sheets.* Her short fiction has appeared in print in *Prometheus, Mammoth Book of Best Erotica, The Mainline,* forthcoming in *Best Women's Erotica,* and also in various Internet magazines. She lives in New Orleans.

HEATHER CORRINA is the founder and Editor of *Scarlet Letters* (www.scarletletters.com), *Scarleteen* (www.scarleteen.com), and *Femmerotic* (www.femmerotic.com).

RAPHAELA CROWN is a connoisseur of fine produce who lives in Jerusalem. "Zucchini" was her first public piece of erotica. Her erotic fiction appears in the anthologies *Best Women's Erotica 2002* and *Bedroom Eyes*; she has also published poetry and prose in *The Paris Review, The New Republic, The Massachusetts Review, The University of Pennsylvania Law Review, Seventeen* and *Agenda,* among other places.

NAOMI DARVELL is an Articles Editor at *Clean Sheets.*

WILLIAM DEAN is a long-time writer and journalist, artist, performer, and award-winning media producer. His interests include collecting books, Hollywood memorabilia, herb and spice cultivation, gourmet cooking, and literature. He is currently Associate Editor for *Clean Sheets,* monthly columnist ("Into the Erotik") for the *Erotica Readers Association,* a Feature Writer for *Mind Caviar,* and hosts the "Erotik Journeys" column at *Adult backwash.com.* His work has been published online and in three anthologies.

JANE DUVALL is the creator of JanesGuide.com—a Web site that has reviewed porn and other adult material of all kinds since mid-1997. In addition to JanesGuide, she runs a personal Web site that is home to her own pornographic non-fiction, as well as an ever-growing collection of photo galleries. She also does the occasional speaking engagement on the subject of the adult Web, and is active in the local BDSM community. She makes her home near Seattle, Washington with her husband and three children.

JAMIE JOY GATTO is the author of *Unveiling Venus* (2001), *Suddenly Sexy* (Brilliant Smut Press, 2001), and *Sex Noir* (Circlet 2002). She is Editor-in-Chief of *Mind Caviar* (www.mindcaviar.com). Her work has been included in dozens of projects, including *Best Bisexual Erotica 1 & 2, Best SM Erotica, Unlimited Desires, Guilty Pleasures, Of the Flesh* and more. She is co-editor with M. Christian of *Villians & Vixens* (Black Books, 2002).

SHANNA GERMAIN (shanna_germain@hotmail.com) is a writer, editor, photographer, and sexy bookworm living in Portland, Oregon. By day, she masquerades as a demure newspaper reporter. But at the first sign of a telephone booth, she strips and begins to scribble erotica on her skin in red lipstick.

J. HARTMAN is a writer, editor, generalist, and native Californian, who has written software documentation, fiction, and reviews. (*Clean Sheets* has published some of the reviews and fiction, but not the software documentation.)

JAIE HELIER has worked for the past thirty years in theatre as actor, director and playwright, and earns a reasonable living this way. He currently lives in northern Australia with his partner, Daphne, writing erotica which is published in Australia and the US. Jaie recently started painting and drawing, which he now loves passionately. Jaie was a fiction editor with *Clean Sheets* for its first two years.

DONNA MICHELE HILL lives in British Columbia, Canada with her three sons. She has been seriously writing poetry for a few years now, drawing much of her writing style for realism from life around her, her family, and her work as a child educator. She currently is poetry editor of *Erosha* (www.erosha.net), an online literary journal of the erotic. Donna's poems have appeared in print issues of *One Dog Press, Poems Niederngasse, Poetry Motel,* and *Peshekee River,* and have also been published by numerous literary Web zines. Her first book, *Dimensional Dreams,* will soon be available through emailing her at dmhill@shaw.ca .

ANNETTE MARIE HYDER (freshink@subjex.com) is a writer with kinkily curly hair and an equally convoluted mind. Her work, journalistic and literary, is published throughout the United States and internationally. She sees life as a poem that is constantly altering its form to accommodate one's world view/experiences: sometimes a sonnet, sometimes haiku, sometimes graffiti on a wall. She believes that in love you should not say it with flowers, you should say it with words. Diamonds, however, are always acceptable.

SUSANNAH INDIGO (www.susannahindigo.com) is the Editor-in-Chief of *Clean Sheets Magazine*, and also the editor and founder of *Slow Trains Literary Journal* (www.slowtrains.com). She is the author of *Oysters Among Us: erotic tales of wonder*, and her work has been widely published, including *Best American Erotica* and *Salon Magazine.*

MIKE KIMERA is fascinated by the way sex and lust shape people's lives. His stories, which range from the tender and intimate to the dark and dangerous, have been posted widely on the Web. He is a member of the *Erotic Readers Association* (www.erotic-readers.com) where like-minded souls help him to improve his writing. Mike works as a management consultant (it's an easy job and someone has to do it), and lives in England and Switzerland.

CHER LADD-VUOLO is a self-proclaimed goddess who is obsessed with world domination. Affectionately known to her paramour as "Munchie," her work can be seen online at *Clean Sheets, Ophelia's Muse, Dark Poetry, Niederngasse* and *Passion Village*. She was also a featured writer in *Latte Magazine* and *Note Bene*. When she isn't writing, she is running with scissors, eating paste, or chasing her two children, who are usually doing the same.

DORIANNE LAUX is the author of three collections of poetry from BOA Editions, *Awake* (1990), introduced by Philip Levine, *What We Carry* (1994), finalist for the National Book Critics Circle Award, and *Smoke* (2000), finalist for the Oregon Book Award. She is also co-author, with Kim Addonizio, of *The Poet's Companion: A Guide to the Pleasures of Writing Poetry* (W.W. Norton, 1997).

PATRICK LINNEY is English. Under another name, he writes mainstream fiction and drama. It is only thanks to the encouragement of Susannah Indigo that his "Blue" stories are seeing the light of day.

ALLISON LONSDALE makes a living as an editorial assistant, and makes the living worthwhile by inventing new genders, rehabilitating domesticated memes for release into the wild, and singing her original songs about sex, science, and God in coffee-houses. Her fiction has appeared in *Clean Sheets,*

ScarletLetters.com, *Anything That Moves*, and the upcoming anthology *Best Transgender Erotica* from Circlet Press. She is the founder of the First Church of Sex & Poetry.

GWYDION MCCARTHY is the pseudonym of a writer living in a major Southern metropolis in the US. By day he is a mild-mannered IT professional. At night, the inanities of the day give way to erotic dreams and disturbing visions. A loving Daddy and devoted to his darling Belle, he is certified pansexual, an enlightened hedonist and pagan heretic.

GARY MEYER is retired from information systems project management, and now has a career in service as butler, chef de cuisine, cookie chef, and head cat wrangler. This transition coincided with a move from the Big Apple to the Biggest Little City in the World. He remains a practicing hedonist. In between hikes in the high desert, he collects and reviews transgressive literature and sexual shenanigans.

JAMES MOGUL is a 30something bondage educator, photographer, and artist living in Seattle, Washington. His images draw heavily on his intimate relationships with the models, creating a very personal type of erotic imagery. His Web site, NawaShibari (www.nawashibari.com), is devoted to his own blend of Japanese style rope bondage and pornography. He is also the creator of ArtBound, a series of live performance-art bondage presentations.

MARY ANNE MOHANRAJ (www.mamohanraj.com) is the author of *Torn Shapes Of Desire*, editor of *Aqua Erotica* and *Wet* (forthcoming 2002), and consulting editor for *Herotica 7*. She has been published in a multitude of anthologies and magazines, including *Herotica 6*, *Best American Erotica 1999*, and *Best Women's Erotica 2000* and *2001*. Mohanraj serves as editor-in-chief for the speculative fiction Web zine *Strange Horizons* (www.strangehorizons.com).

EMILY NAGOSKI is currently a Master's/Ed.S. student in Counseling Psychology at Indiana University, where she administers the Kinsey Institute Sexuality Information Service for Students (KISISS). She will enter The Real World in May 2002. When she grows up, Emily would like to be the Playboy Advisor, and live anywhere with a beach and great swing dance scene. Emily believes that good sex is the key to world peace.

BILL NOBLE is a fiction editor at *Clean Sheets*. This is the realization of an adolescent dream: reading sex stories and disguising it as an adult responsibility. In the time left over, he practices being Dad, saving the world, surviving long meetings, or being otherwise actually grown-up. He occasionally has sex, or writes. He's received national recognition for his poetry, and is widely anthologized as a fiction writer.

SHAILJA PATEL has had work published in *Trikone Magazine, Sow's Ear Poetry Review*, and the *Emily Dickinson Award Anthology.* She won the 1999 Outwrite Poetry Prize, and judged the contest in 2001. Her manuscript, *Dreaming In Gujurati*, was a semi-finalist for the 2000 Nicholas Roerich Poetry Prize. She is a recipient of a Serpent Source Foundation Grant and Voices Of Our Nations Arts Foundation Poetry Scholarship, and she was the 2001 Lambda Slam Champion, Santa Cruz Slam 2000 Champion, and represented Team Santa Cruz at National Slam Championships 2000.

BRIAN PETERS is managing editor of *Clean Sheets Magazine* and the Web designer for *Slow Trains* (www.slowtrains.com). His inclusion in this anthology is entirely unrelated to the fact that he's the co-editor. Really.

SCOTT POOLE (www.spocom.com/users/spoole) is the Assistant Director of EWU Press. His first book of poetry, *The Cheap Seats* (Lost Horse 1999) was a finalist for *Foreword Magazine's* book of the year awards. He reads his work every Monday morning at 7:50 a.m. on KPBX, Spokane Public Radio, which can also be heard live at KPBX Listen Online. His second book of poetry, *Hiding From Salesmen*, is forthcoming from Lost Horse Press in 2002.

ALEX M. QUINLAN lives on the East Coast of the United States with spouses, pets, and children, of both the two and four-legged variety. Her work has been published in *Unlimited Desires: an International Anthology of Bisexual Erotica* and *Clean Sheets.*

JONAH RASKIN is the author of *Jonah Raskin's Greatest Hits* and *More Poems, Better Poems.* He performs his poetry with live jazz musicians. He is also the chairman of the Communication Studies Department at Sonoma State University, and he is now writing a biography of Allen Ginsberg.

HELENA SETTIMANA lives in Toronto, Canada. Her stories have appeared at *Clean Sheets, The Erotica Readers and Writer's Association* (where she serves as Features Editor), *Scarlet Letters,* and *Amoret Online,* and in print in *Best Women's Erotica 2001* and *2002* (Cleis Press), *Best Bisexual Women's Erotica* (Cleis), *Erotic Travel Tales* (Cleis), and will appear in and *Herotica 7* (Down There Press). She has extraordinarily fond memories of her travels in the Greek islands.

H.L. SHAW (users.lanminds.com/gryffyn) is a transplanted Midwesterner now living in the Bay Area and loving it. She has published short fiction, poetry, and articles. She also works for a sex-toy catalog, which is more fun than you can imagine. Her ongoing goals are to write and publish fiction, maintain her online journal, and read, read, read.

SOUVIE is a college student at a state university in East Texas. She's always dabbled in writing, but it's only in the past few years that she's started writing seriously. She's an avid reader, and believes it's her love of books that got her started writing in the first place.

DAVID STEINBERG writes frequently about the culture and politics of sex. His books include *Erotic by Nature: A Celebration of Life, of Love, and of Our Wonderful Bodies; The Erotic Impulse: Honoring the Sensual Self*; and the forthcoming *Photo Sex: Sexual Photography Comes of Age*. He lives in Santa Cruz, California.

NOLA SUMMERS (nolasummers@yahoo.com) was born in Scotland, spent her formative years in Northern Ontario, and now works, reads, and writes in Toronto. She is a Galley Slave and Contributing Editor with *Clean Sheets.*

DAVID SURFACE played in rock and roll bands in Kentucky for ten years before moving to New York City to write. His fiction and essays have been published in *DoubleTake, North American Review, Crazyhorse*, and elsewhere. He leads fiction writing workshops at the Hudson Valley Writers Center in Sleepy Hollow. He is currently at work on *Tuesday Night When It's a Full Moon*, a collection of stories about sex, alcohol, religion, and other fun facts of growing up in the South.

Clean Sheets Magazine

www.cleansheets.com